River Of Fire
And Other Stories

River Of Fire
And Other Stories

Ed Robison

ISBN: Softcover   978-1-4628-8715-6
             Ebook   978-1-4628-8716-3

To order additional copies of this book, contact:
Xlibris Corporation
1-888-795-4274
www.Xlibris.com
Orders@Xlibris.com
100989

HER OWN SWEET LOVE was previously published in *Tidepools* June 2011.

CONTENTS

In Memoriam Marlene Robison

For Janet and Nicole

RIVER OF FIRE

I

We were just a bunch of guys sitting around
In my house talking—three of us.
You know how that is,
Being philosophical, talking about nothing, really.
Philosophy 101.

One of us got on to something and didn't know
For sure, where the hell he was headed.
Someone else raised the issue of breaking promises.
Important promises. In which a moral issue was involved.
It *sounded* heavy. Skirted heavy *seeming* issues—Death.
Whether that mysterious light at the end of the
Tunnel of Death might just be a cluster
Of random-firing neurons, self-generated,
In your own brain.
Things like that.

Memory was part of it. That certain aspect of the mind.
Memory. It's what?
Something generated in an electro-chemical crucible—
The brain—
Which creates, and imperfectly stores experiences, and
Which, when they are recalled,
Become recollections—memories.

One of my friends had fought in Vietnam.
Another friend participated in that
Dirty little Middle-Eastern dustup,
The Gulf War, in the Nineties.
Me—Korea.
Three guys. Three wars.

Look at that damned fly on your fingertip,
Someone said. How can you stand it?
I turned my finger as if
Entwining a drizzle of honey.
It was an enormous horsefly, fat and lazy,
A big leftover, winter, kind of fly,
A winter relic—moving slow.
I rotated my fingertip and watched as the fly walked
Round and round it,
Staying always on top, as if it were
On a log, or a barrel in the water—
As in a log-rolling contest, maybe.
Like a logger in the Pacific Northwest. You've seen them.

But the rhetorical question about
Breaking a moral promise
Syruped around inside my brain like molasses
And, like the fly, wouldn't go away.
Oh, come on, somebody said, get rid of that damn thing—
How can you *stand* it? You don't know where in the hell
It's been, after all. Germs.
I held the sluggish horsefly up to my lips
And blew slowly
Against it.
Its isinglass wings flexed,
Resisting.
Just as I had done once.
They could all see it from where they sat,
It was that *large* a fly, if you can understand
Something like that.
It dug in its many sticky feet and held on against my
Breath.

Oh, come on—*disgusting*—somebody said.
I breathed deeply and, pursing my lips, I sent a
Blast of air from deep inside my lungs toward the
Huge insect.
The fly was dislodged and we watched as

It headed slowly toward the golden shaft
Of hot air above the silken,
Amber-colored lampshade on a Stiffel brass lamp.
It circled lazily there,
Like a hawk on a desert thermal, and then
Disappeared into the kitchen, buzzing.
None of us moving, we watched the little beast
With amused fascination.

The *Times* lay, folded in half,
On the table. A headline invited reading.
There we were, just over the brink into the 21st Century.
North Koreans, still dyspeptic,
Sending in sappers in two-man subs to scout
(With envy?) their brethren to the south.
I continued to watch that fly,
Reminding me, for some reason of
When I was in Korea.
I mentioned it without quite knowing why—
That fly, maybe—
An F-86E on its way to MIG Alley. Possibly.

My forefinger was still poised
In front of my lips
As if I half-expected the hirsute insect to
Fly back in from the kitchen
And perch there upon it once again.
My two friends settled more deeply into their chairs
And looked comfortably receptive.
Somebody cracked a beer.
It was raining.
They were younger than I was,
Two wars younger
And they exchanged glances,
Deferentially encouraging me to continue.
Korea? one of them asked.
Yes.

II

I remember that I first met Lieutenant Park
At the war-ravaged Kimpo airport.
A shy and scholarly Republic of Korea officer,
A ROK officer,
About my own age,
He was to become my friend
And a key translator in my military workplace,
Radio Intercept Operations; encryption; decoding;
Things of that sort.
I descended the ladder of the C-119 Flying Boxcar,
That workhorse of Korean War air supply drops,
With its curious double booms. The hop
Over to this new assignment from Kyushu,
That beautiful southern island of Japan,
With its warm and dazzling blue seas,
Didn't take long.
Would I miss the home of *Konohana*,
The Goddess of Fujiyama?
As it turned out, probably.
Lieutenant Park motioned me,
From the edge of the hastily repaired tarmac,
To the front seat of the jeep,
Next to the driver—
And he himself climbed into the back.

As I remember
It wasn't just the rough jeep ride to my
New assignment that
Shook me up.
An enemy saboteur had apparently
Ignited a floating fuel depot
Somewhere near one of the Han River bridges.

As we approached it,
We could see a dense pall of smoke
Drift downwind from us.
Just like those in the worst WWII newsreels a
Mere five years earlier.
We joined a line
Of military vehicles, and
Everywhere we looked—the dispersion
Of the volatile fluids had
Turned the Han River into
A river of fire.

Below us there was the noise and tumult;
The terrible screams of victims;
Sequential explosions,
And the *dwoop-dwoop-dwoop* of sirens.
Above me, just in front of our jeep,
The rotting corpses of three *NKPA*, North Koreans,
Twisted silently from their garrotes,
Suspended from a bridge girder,
Phasing in and out an undulant curtain
Of foul petrol smoke.
My driver, fresh from a Midwest vocational
High school, leaned over to me
And bummed a cigarette.
He was laughing. Commie saboteurs, he said,
Pointing to the corpses twirling languorously
At the end of those garrotes.
Infiltrators, this blond American shouted
Over the tumult—terrorists
You'll get used to it,
He advised me. He thrust his chin
At the gyrating sappers. They had been there
A week—as a warning—he shouted.
ROKs won't let us take them down.
General Ridgeway, he don't care. It's
War, buddy. War.

Take a look at that down there. He pointed
To the flames and to the roiling black smoke below us.
The heat from the fire was intense,
Rising up the banks of the river
To the line of camouflaged
Jeeps and trucks queuing
To cross the bridge.

I looked over my shoulder at Lt. Park.
His composure had an almost menacing air to it.
He nodded impassively, his eyes, slitted.
It was hard to imagine what he might have
Been thinking about this sacking of his city,
This serene, and once-lovely setting of beautiful temples, with
Its venerable culture frozen in a Confucian
World, unchanged for centuries, until
The years of the rapacious Japanese occupation
From 1910 to 1945.
And then, the commies; the Chinese;
The Russians; and, those most bitter
Of enemies, the North Koreans themselves.
And now, a hundred thousand UN troops were
Overrunning his
Land of the Morning Calm.

There was much grief and
Sorrow on all sides of us.
Peasants with neatly tied bundles of
Possessions perched on their heads, or
Balanced on bicycle seats—carts—
Anything with wheels—
Formed long silent lines of exodus
From Seoul, heading south into safer territory.
Other, more desperate peasants, with no possessions,
Their frozen feet wrapped in straw and rags,
Struggled to find a place among them.
An MP motioned for us to make a run

Across the bridge. My driver
Flicked his cigarette out of the jeep
And floored it, smoothly slipping through
The succession of gears as if
He were showing off for a
Saturday night date—on an interstate in Iowa.
That river of fire was soon enough
Behind us and under the supervision
Of a swarm of raucous H-19 rescue choppers
And gunboats,
Trying to get a handle on
It all.

After a thirty-mile, gut-wrenching,
White-knuckle ride, over dusty hardpan;
Past Syngman Rhee's trashed presidential palace;
Past a couple of dazzling, but damaged, temples;
And through the hills beyond,
My driver announced that we had arrived.
Here it is, he said. No place like home.
Six weeks ago, this
Place was in North Korean hands, he said.
I tossed out my duffel bag, and he
Headed for the motor pool. An enigmatic
Lt. Park smiled and accompanied me
To the office of the C.O.

I had been assigned to a sensitive radio squadron,
Twenty-five tekkies and a support group,
That was billeted in the rubble of a venerable
Girl's college. Chosin Christian College.
CCC. The buildings comprised an eccentric cluster
Of bleak granite and brick,
Safely Calvinist in their conservative
Architecture. The founding
Patriarchs must have been hugely pleased, you know,
To set up this gloomy, cheerless, pinstriped,

Ecclesiastical esthetic of the Occident,
In opposition to the silken grace, and elegant beauty, of
A nearby ancient and pagan temple—an edifice
Which must have seemed to them, little more than
A heathen, Brobdingnagian incense burner.

In the main courtyard of this
Magisterial, colonial monument to Western
Scholarship and monotheism,
The very large bronze statue of the school's first
President had toppled face-forward,
One hand fingering his lapel,
And the other clasping his scroll of office.
Fresh out of college,
I thought of
Ozymandias,
Covered by the shifting sands of time.

The college buildings had been badly
Damaged by the impact of rockets, mortars
And machine-gun bullets.
Decorative acanthus cornices had shattered
To earth, destroying the landscape shrubbery.
There was no glass in
The windows. Tarpaulins were nailed
Over the openings to dull the chill.
Adding further to the grimness
Of this duty assignment,
The trees in the quadrangle,
Plundered for firewood,
Were reduced to scarred stumps.

III

The accommodations at the college
Were Spartan, but certainly luxurious,
Compared to the frigid foxholes in the field.
My cot was barely satisfactory for my lanky body
But I could live with it. This was war.
Khaki mosquito netting was draped on a frame over each bunk
For what reason, I couldn't imagine.
It was winter in those frosty rooms,
And any mosquitoes long gone.
But you could lower the netting,
That khaki netting, on all four sides of
Your bunk and have, maybe,
A *semblance* of privacy,
Like a porch screen—a widow's veil.
The netting conveys:
All my systems are off.
I want to read.
I want to sleep.
I want to dream.
Bug out, dude!
The dorm had been a schoolroom before the war,
And pictures of the English alphabet, with simple
Graphics, Apples to Zebras,
Started on the wall over the door—A for Apple,
Scripted their way across the front of the room,
And turned the corner at the shattered,
Tarpaulined windows—
Stopping there—Z for Zebra.
Alpha and Omega.

A thousand college-age Korean women
Learned their rudimentary English
In that austere space,
Just as younger school children learned
English in the States.

Up front, a slate chalkboard,
Cracked and crazed,
Riddled with an arc of tracer bullet holes
Had a bit of familiar Korean calligraphy
Still on it,
Not quite erased—
And beneath that, in a fine
Spenserian script,
Were these English words: *The quick brown fox*—.
Propped up, my pillow rolled beneath my neck,
I contemplated these matching
Linguistic fragments—
Little arrows drawn correspondingly
From here to there, English to Korean,
A *Rosetta stone*, which could be,
In a reach of the imagination,
God forbid, the only
Clue left to future archeologists
Of two civilizations, East and West,
Which having run amok—destroyed each other.
The quick brown fox—

I shared my room with Chuck Dasso;
Archie Lear, I think his name was; and
Kyle Knight, all of them buddies from fried
Green tomato country, deep in North Carolina.
We toiled, with other fellow radio intercept operators,
In the labyrinthine basement below
The main wing of the college,
Supporting UN soldiers and aircraft
By analyzing WX and troop movements.

A small, orphaned Korean boy, ten years old,
Was our orderly and he kept our boots glistening
While he learned English cuss-words and
Accepted the unimaginable largess of
His rich patrons:

Candy, cigarettes, money, clothes.
We called him *Skoshie*,
Which meant in Japanese, I think,
'Shorty' or *'Little Buddy'* or something like that.
(Did *Skoshie* muse on the irony of his having
A Japanese nickname? I don't think so.)
Each of us had a burp gun hooked over the
End of his bunk, and
Each of us had been issued a holstered .45 caliber sidearm
With a web belt.
It all seemed very melodramatic.
I couldn't wait to swagger around
With my pistol.
But swagger for whom?
The front line was a dozen miles
Walking distance. (Listen—the guns of battle—
Just north of Seoul—the enemy was *that* way.)
I cocked my head to hear.
I couldn't wait to get up there, check it out,
And posture with my sidearm,
As if I were a dogface in the field,
And not assigned to the relative safety
Of a radio intelligence squadron.
Dry with a roof over my head.

The ROK staffers assigned to my unit had
Separate quarters from the GIs.
We were squirreled all about the college
Corridors. Lt. Park and the other ROK
Translators slept in similar schoolrooms
Down the hallway.
We ate in the same mess hall. GI chow.
The usual fresh vegetables flown in from Japan,
Reconstituted milk
(Bluish, tasteless, watery),
And, for breakfast, the always-obnoxious SOS,
(Ground meat in thick white sauce, on toast).
And chicken, chicken and more chicken.

I gave Lt. Park a large container of
Chocolate chip cookies, with walnuts in them,
From my girlfriend in the States, Jeannine.
Lt. Park was my friend for life.
We will go into Seoul tomorrow,
He said to me.
And we did.
We took a motor pool Jeep into the city
And Lt. Park and I went to the black
Market, and walked many miles up and
Down crowded alleyways,
Incongruously picturesque,
Teeming with
Frightened refugees and
Those daring merchants who had
Something to sell.
American country western music,
Cold, Cold Heart; Tennessee Waltz;
Your Cheatin' Heart; all of those—
Courtesy Armed Services Radio,
Throbbed from every grenade-shattered whorehouse doorway.
Honey bucket censers, pulled by oxen,
Eased their way through the narrow
Market transits, commingling
The shocking smells of night soil,
With steaming cabbage, kimchi, garlic, and
Aromatic charcoal smoke.
Elderly men and women, unable to flee the city,
Stoically tended thousands of
Warming brazier fires
To ward off winter's bitter, biting, bone-chilling cold—
And they traded tiny treasure troves of this and that
For bits of food—and this and that.

GIs and other UN troops from 11 nations—
Scotland, England, Canada—even Turkey,
Were ubiquitous, and the offerings of the marketplace,
Rich, exotic and varied, vied for their attention.

Ancient brass coins pierced with Chinese characters;
Traditional Korean horsehair hats; cloisonné boxes;
Tapestries; oil portraits on silk of your stateside sweetheart—
From your wallet photograph—while-you-wait—
Souvenir military gear from
China, Russia, Korea, and the U.S.
For the connoisseur, live hand-grenades, and even
75mm recoilless rifles. And yes, *Kalashnikovs.*
AK-47's.

Lieutenant Park, a dignified and cultivated man,
With great patience, and gentility,
Did his best to explain everything to me.
The UN troops who had come to save his
Country, he told me quietly, were the object of
Immense gratitude.
But he advised me that I must, philosophically,
Overlook the occasional rudeness
Of the few Korean merchants here and there,
Who resented the presence
Of foreigners, and cheated the GIs.
He regretted it, but we both
Agreed that it was probably inevitable.
Fortunes of war.
I admired the quiet balance of his outlook.

That night, after my shift ended, I fell
Into the sack and into a deep sleep.
Archie was out like a light,
And the other two, Dasso and Kyle,
Were on shift in Operations and
Would be there until daybreak.
Skoshie was asleep in a corner,
In his much cherished GI sleeping bag,
His sugary treasures lined up, with
Evident pride of ownership, on
The oaken floor beside his drowsy head.
Snickers. Baby Ruth. Mr. Goodbar.

Sometime before dawn, all hell broke loose.
Explosions ripped through the mess hall
And the dormitory wing of the college.
Flames erupted from everywhere.
I leaped out of the sack immediately
And pulled on a jump suit.
There was a tremendous amount of racket.
I checked Archie. Man, he shouted, *incendiaries—we been hit.*
Sure enough, the ceiling over his bunk
Had caved in and a good fire had got started there.
I looked for *Skoshie*.
A fragment of phosphorous was burning the
End of his sleeping bag.
Quickly, I grabbed the stunned kid,
And then my burp gun and my .45,
And headed for the doorway.
Archie screamed out to me: Outside, man—*outside.*
He raced down the stairs, and part of the ceiling
Collapsed behind him.
I didn't know then, whether he got clipped or not.
There was a tremendous implosion, and I didn't hold
Out any hope for my bunkmate.
Lt. Park suddenly appeared in the hallway.
It was filled with smoke.
He shouted to me:
Come this way. *Come.*
The stairway had collapsed.
We had no light except from the
Incendiary fire itself.

Lt. Park led *Skoshie* and me down another long corridor
And into the college library, a hundred
Yards away from the dormitory wing.
Once inside, *Skoshie*, who was quaking in my arms,
Struggled and kicked,
To free himself, so that he could
Reenter the smoke-filled hallway.
He was screaming desperately.

Lt. Park, I shouted, what is he saying?
He wants his sleeping bag, Lt. Park shouted.
He wants his things. His candy. Now he have
Nothing, he say.
I could barely hold this child.
Lt. Park, I screamed out to him,
Tell him, I'll get him another sleeping bag.
Skoshie quieted down.

The great library room was nearly dark,
But a quick glance in the half-light,
Revealed that thousands of books lay in
Heaps all over the room.
The oaken tables and chairs had long since
Been burnt for firewood.
The image of those damaged books,
That I'd been conditioned to cherish since childhood,
Seemed to symbolize the end of civilization,
As if the *Lascaux* cave paintings themselves, had
Crumbled into *chalky, limestone nothingness* before my eyes.

This same thing happened last month, too, Lt. Park told me.
Before you came. Enemy plane
Flew over to drop incendiary bombs on this installation.
How's that possible? I asked.
What aircraft could get past
Our guns—our fighters?
I had much to learn.
They fly low, he told me. Below the radar.
They fly slow, he said.
He was on full alert,
His eyes, black and electric,
The former laconic and philosophical
Lt. Park of the black-marketplace
Was gone.
Suicide mission, he continued.
Pilot already dead.
They target this intelligence unit
Second time, now.

I pulled the tarpaulin off the window
And looked over at the next wing of the building.
There was fire everywhere.
The weather was freezing
And fresh snow blanketed the quad.
If there had been fire hoses
They'd have been useless.
Frozen solid.
A pale dawn had started in the east.
I shouted below to my buddies for assistance.

I looked back into the library,
Illuminated by the flickers of the firestorm,
At the books wet with rain and frosty leakage;
Ruined by mold and weather and destructive ph.
Many of them had been spirited away
To be used like starter logs—
To yield up their life-saving warmth.
So much for culture—the printed word.
I leaned down and salvaged a smallish fan-folded
Volume with sewn signatures.
It was very old, I'm sure.
Lt. Park was directing the placement of the tip of the
Rescue ladder to the outside of our building
And up to the library window.
Flames had spread from the roof and hallway,
And were now licking
At the piles of irreplaceable books.

Archie was down below on the fire-fighting team.
He'd made it safely out of the dormitory wing.
When he saw us,
He whooped a wonderfully silly, hillbilly
Exuberance—a rebel yell—or something,
That put us all at ease, this so cool,
North Carolinian.
I threw my fatigue jacket over the
Shivering *Skoshie* and

Stuck the little book I'd picked up into my fatigue pocket.
We descended the escape ladder by
Dawn's early light. I could
Feel the same sense of shared pride
Over our rescue and survival
(heavy with the youthful stirrings of parade-ground patriotism)
That I felt marching
On the drill field in
USAF tech school. We're all in this
Together, I reminded myself.

Well, we pretty much got out okay.
There were some injuries.
Nobody killed.
Our intelligence-gathering must continue unabated.
Our work was critical,
Make no mistake.
Even though the official situation in Korea,
As the pundits reported in the press,
Seemed to be *fluid but hopeful*,
The question of the day was: Were the Soviets
Launching the Chinese in a major
Counter offensive against the 8th Army?
Who?
What?
Where?
Why?
When?

After the air strike,
Our hard-working tekkies put us
Back on the air in short order
To help answer those and other
Strategic questions regarding this
This furiously imploding Korean Peninsula.
We renewed our intercept of enemy messages
And stuck pins into our maps.
Cartological acupuncture.

The aircraft which had targeted us
Crashed and burned not far away.
Afterward, we went over and scoped out
The still smoldering wreckage.
It was a Mickey Mouse operation,
A one-shot, canvas-and-baling wire disaster,
A crop duster, really.
A vintage bi-plane—
Someone said.
A Sopwith-Camel—
Miraculously reconstructed from the past,
For this solitary bombing raid.
It took planning and guts
For a highly motivated enemy pilot
To pull it off. He sacrificed himself
To his *system*. Would I do the same?
Was I even then, maybe? Sacrificing?
I had plenty of admiration for
The incinerated, suicidal pilot—
Whoever he was.

Omar Bradley called Korea
The Ugly Little War.
Wrong war.
Wrong place.
Wrong time.
Wrong enemy.
He got it right—
A stubborn war
Of hilltops and ravines,
And low-flying, suicide,
Antique Sopwith-Camels.
F-86s.

IV

I paused and looked at my friends,
Remembering another specific incident.
I continued.
One day in particular, for some reason,
I told them—a week later. Yes.
A week. I shrugged.
You'd think I'd put all that behind me.
It was the dawn of dawns. White and icy terrible.
Icier than hell, you know,
Not a hint of yellow, or the golden tints, which come with dawn
In the temperate climates where I was raised.
Somehow, you knew you would never again be warm.
The freezing days of that then inhospitable
Korean Peninsula, in those rocky hills,
Knee-deep in snow, seemed interminable.
Frozen Chosin, we nicknamed it.
Hell is fire—flames. Chosin is—ice.
Frozen Chosin.

F-86E and F-86F fighter jets scrambled
Against MIG-15 fighters.
They hung overhead, tiny and silent—
Nearly motionless saber tips—their white contrails
Chalking up the blackboard of the sky
Into vast, geo-political sectors,
One of which would soon enough become the DMZ,
The 38th Parallel.
They were aimed now toward the Yalu River,
To rendezvous there in MIG Alley
In spectacular aerial dogfights with
The Yellow Horde, piloting Soviet aircraft.
You know,
Even though you could see them up there above you,
In one of the glory jobs of the war,

Piloting a jet fighter,
You couldn't really hear them.
Well, not *quite*, anyway.
The black and white magpies squabbling, cracking at, and
Pecking through the icy stubble in the frozen rice paddies,
Seemed more real, and more immediate,
To me. Them you could hear. Them, you could see.
Those magpies.

Well, as I mentioned, I was on a hilltop aerie,
Stickered with denuded winter trees,
To which I had impulsively hiked, just
To get away from the crowded barracks atmosphere—
And the jitteriness I'd felt—(because of the
Unsettling attack on our billet.)
I just wanted to check out the neighborhood.
The terrain. Reconnoiter. Escape.
It was quite a climb and my breath
Unfurled from my lungs like a spring-loaded,
Paper party-favor, or the thick tongue of an iguana.
Looking about me in that calm and silence,
I could see proof all about me, that this hilltop bunker
Had been a strategic promontory, just a few weeks prior.
It was just as the Jeep driver had said.
I didn't have to be a West Point graduate to see that—
Or a rocket scientist as they say today.
The Chinese held all the high ground
With their machine gun nests.
And why not? They *had* got there first, after all.
King of the Hill.

A battle had been won or lost upon this hill,
Depending upon which side you were on,
If you get my drift.
And in that freezing—that sub-zero cold,
In that screaming wind from Siberia,
That could freeze you solid,
You could see the evidence all around you

Of a hastily abandoned machine-gun nest,
A mortar emplacement, really.
I spread my fingers,
And then made a semi-circle in the air around my chair,
To suggest this terrain to my friends.
They nodded, and clearly,
They could see it in their minds' eye.
The site had been hastily abandoned, I told them.
It was obvious.
Rice bowls, wooden spoons and cups, scattered,
Were captured in *death grips* of frozen rain—
The personal mess issue—kitchen minutiae of wasted lives,
Depicted briefly until the next thaw,
In *Daguerreotypes of ice.*
It was that cold and bitter a winter.
And I can recall that, as if it were yesterday,
You know.

Well, I picked up one of these humble eating implements—
Of a Commie soldier—part of his issue—
I'm sure of that—and it *was* a spoon—
Looking hand-crafted from bamboo, I speculated,
But flat and fairly wide, with a very shallow bowl,
And I realized, with a sudden shock of heightened awareness,
From simply standing on this
Promontory of Death—
As I now began to think of it—
An awareness that powerfully disturbed me—
That at one time—this—this—that—
Crude wooden spoon—*a peasant spoon,* had
Actually been inside the mouth of an enemy soldier—
With a bit of rice—a bit of garlic—*kimchi*—perhaps—
Perhaps a bit of sauce—
Some tiny mealtime reward
In exchange for a life, up to then,
Philosophically nourished by a flawed political ideology—
But soon to be snuffed out by a mortar from
One of our guys—you know.

In a meditative manner
I slowly touched that wooden spoon
To my own lips.
A giddy thrill of contact swept over me.
To savor the essence of that fragged soldier
(Who lay about me in snowy pieces)
On the lip edge of that humble wooden instrument
Overwhelmed me.
Guiltily, I pulled the spoon away.
A taste of battle?
Never before had I ever felt so strongly
The presence of what we might call ghosts.
So help me, I don't know what else to call them—
Ghosts.
Ghosts

Well, impulsively, I tucked that frozen,
Wooden spoon into a pocket of my field jacket,
Knowing that as it warmed up,
Or defrosted, as we say these days,
The ancient cooking scents of garlic,
And fire-peppers, which
Had infused it, would now be released
Into the pocket of my khaki field jacket.
The younger men to whom I was telling my story
Nodded at that minor revelation
With a certain grave understanding.
I have that wooden spoon today, upstairs, I told them.
In a foot locker. I don't know why.
One young man raised his hands in a sympathetic gesture
And then dropped them resignedly
Back into his lap.
The other nodded as well.
I'd like to see it, he said,
That spoon.

I continued my story, telling them that
My attention was drawn to the shattered peasant homes
That lay scattered below me among
Checkerboard fields.
Fields which, for centuries, had been passed down
From the dead to the living, according to complicated rules
Of custom and primogeniture.
I knew, as I observed the farmers there below me,
That it would take a lifetime
To understand the mysterious practices
Of their lives and routines, but I nevertheless
Watched with great curiosity,
Committing much to memory of what I observed.
A khaki-clad ROK Soldier, exhausted and
Heavy with knapsack, trudged below me
On the boards of this
Impromptu outdoor theater,
Entering from stage left, so to speak,
Along the zigzag pathways between the frozen rice paddies
And the fallow sweet-potato fields.

I leaned forward, my boot upon some piece of gray schist,
And I watched as an emotional welcoming,
A hue and cry,
Gained volume down below me, there in
That battered village,
Each time this soldier passed a hut—
Reminding me of the cacophony
Of the competing choruses in
Carl Orff's *Carmina Burana*.
A growing gaggle of scrawny children
And aged adults
And bone-thin dogs
Followed this ROK soldier as he made his way to a dwelling
On whose war-shattered roof-tiles,

Drying, fiery, blood-red peppers gave up their moisture
To a weak and pale and wintry sun. A tableau.
This ROK soldier spared from further battle,
Because of wounds, I supposed,
Had returned to this homely center of
His spiritual universe,
His sanctuary—his hearth.
As I watched, he
Limped from door to door, searched for,
And was clasped by an ancient crone,
And then surrounded by a throng of
War-weary and spent villagers,
Skinny dogs and foraging pullets.
I witnessed an outpouring of emotion
That no poverty, starvation or
War-pillaged food supply
Could diminish.
Home from the Crusades.

I certainly wished then,
And, as I think back on it now,
As you might imagine,
That I might be next to appear on *my*
Fifties street—neighbors calling out to *me;*
Children running to carry *my* duffel bag;
Dogs at *my* heels;
Grandma at *my* front door screen, smoothing her blued hair;
My Fifties mother in bouffant; lipstick; pumps; and cinch belt,
Dividing daffodil bulbs in the potting shed;
My Fifties father pruning the laurel hedge
In loosened tie, in suspenders,
In dress slacks, and wingtips;
(As they dressed then),
All of them caught unawares by my arrival.

You can understand the feeling I had, can't you? I asked.
The young men before me nodded in agreement.
I warmed to my subject.
However strange the customs of those exotic Asian peasants,

I *needlessly* instructed them,
Those feelings of home and duty, unspooling there below me,
Were the universal, if tenuous, threads
Which connect all of us to
The fabric of our collective past
From the *Red Badge of Courage*
To Homer's *Ulysses.*

But, how to express what happened next?
I can only tell you that
The *sense of death* in the desolate wasteland
Of those Pork Chop Hills was very
Nearly palpable—
So that when I first glossed around
And saw this skeletonized arm
Sticking out of a pocket of cold, snowy-beige earth,
As if *beckoning,*
It barely gave me a start,
I had so reigned in my feelings
As a form of self-protection. Denial?
Probably as a mortician must, you know.
At first,
I looked dispassionately at this arm,
Barely encased in its shredded sleeve
Of quilted khaki,
And then I looked with clinical fascination.
That arm had to have been picked clean
By foxes and magpies,
So pure and white was its tone—
One of those thousand shades of off-white,
Between chalk and old-ivory,
That only interior decorators
Can give a name to.
How long it had been there, I could only guess.

Is it possible, I wondered,
To know anything of a man
From a bleached skull, say,
Or a clutching of frosty metacarpals?

I shuddered somewhat, to reach out to these
Mysterious and touching remains,
But it seemed the *decent* thing to do, you know,
To scuff those bones, *awkwardly*,
Into a frozen depression,
And then kick a snowy shroud over them.
How had they been missed by their corpsmen?
In other, more *ordinary* wars, you know,
The abandonment of dead or wounded comrades
Was *unthinkable*.
What say you, *Horatio*?

But this was a new kind of war and
It would extort a heavy toll from the
Conscience of many young men.
The new term, *brainwashing*, was invented,
And defined itself, here in
These hills and ravines, and commie POW camps.
What were these bodies doing here?
I kept asking that question of myself
Just to keep up my spirits,
Made so uneasy
By the reaching toward me of
This apocalyptic *Arm of Death* that seemed
To want to *clasp me to it.*
I had to get angry to get through this grim task of
Burying the bones of him, my *unwanted dead companion.*
Red Chinese, was he? North Korean?
A ROK?
There was nothing about those graceful,
Picked-clean bones to give me a clue.
I wanted to grieve. *Really*
I did—and if you had been there with me,
You would have wanted to grieve, too,
For this Unknown Soldier
With the garlic, *kimchi*-flavored spoon.
You would have wanted to say

Exactly as I did
Looking at those bones,
That it was just a
Terrible damn shame.

Was some mother or father or wife or child,
Even now weeping for news of this fallen warrior,
(This son? This husband? This father?)
In some *other* checkerboard of rice paddies,
Somewhere else in that far Far East?
My friends nodded supportively
And with complete understanding.

You know, I felt compelled to say,
In another time—another place,
To find an arm-bone with a clutch of fingers attached,
Is to call 911, the police,
To lose a night's sleep,
To raise hell until those bones are
Reunited with the rest of its skeleton;
Identified and placed at rest.
But, this is now,
And that was then.
Well, I tried to put all of this into perspective—
This dead enemy soldier—
The bleak location—
The insensitive abandonment of his corpse.
But a kind of angry self-righteousness prevailed.
We were, after all, on the Korean Peninsula
With the full *moral authority* of the
United Nations fighting *international outlaws*
Of whom this corpse was one.
General Ridgway had said it was war.
MacArthur declared it a war.
The American public called it a war.
Congress proclaimed it a war.
But Harry Truman—get this—to his detriment—
Wouldn't be bullied by congress—
He called it a *police action*.

Crazy. Never lived that mistake down.
Did you, President HaryTruman?
A war—well—by any other name—*well*.
How many GI's lay decomposed and frozen,
Killed to death,
By wave after wave of yellow
Automatons? Oh, yes. Look it up.
The information is there.
It's all documented.
Missing in Action?
Try 8,100 for *starters*.
Oh, what monstrous horrors
Would these melting snows reveal?

I lifted up my eyes to the sky.
More F-86F's whistled past
In a crucifix-shaped, flying formation
To play ominous tag,
Up there somewhere—up by the Yalu River.

V

Then, *really*, I don't know when it hit me—
The realization that perhaps this bunker where I stood,
Might have been completely overlooked by
All of the military involved
And, that, you know, for crissakes,
I might even then be standing in a minefield.
It was common for
Those *gooks*—as we called them
Then,
An insensitive term—
Which of course I
Would *never use* today, and really
Never did then, you *must* understand.
It was their procedure to plant those
Anti-personnel mines—the *Bouncing Betty*—
Around their foxholes and their gun emplacements,
And those mines would help take
The brunt of any surprise assault
By night or from the rear.
Of course—they—those Chinese commie soldiers,
Had memorized the location of those anti-personnel
Mines—that could blow off a foot—you know—
A leg.
Blow out your crotch.
Disembowel you.
Kill you quick.
Kill you *dead and messy*.
Anti-personnel mines,
Buried just beneath the surface of the soil—
With leaves on them, soil and dust, you know.
Invisible to the naked eye.
Anything could set them off.

Pressure detonation. Pressure release.
You would never attempt an assault on one of those
Pork Chop Hills, those Heartbreak Ridges, at night.
Suicide, I'm telling you—*pure suicide.*

Suddenly, it was obvious
That the bodies around me, there
In that mortar emplacement,
That I'd stumbled on really by accident—
There could be how many?
Two, three, ten? Now, it looked to me
As if they were taken out
Either by an air strike, or maybe
A lucky mortar or two, from one of
Our guys.
There were pockmarks, those depressions caused
By explosions—shrapnel. Sure, the snow
Had deceptively softened their edges
Into innocent-looking, vanilla ice-cream-scoop outlines,
But they *were there*, and obvious enough
To chill the sensibilities of
The trained military observer.
The rape of a hillside.

Well, perhaps, the cleanup of this snowy mess, I speculated—
The body parts—
By medics and so on,
Maybe that would come later—spring possibly—
The see-saw of battle making an orderly
Gathering up of those dead—*simply out of the question.*
So, with all this going through my head, you know,
Suddenly I realized that
I had no business here on this snowy redoubt,
That I might even then be standing in
A treacherous field of unexploded ordnance.
But God was with me and
By some miracle—yes?
A *miracle*—no other word for it—He had allowed

Me to hike up there
Without somehow getting
Blown apart. Running through the raindrops,
As they say, *without getting wet.*
My two companions nodded empathetically.

Well, naturally, those *gooks,*
(Those *Chinese,* those *NKPA*),
Would not
Have placed *Bouncing Betty,* anti-personnel mines
On their *own* footpaths—
That was my hope at least—
My *rationale,*
But unfortunately, the snow had completely covered
Those paths up. The terrain was hardpan and crusty.
I couldn't really read it,
If you get my meaning.
On impulse, and to test my theory,
I picked up a length of tree branch,
Defoliated by war or nature, I couldn't tell,
And looking around me,
I tried to put myself
In the place of the dead commies
Buried so ineffectively around me.
I walked gingerly back to the gray schist
From where I'd earlier viewed, so far below,
The peasant soldier's homecoming tableau—
And I tossed the branch,
Oh, five meters long, or so,
Tossed it lightly
Downhill from where I was—
Down a shallow slope leading to a
Precipitous escarpment.
There was a tremendous explosion
And the impact and the power of
It hurtled me backward onto the
Rough grave that I had just
Made for the commie soldier.

Protected somewhat by the schist outcropping,
I knew that I was not badly hurt.
The concussive effect of the blast
Lasted for a few moments only.
But I tell you—
Those moments *passed like an eternity.*
I was somewhere in an idyllic state
Between torpor and death, until I roused myself.
I was not hurt, but rather effectively stunned.
I noticed that the roughness of
The explosion had loosened
More earth and snow, and revealed additional
Body parts of *other* soldiers.
Strangers.
I was *too horrified,*
A ghoulish grave robber,
Lying among them—their body parts—you know, and
I knew that I could not provide any of them
The voluntary grave detail
That I had already earlier performed for the one,
Who, by now, had become in a ghastly way,
Almost a *familiar*—an intimate.
I was in shock, I suppose, and
I had to run, a coward, from that place of the dead
On that Pork Chop Hill;
And, feeling myself all over
For bruises and blood,
I, in a way that I now realize
Was very nearly *irrational,* ran back down that
Land-mined
Mountain,
Retracing,
Placing—
Each of my boots in my own prior
Bootprints
In
The
Snow.

I finally stumbled back down to
One of the main trails which
Merged, more or less,
With the roadway into the village,
Myself a walking dead man,
Eardrums, bursting, blasting, ringing,
From that blast—and from there,
Like a frightened prairie dog,
I scuttled deep into the
Basement of the college dormitory building
In which my squadron was billeted.
And I must tell you this—
An ominous *Stygian* gloom,
As if a *live thing*,
Seemed to follow me down that
Mountain trail, as well,
Elbowing its way
After me, into the dank,
Subterranean corridors of my cement bunker,
Burrowing its way *deep into my subconscious.*
It was only by the most diligent
Concentration upon my military tasks that
I was able to shake the bleak depression
That had crept over me and
Finally dispel those phantoms of death,
From that haunted, Pork Chop Hill,
Who had dug so deeply
Into the foxholes of my mind.

VI

Well, after a time, the noises of war
Began to recede like the sounds
Of distant thunder, and the spring sap
Began once again to flow,
Forcing wild Asian forsythia,
Almost against its will, in this forlorn
Wasteland, into timid yellow blossom.
The Marxist demon seemed to be at bay and
Pax Koreana
Was being hammered out
On the peace tables in Panmunjom
(A village in the DMZ).
The two Koreas, Pyongyang and Seoul,
Seemed about to be cast into political bronze,
Tentative and squabbling, yet,
But the thing *did seem done.*
Well, all right. Not peace,
But a *shaky armistice.*
North.
South.

Accordingly, FEAF now had the idea
That the covert operations of which I was a part
Should relocate to Okinawa, that new
Island fortress, and electronic listening post, for the
USA. There were other hot, Cold War assignments.
South Korea would pick itself up and
Dust itself off. One could feel it in the air,
Even then, the emergence of an economic
Miracle which would soon astonish the world.
An industrial behemoth.
Isn't that right? I looked at my buddies.
They would have been too young to know that.

I remember that I was sitting in the weak
Sunshine with Lieutenant Park, going through some of
My gear. Culling. I'd miss him,
And I think he'd miss me.
Our friendship seemed quite genuine.
I bought him a Coke in one of those
Green Coke bottles.
Before aluminum cans, you know.
Collectibles, now.
We each had a Coke.
Lt. Park loved those Cokes—
And I had noticed that in the four months of our
Acquaintance, his body-weight seemed to have
Doubled on the diet of rich GI mess. The
Gravies, the hotcakes, the mashed potatoes;
Those sugary Cokes.
Most Koreans were quite slim on their
Wartime diet of rice and the odd
Piece of chicken, you know.

I tossed a couple of paperbacks over
To Lt. Park. Like most GI's, I read a lot, and
I'd read some books several times each.
I gave him some Hemingway. Some Mailer. Faulkner's,
Absalom! Absalom! And, *As I Lay Dying.*
Whitman's *Leaves of Grass.* And so on.
A bunch of *Time* magazines and *Arizona Highways.*
He was cheered, and delighted to have them.
Read these, I told him. You'll learn all about Americans.
Maybe that will be a good thing, I said.
(Maybe not,
I thought.)
But maybe.

I have a question for you, Lt. Park said.
Not really listening, I pulled some more things
Out of my zippered bag.
A Swiss Army knife; the wooden spoon I'd found

Up on the ridge, which so intrigued me;
A couple of enemy flags—coins.
Lt. Park examined the spoon and confirmed
That it was probably *NKPA* issue. He handed it back.
I put it into my bag along with the flags.
I slid the Swiss knife over to him as a gift,
But he pushed it back across the rough table which
Separated us.
Please, I said, I *want* you to have it.
He thanked me and opened up some of the blades,
The little scissors, the awl, and so on,
And examined them.
I could see he was very pleased.
I want to go to the States, he told me.
Southern California, maybe.
Many Koreans there.
I want to go to university—UCLA School of Medicine.
You want to be a doctor? I asked.
He nodded in a serious manner. Yes.
Well, I joked; you could use that Swiss Army knife,
And I made a motion as if I were cutting a
Tumor out of a diseased intestine.
He made a weak smile.

Something else was on his mind.
He held up the Swiss knife and worked the scissors
With his thumb and forefinger.
I'll need a sponsor, he said, to enter the States.
Will you sponsor me?
Me? I asked. I was momentarily dumbed
By the magnitude of the request.
Yes, he said. I will need an American citizen.
I passed the flinch test.
Sure, I said. Sure. I'd be happy to sponsor you. I meant it.
A great idea.

I don't know what else I said, or what else he said,
Or what plans we made to clinch my commitment.
I certainly gave the address of my parents to Lt. Park.
Lieutenant Park—Language Specialist.

I *remember* that. I wrote it on the inside cover
Of *Tender is the Night*, by F. Scott Fitzgerald. A great book
To learn about the American mystique? Hmmm.
Hemingway and Fitzgerald were very best friends,
I told Lt. Park. He nodded. Friends for a *while*.
When you read these books, try to remember that,
I told him. And we talked some more about American
Writers, after which, I gave him a comprehensive reading list.

Did you ever hear from Lt. Park? one of my friends
Asked me. Well, here's the thing, I responded.
I was transferred to Okinawa. My hitch there was *what*?
Six months. Seven? Like *that*. Afterward, I was reassigned to
A sprawling crypto center in Texas for a year or so.
(Russian radio traffic was now the hot assignment *du jour*.
It was the beginning of the burgeoning Cold War.)
And after that, to some secret base in California for
Six months. I don't even remember
The names of these places, anymore.
That was all *years* ago.
But, *yes*. After I was mustered out of the Air Force,
I decided that I had to make
My obligatory—my ritual—
My Hemingway-esque—Grand Tour of Europe.
Paris, you know. Piaf. The Left Bank.
The sound of the button accordion. All that.
Le Cafe Les Deux Magots and so on.
I'd read *The Sun Also Rises*. It blew me away.
All that stuff about Gertrude Stein and Alice B. Toklas;
And Picasso, and James Joyce's *Ulysses* and
Shakespeare & Company, in Paris, and I just knew
All of that was for me. I wanted to write, too,
And drink red wines, and inhale my fancied ambience of
This *literary* Paris—run
With the bulls in Pamplona;
Fish the streams of Portugal, and learn to
Sing *fado*. I wanted to be blown away by
All that stuff.
Flamenco. Gitanas.

Do you know that great black-and-white
Photograph by Doisneau? The French street photog?
Robert Doisneau?
It's called *Le Baiser de l'Hôtel De Ville*?
Two lovers kissing in front of a street cafe?
Arms at their sides—fingertips touching?
Everybody knows it.
That's it.
The *essence* of my quest.
(It all seems so innocent, now.)

My friends nodded at this perfervid litany of
My romantic Everests. (It had become
Cliched in the years since the
Korean Police Action. My
Little daydream had become the daydream of
Millions, and Europe was crammed with ugly-Americans,
Choking the alleys of Pamplona—
Clogging the Spanish Steps—*Menilmontant*—
And the jails of Turkey, for that matter.
But *then*, the concept was fresh and new and exciting.)

I bought an oversized wallet, I remember,
For those passports, and francs,
Deutschmarks, lira and pounds.
And I had my
Europe on Five Dollars a Day paperback.
(There was no *Euro* dollar in those days. Not then.)
I had my shots—one foot on the gangplank.
All of that,
Leaving for New York, the next day—
Ticketed for some steamer whose name, I think,
Was the *Toulouse*. French.
I was only 24-hours away from this
Important event in my life.

My Dad came down the walk from the mailbox,
Alongside the laurel hedge (which, you remember,
The trimming of which
Was his lifetime project,)
And he handed me this thin airmail letter from Korea.
I had no idea what it was.
Korea was not even near
The *middle* of my consciousness.
It was as if I had *never been there*,
But this stranger whom I did not know.
You see what I mean? This stranger—this other self
Who used my name—
Impersonating me.
You understand?
A trick of the mind.
Oh, It'll happen to you one day. Don't laugh.

Well, I slit open the envelope and extracted the letter
With no expectation *whatever*
Of knowing who wrote it, or
What its pages might convey.
There, in a beautiful and refined script,
Stunning in its meticulous draughtsmanship,
Was the letter I'd thought never to see.
A letter which was
Elegantly composed in the slightly
Stilted manner practiced by persons
For whom English is a second language.

You know who it was from, of course.
The now Mister Park. Civilian. He had written to
Remind me of my commitment.
My promise.
I barely remembered his name.
Visions of *Euroail, Euro*-this, *Euro*-that—
And youth hostels,
Which danced in my head, nearly lost their
Footing. You bet.

So, what did you do? one of
My friends asked me.
What did I do? I did the only thing I could
Do. I stuck that letter
From Korea, tissue paper thin,
And, apparently, as thin as the promise
I'd made to Lt. Park,
(And I recognize that now,)
I stuck it inside the little book
I had saved from the burning college library. You remember
That little book? The one I'd saved
After the fire-bombing of the girl's
College in Korea? The letter is
Inside that book, now, as if it were a book mark,
In a book I cannot even read, because it's written
In some ancient Korean mode that
Only scholars can interpret.
I had that book evaluated
At university—the Asian Lit Department.
They were quite excited by it.
They wanted that book. But I told them, No,
I was going to send it back to the
College after the war.
Back to its rightful home.
I've not done that—yet.

And then, at dinner, my mother says:
So, *honey*, daddy says that you received
A letter from Korea. How interesting.
There was no *e-mail*, then. No ubiquitous cell-phones.
Uhmmm, *yes*, I said.
Her hands fidgeted nervously with her sterling salad
Fork. Yes, I said. A friend.
A girl friend? my father asked, winking at my
Mother—I know my son—no little *announcement*?
He tapped my plate with his knife
In a chillingly over-hearty, father-son fashion.
I really couldn't believe what I was hearing.

That's what they *do*, my dad said. That's their
Ticket to citizenship in the good old
U. S. of A. Spring a *kid* on you, those *gooks*.
I wanted to leave the table.
Leave the house.
I thought I might be sick.
Not even *your* kid, he added. Paper's *full* of it.
A scam.
Then he winked at me during this *Last Supper,*
Before the *Toulouse* sailed for Europe,
And asked for more of his favorite dish—
(A festive compote of mushroom soup, string beans,
And canned, French-fried onion rings.) Ugh.

Dad, I've been home for *three years*, I told him.
My mother said, *Daddy, stop it.*
Well, so who *was* the letter from? she asked me,
Daintily wiping the corner of her lip
With a linen napkin.
Pardon? I said. The letter?
Well, *yes*, dear.
Oh, nobody, really.
I did say that.
It was an ugly thing to say,
And I admit that. Mr. Park was *not a nobody.*
But you can see here, can't you?
It's all laid out
Nice as pie.

In those days, you know.
Prejudice, right?
Arrogant racism. Homegrown variety.
Ethnic partitions were still
Very sharply drawn in the U.S.
In *those days.*
For me to even *think* of sponsoring
An Asian or, as we called them then,
Orientals—
Walk around the neighborhood, and so on—

With an Oriental—well—the corollary
Would have been—say—to
Marry a Negro.
Unthinkable. That would all come later.
After MLK.

After that dinner, some buddies came by.
My date, Jeannine.
Tomorrow was the big day.
My bags stacked by the front door.
I was outta there in the morning.
Off to New York and the
Maritime *Toulouse.*

I told myself that I'd send
Mr. Park a cable from Paris.
I'd meet him in the spring
In front of the American Express office,
On a day of his own choosing.
Or, maybe in front of *L'Hôtel de Ville*—
The city hall.
I'd be sipping a Pernod or a Perrier or a Pepsi
Or *something*—a sprig of forsythia in the
Buttonhole of my fly-fishing vest.
Paris, so far away from the restless, spiky, truce
Struck between the reps of the UN
And the North Koreans, July 27, 1953.
Appropriate.

And so, one of my friends
Asked me: Did you wire him?
Did you cable Mr. Park?
Well—no, I said, as a matter of fact, I didn't.
I *didn't* wire him. When I got back from
Europe—a year-and-a-half later, you know,
I thought of it again and I did drop him a line.
There was no reply, as I knew there wouldn't be.
And Mr. Park now?
Did he get to the U.S.? To UCLA Med School?

Did he have a backup sponsor?
Did he become a physician?
To whose illness does he now attend?
Some flabby, white, middle-aged ex-GIs
In Southern California,
With medical insurance and prostate problems?
Is he writing prescriptions for Viagra
For the erectile dysfunction set?
Does he have a clinic in rural Seoul?
Does he work for an HMO in West LA?
Did he lose faith in America?
Americans?
Because of me?
I don't know.
I'll never know.

We'd been talking earlier about denial—selective memory—
Broken promises.
All that. Well, I'd blocked a lot of this out.
God, for how many years?
I know that now. Freud and Jung gave
Us the words to describe this phenomenon, I think.
In the old days we were said to be
Lying to ourselves.
Delusional.
Now, it's called *denial*.
Different words. Same story.
But all that denial, I told my friends,
Never exorcised the picture I
Have in my mind of Lieutenant Park
Leading me and that little *Skoshie*,
Down a choking, smoke-filled hallway,
To the safety of that
Scavenged library room
And to our rescue.
History—or time
May have dulled
The memory of my Korean tour
A bit, however,

As I brooded before them,
I could promise that
That episode
Would
Never
Be forgotten.
Like the sappers in the two-man
Sub, they'd keep trying to get at me
And my sub-conscious.

There was a long silence and I thought
I felt the sting of a wordless rebuke
From my friends.
I was sure of it.
I'd somehow been found wanting.
By my own confession,
I'd let Mr. Park down.
Blown my personal integrity.
But, you know what one of them said to me?
Don't blame yourself, he said,
I'd have done
Exactly
The same thing you did.
That's what he said.
My other friend said: Well, what's done is *done*.
It is what it is.
Of course, each of them said
Exactly what I wanted to hear.
After my confessional.
What I needed to hear.
What's done,
Is done.
It is
What
It is.

Well, look at that, I observed.
My little furry friend,
The wintering-over fly,

Tired of the kitchen,
Slowly buzzed its way
Past the Stiffel lamp,
And returned to the area
In front of my face.
Somebody cracked another can of beer.

I lifted my forefinger
And hoped for the fly to land there
Once again.

The End

THE ELEPHANT PIPE

"Maybe it *would* be good for you to move away," Marty had suggested to him. "You know, put the house in the hands of a good property manager. Rent it. Lease it. Go to Provence for a year. Take your mind off Frances. What could it hurt? It's been a year, already. Travel."

It was nice of Marty to care and to voice his concerns. But why did everyone who knew about Frances' death think that he was still grieving? He was a bit more withdrawn, sure, who wouldn't be? Contemplative. But he enjoyed his aloneness. He'd thought about subscribing to the Internet sometime—maybe to shmooze with someone like himself out there in electronic never-never land, an anonymous, information highway soul-mate in a chat room for the grieving-challenged. But he never got around to it.

The night light in the den reflected off the beveled mirror and sprayed the wall with some delicious geometrics. Hastings walked into the kitchen, emptied the dregs of his wineglass into the sink, and popped it into the dishwasher. He'd saved and rinsed the dishes for three days without washing them on *Full Cycle*. He shot a glance at the clock. It was twelve-twenty. He couldn't channel-surf between Letterman and Leno any longer. Forget Conan. *Coco*.

Hastings filled the soap cups of the dishwasher and pressed *Heavy Wash*. He flicked off the overhead lights and listened as the machine clicked and ratcheted to some starting point in a long sequence of instructions. He heard the sound of hot water filling the reservoir at the bottom of the machine and he watched the diode over the words, *Heating Water*, light up to inform him what task it was about. The perfect servomechanism. Now, if they would just invent a machine that could put him to sleep for eight hours. Something besides booze or a chemical sledge hammer.

The partnership, Shumate, Hastings & Brooks, had given him a year's sabbatical. It was just in time. In his sleep and before the shaving mirror, and at the breakfast table, he'd been composing hard-hitting, emotional, closing arguments against imaginary sociopath scum. He knew he was headed for the edge. Sleep had been fragile for a couple of years—the night increasingly fractured into two-hour alternations of restless tossing and deep slumber. Young, healthy Dr. Brett drew a bell curve with a base line marked in decades, on the waxy tissue paper of the examining table. His expensive white running shoes telegraphed his own secret agenda. Jog, he told Hastings. Get some exercise. Run. Row. Swim. He jabbed at the bell curve with his ballpoint pen. "You're right *here*," he said. "Men your age typically have a bit of trouble sleeping." Sure, Hastings told himself, and a man with an aluminum foot might have trouble jogging, too. "Sorry," young, healthy Doc Brett said, "but, let's wait a while before we get into sleeping pills. We don't really want to get into pills, do we? Not yet." He should know. A friend of Hastings at the clinic told him that Doc Brett was in court-ordered drug rehab. Dope, AIDS and alcohol—the flames of a hedonist *Gotterdammerung*—a worldwide phenomenon, taking with it a generation of the best and the brightest.

Hastings lit a last cigarette in the darkened room and rested his elbows on the windowsill over the kitchen sink, nesting his cheeks in the heel of his palms. The sharp angle of his nose glistened against the blackness of the pane. The dishwasher whumped into action with a start and then purred softly, swishing clean his three-day accumulation of dishes, pans, and cutlery. As he looked into the night, he saw a light turn on in the kitchen of the house next door. How times had changed. His family had lived in this once lily-white, upscale neighborhood since the turn of the century. Yuppie Blacks and Asians slowly moved in, creating a pleasant ethnic mix. Nothing menacing. The old First Church of Christ Scientist at Oak and Hillcrest sold to a Korean Baptist group. Down in The District the discreet *sushi* takeout shop or *dim sum* restaurant surfaced here and there. A whole section in the video store was now devoted to Asian art films. Hastings had watched several of them himself. *Raise the Red Lantern, Red Sorghum* and, *The Scent of Green Papayas*. They were excellent, and a far cry from the old phony Pearl S. Buck Hollywood tearjerkers. A few things like that suggested the new multiculturalism of his Doheny Park neighborhood.

Hastings continued to observe the kitchen next door. Except for the one six-foot replacement plant, a long row of mature fifteen-foot golden arborvitae sentries, and a driveway, separated the two houses. Marty Chang's BMW and Mae Chang's 3-year-old white Jaguar parked there. Blue plastic tarpaulins covered their two unused Kawasaki jet skis in the back of the house, next to last year's, gotta-have-one-of-those lap pools—also unused. Hastings had personally removed the dying tree that divided their properties, as if it were a bad tooth and inserted the six-foot replacement hedges. It was the only place from his house to the pink stucco Chang house next door that one could easily see anything at all of his neighbors. Lazily watching the Changs in their kitchen was a guilty pleasure that Hastings sometimes allowed himself. It was all very ordinary. Opening cupboards. Closing cupboards. Stir-frying. Fixing sandwiches. Filleting orange roughy. He knew he would look away if anything untoward happened. He was like that. He could trust himself to do that. He was not after all, a *voyeur*, he told himself. A *sicko*. He took a drag on his cigarette. Hell, he thought, Neighborhood Watch. And the Changs could certainly look into his kitchen if they cared to. Fair is fair.

Tonight, the old woman that Marty had referred to as Aunt Chang, entered the room and sat down at a large glass kitchen table. Everyone else appeared to be asleep or away. It was hard to tell. Marty and Mae traveled a lot. He assumed that the old woman couldn't sleep either. As he watched, Aunt Chang filled and then lit a beautiful ivory pipe using a Bic-style lighter. He had seen a pipe like hers somewhere before. Probably in Vietnam. Somnolently, she held it up to admire it and feel its warmth in her tiny, perfect hands. It looked to be a row of ivory elephants hooked together, tail-to-trunk, trunk-to-tail. The tobacco seemed to go into the head of the largest elephant farthest from her lips. The tusks, like two scimitars, protruded elegantly from this ivory head to create a graceful finial. Aunt Chang's forefinger nestled securely between them. Hastings wished that she would hold up the pipe again to admire it so that he could get a better bead on it. He wondered what it would be like to smoke an ivory elephant pipe.

Aunt Chang pulled on the carved pipe again, and took in only a bit of the smoke. He'd inhaled pipe smoke. It smarted corrosively. She couldn't be inhaling, he thought. She paid out pale wisps, and appeared to be contentedly murmuring to herself, moving her head from side to side as if conversing with someone he couldn't see. Hastings drew on his cigarette and exhaled a thin stream of smoke as well, pacing her. They were, really, somehow together. Fellow insomniacs. Practically sitting at the same table. Or, maybe strangers at the same picnic. Smoking. Daydreaming. Smoke dreams. Pleasuring in one another's silent companionship. Hastings wished that she were aware of him. Mrs. Chang was really quite beautiful, he thought. She had lovely high cheekbones and the finely articulated lips of the highborn. No one would ever mistake her for a peasant. Her hair was loosely cut in a trouble-free flip with bangs. An easy maintenance-do, he supposed. He guessed that she was somewhere between fifty and sixty years old. With Asians, one might never be sure. What did she think about this New World to which her nephew, Marty Chang, had brought her to live? What *must* she think of it? Marty was a partner in a West L.A. brokerage house. He was very successful. Very hip. A retirement portfolio specialist.

"Look, Mike—I'm not soliciting you—but I can get you earnings—you could live in Provence for five years—believe me—I've got a package."

Hastings laughed. "I'll think about it."

"You'll bring yourself back a French wife—French cooking—hey, you speak French?"

"*Oui.*"

"See," Marty said, "done deal."

Marty's wife, Mae, had her own textile design firm in the garment district with a staff of superb Mexican artisans. Neiman Marcus had picked up her bath towel sets for its fall catalog, and Bergdorf Goodman was sniffing the air for a line of Mae Chang scarves and throws. Mae Chang's fall colors married brilliant plum to a neon-jade, a combo that she had developed on her Apple computer. Sharp kids—both of them.

They'd known about his Aunt Chang for several years, Marty told him. He and his late mother tried everything to get her out of Saigon. When word arrived that she had been located and would be free to emigrate, Marty and Mae flew to San Francisco to greet her. It was a memorable moment that they accordingly preserved forever on a videotape that they showed repeatedly to the delighted old woman. Mrs. Chang's sister, Marty's mother, had died just a month before her release. Aunt Chang was devastated, of course, but confided that she barely remembered her sister. She had not, after all, seen her since just before the French turned *Indochine* over to the CIA.

When Mrs. Chang moved next door into the beautiful 14-room pink stucco house of her nephew Marty, she became heir to all of her sister's expensive clothing and personal effects. Her lovely bedroom suite with the finest down comforters and California queen-sized bed seemed luxurious beyond belief. The walls were covered in Mae's beautiful textiles, and the drapery and swags were one-of-a-kind designs executed by her Mexican staff-artisans in her MAE CHANG LTD. loft, in the LA garment district. Mrs. Chang was humbled by the luxuriance of the new setting into which she had stumbled.

"She spent the past 35 years sitting in a tiny Saigon doorway selling cigarettes and candy bars to American soldiers, Viet Cong, Russians and Aussies," Marty told him, "to say nothing of Frenchmen. Her husband and her sons—cousins I never met—uncles—were all killed in a whole damned series of wars from Dien Bien Phu and the Plain of Jars to the Tet Offensive. I mean, really, Mike, she's so bummed out by her personal losses—by the enormity of them—it's never quite hit her. She's in—you know—denial. She can hardly remember anything."

"So, how did you find her?" Hastings popped another beer for Marty.

"We finally tracked her down using the leads provided by my mom and when the confirming photographs, showing those two identifying moles on auntie's jaw-line arrived from the Red Cross investigators, we just knew we'd hit paydirt. Mae and I immediately sent the required papers and the bribery money—hey—the equivalent of twenty-one thou—*US*—to the proper corrupt officials and just began waiting for her exit visa to be issued. The wait took over three years."

"For that kind of money you still had to wait three years?"

"You bet. It was the stress that killed my mom. The suspense of meeting her baby sister after all that time. It was simply too much for her." He shook his head. "If only she could have hung on for another month. You remember?" Hastings did remember bits of it here and there. It was fuzzy. Frances, his wife, had been terminal then.

Marty's aunt, who had worked from dawn-to-dusk all her life suddenly had to face the fact that there was, quite simply, nothing for her to do. She was completely intimidated by the mysterious gadgetry in her nephew's kitchen. Microwave ovens. High-pressure latté makers, stainless steel ice-crushers, waffle irons, juicers. Electronically controlled ovens. Automatic bread makers. The quarter-mile of stainless steel countertops looked forlornly morgue-like. There was not a crumb, not a single drying, homemade noodle, not a steaming stockpot anywhere in that sterile laboratory of a kitchen. No chicken in a cage by the back door waited to have its neck wrung, scalded, and plucked for the evening meal. No pig carcass hung from the rose trellis, dripping blood into the yuppie loam. No sow squealed outside in slops and offal. Mae's Chang's proud, island stovetop with its glimmering black Ceram burners looked as if it had been borrowed from a bad dream, with no hint as to its source of heat. Everything gleamed surreally. Mrs. Chang peeked at Delilah, a large black woman, as she polished the appliances with a mysterious milky substance, from a bottle with golden stars whooshing across the label.

"Hello, there, honey—" Delilah addressed her in a warm contralto, "you like it here in Doheny Park? Your niece, she says this be *something different* for *you*. Yes, *ma'am*."

Mrs. Chang didn't understand a word she said. Gingerly, she set down a piece of toast that she was nibbling, as if she had been a child caught at the cookie jar, hoping to reclaim it later. Delilah whirled around, towering over the tiny Asian woman. "Oh, "she said," Miss Mae, she don't like any crumbs on her countertops. You through with this?" Mrs. Chang nodded politely and then disappeared from Delilah's line of vision, watching her in the reflection of a mirror, as she enshrouded the toast and crumbs into a crumpled paper towel and continued buffing the refrigerator to a high-gloss finish. The vaguely sweet chemical scent of the appliance cleaner left Mrs. Chang with a slightly queasy feeling. Petroleum distillates. Bleach. A kitchen should smell like herbs. Lemon grass. Cilantro, for instance. Oranges. Chicken broth. Charcoal smoke. Shredded cocoanut. This kitchen of Marty and Mae repelled her. Every vestige of food was stored forbiddingly behind cabinet doors—doors with hidden magnetic catches, doors with no pull handles, inviolable, as if warning her not to examine the contents—not to inspect.

.. ..

Just as Hastings pulled into his driveway, he glanced up Marty's adjoining drive. There was Mrs. Chang, like a day laborer on a lunch break, sitting in the sun upon an upended blue plastic milk crate. She was smoking a cigarette. Hastings waved at her and lightly touched the horn of his Honda Prelude. Mrs. Chang returned a small wave and frugally pinched out her cigarette. She rose and slipped through the arborvitae like a tiny foraging bird and into his driveway, handing him a small package from the UPS driver who had, in his absence, given it over to her care. He thanked Mrs. Chang and stepped from his car. Mrs. Chang made a small polite bow and it was then that she noticed, for the first time, that Hastings had a prosthetic device for his left foot. He tucked some packages from the front seat under his arm and popped the trunk to retrieve some groceries. Mrs. Chang stepped quickly back to the trunk and removed a couple of the heavy plastic bags. Hastings remonstrated with her, but she carried them up the stairs to the back door without acknowledging him.

"Well," he said, "*many* thanks. I could have managed. You really didn't have to trouble yourself." Mrs. Chang smiled affably and gave another, old-world courteous bow. Hastings slipped the key into the lock and opened the door. She said something in Chinese. Hastings could only guess at what it was. He watched her as she hefted the groceries the rest of the way into the kitchen, passing through the back porch. He found himself somewhat embarrassed.

"Oh, well, thank you, again—very *much*, Mrs. Chang." He smiled at her. "You really didn't have to do that." He thought to offer her a soft drink, which she declined.

As she looked around, she noticed a very different environment from the sterility of the Chang house. A half-consumed cherry pie, in a clear plastic container, sat on the draining board and wine bottles and diet drink cans were stacked conveniently on countertops. Boxes of crackers and cans of cat food perched conveniently about. Mrs. Chang liked the feel of it at once. Her glance took in the kitchen table, with its messy scattering of spice jars designed to perk up almost any bachelor dish from Denver omelets to canned hash. A loaf of raisin bread sat comfortably near the toaster, and an uncovered tub of whipped butter, with crumbs still in it, bore silent witness to Hastings' eating habits. Quickly he grabbed a kitchen towel and flicked some particles off the oak table, knocking a deck of Bicycle playing cards to the floor.

.. ..

Hastings had no idea what it was he might have done that day, but it appeared that he had struck a sympathetic chord deep within Mrs. Chang. Afterward, he frequently arrived home to find that she was either raking up the odd leaf fall in his yard or watering his lawn with a hand sprinkler. When his jacaranda tree began its seasonal rain of pale violet blossoms, she swept them up so that the wheels of his Honda did not crush them and stain the brick driveway. She took it upon herself to dead-head the roses and hibiscus, carrying the defunct blossoms back to her own house and mysteriously tossing them out in Marty's trash. Always, she smiled and bowed sweetly. Hastings was at a loss to account for her attention and he was concerned that the Changs didn't seem to know about it. Whenever she heard their automobiles enter their driveway, she quickly slipped back home through the hedge and puttered about Marty's yard as if she had been there all day. Hastings sensed that she did not wish to be seen working at so-called menial tasks at his house. Marty had gardeners, pool service, and Delilah, his four-day-a-week maid.

After a time, Hastings was disappointed to come home and not see Mrs. Chang performing maintenance about his place. She seemed to enjoy sweeping his wide porch; beating the dust out of the cushions from the Adirondack chairs with a bamboo rake; trimming the dead asparagus ferns from the hanging pots; polishing the brass on the front door, or picking off lame fuschia blossoms.

The one time he went over to chat with Marty Chang about what he conceived as, The Problem, Mrs. Chang was in the driveway standing just behind Marty. With the sixth sense of a guilty child, she pretty much knew why Hastings was there. She motioned, by pinching her lips together, for him not to say anything to Marty and Hastings quickly changed the subject.

"Well," Marty told him, "Aunt Chang does speak Mandarin. But, Jesus, I can hardly understand her. You know," he said, "there are *four-hundred* ways to pronounce the letter 'A'."

"You mean you can't *talk* to her?" Hastings asked.

"Sure, but not so well. Mae does it much better than I do. The thing is, they all speak Mandarin or Cantonese or whatever over there, right? Even French. But all those crazy accents. It's like—well—here, everybody speaks, English, okay? But look how tough it is to understand Scottish and Irish when they talk—*hell*—even people from Alabama and Georgia. Know what I'm saying? But it's *much, much* more complicated than that—*trust* me." His pleasant Chinese face crinkled humorously.

"Say, Marty," Hastings asked impulsively, "do you think Aunt Chang might like to go to the opera with me? Could you ask her?"

"Hey—I'll try," he laughed. "Ever hear Pidgin English? Wanna hear some Pidgin Mandarin?"

Marty turned around where Mrs. Chang had been standing quietly listening to the two men. Her lovely black birdlike eyes seemed to understand that Hastings had not betrayed her. Animatedly she brushed off imaginary burrs from the arborvitae that she pretended had stuck to her sweater. Marty spoke to her in Mandarin, slowly enunciating Hastings' request. It took a few seconds for it to sink in. Slowly she nodded, as if trying to imagine any possible negative impact. She looked at Marty and nodded.

"Unbelievable," Marty intoned, "—she says, '*Sure*'".

"It's *Turandot*," Hastings told him. "Puccini. The opera. Story's sorta Chinese, right? Sorta sung in Italian, by an American, German and Italian cast. I don't speak Italian. Mrs. Chang doesn't speak Italian. What the hell—we'll both be lost. Level playing field. How about you and Mae? I'll get tickets for the four of us."

"Oh, puhleeese," Marty joked, "not me. I'm still doing the BeeGees. Thanks. Look, Mike, you don't really have to do this, you know. I don't even know how the hell you can listen to that crap. I really don't." Chang's cell phone rang. He reached inside his pocket and snapped it open. "*Please*, excuse me," he apologized with an ironic smile, "cyberspace calling." He turned his back. Mae Chang came out of the house at the end of the conversation nibbling a crescent of cantaloupe. "I'm with Marty," she said. "I could hear you guys. You sure you want to do this?"

"Oh, absolutely," Hastings said." Mae said something in Chinese to Aunt Chang and she smiled dazzlingly at Hastings. He bowed to the older woman in a theatrical, courtly manner. "I'll take care of everything," he said. "Oh," he added, "It's all right to call her Mrs. Chang—not use her married name? It's the same as your last name."

"Oh, sure," Mae explained. In China—the Far East—the father's name goes to the son and the father's surname is retained by the daughter after marriage—so—sure she is Aunt Chang to us. No problema."

.. ..

Hastings looked spiffed up in his tailored dark suit, gray dress shirt and mauve Paisley tie. Mrs. Chang was attired in a beautiful brocade evening dress, which must have belonged to her late sister. The little slit up the side, the classic Mandarin collar with the frog clasp, and the jade dyed-to-match peau-de-soie high-heeled shoes had their intended effect. She fingered her clutch purse and matinee-length pearls with aplomb. No one would have known that, earlier in the day, they had been raking yard debris into large trash cans. With a seasoned sweep of appraisal, Mrs. Chang assessed the posh foyer of the Dorothy Chandler Pavilion, with its glorious grand staircase, glittering chandeliers and carpeted elegance. It was clear she had never seen anything quite like it. Hastings was glad he had not yet turned in his Founder's Circle season tickets after Frances' death. They stood in front of a vendor.

"Would you like a production program, Mrs. Chang?" She was bewildered. They were fifteen dollars. He bought two and he handed her one of them. They looked at the broad staircase. "Let's take the elevator," he decided, guiding Mrs. Chang by the elbow.

Hastings had no idea whether or not Mrs. Chang was going to be bored to tears by all of the loud singing and the unfamiliar sounds of the Western orchestra. There would be no bongs, gamelans—no pentatonic scale, Chinese flutes—no exotic cymbals. During the performance, he rapidly scanned the super-titles projected over the proscenium arch and, whenever he could, he'd lean towards Mrs. Chang and try to convey certain plot nuances. Mrs. Chang was unfailingly polite about these intrusions, nodding courteously in a sideways manner, but her eyes were riveted to the stage. At one point in the plot, the Unknown Prince Calaf challenges Turandot to guess his name before dawn: *Il mio nome non sai! Dimmi il mio nome prima dell'albe—*.

Hastings leaned over to Mrs. Chang and crossed his neck in a direful manner with his forefinger, pointing to the two shrieking principals in the footlights below them. Mrs. Chang nodded politely and then solemnly crossed her own throat with her forefinger. When the tenor sang the shows-stopping aria, *Nessun Dorma—None Shall Sleep*, ending with the fateful, '*Vincero! Vincero!—I shall conquer!*—Hastings looked over at his companion. Mrs. Chang had clasped together both hands and placed them under her chin, pulling her shoulders forward as if offering a prayer for the stressed-out lovers. Clearly she had intuited the plot basics with no help from him. At the conclusion of the aria, the audience, many of whom stood up, erupted in vociferous and prolonged applause. Mrs. Chang moved her tiny hands over her heart and looked at Hastings with moistened eyes. She was deeply moved by the operatic experience. After the performance, Hastings again took her elbow and guided her down the elegant staircase. The wait for the elevators would have been too much. She was floating.

Hastings said to her, "You *like*?"

Mrs. Chang gave her wholehearted assent. "Like, *like*," she answered. And then, she asked him, "*You* like?"

"Yes, Mrs. Chang, I like too."

About halfway down the staircase, Hastings caught the heel of his prosthetic shoe on the edge of the carpeted riser. He quickly reached for the banister and he felt Mrs. Chang stiffen the muscles of her arm supportively and reach over to steady him. The crowd pushed past them, eager to get to the underground garages. Hastings recovered in a split second. He could never have imagined when he was stalking black-pajama clad Viet Cong in the jungles of Southeast Asia that he'd one day be escorting a Vietnamese woman to the opera at the Dorothy Chandler Pavilion. He could still feel the touch of her tiny, helping hand upon his arm. It was a thrill he had not felt in a long time.

After the opera, Hastings took Mrs. Chang to a four-star Chinese restaurant. She tasted a bit of this and a bit of that, sampling, expressing only qualified approval. Suddenly, she said to Hastings, "I cook. I cook." She pointed to him. "I cook for you."

.. ..

Hastings could not wait to get downstairs at first light. He had called Marty for permission to take Mrs. Chang with him to shop in the real working class Chinatown up on north Broadway Street. The thousands of L.A. Chinese had mercantile, import, and manufacturing businesses up there. They did not frequent the tourist traps in the gold-and-red lacquered nightmare called 'Chinatown'. Many Chinese shops up there sold a bit of this and a bit of that. Specialty noodle shops. Tinned foods. Exotic meats. Fresh rabbit and chickens. Exotic vegetables. There were very few Caucasians to be seen strolling along the dozen blocks that comprised that other Chinatown where very little English was spoken. The storefronts were plain, even humdrum. Stucco buildings harked back to the Thirties.

"Auntie says, sure, she'll go with you. She was born to shop, you know. No problem—if you want to. Look," Marty said, "Mae and I are flying to Scottsdale for a seminar this weekend. Maybe you could keep an eye on her in case anything horrible happens. You going to be home? I mean—like I don't know what. We'll call her, you know, but she won't answer the telephone—won't even try."

"Of course," Hastings replied. "So, what could happen, a possum could break into your pool house?"

"No," Marty riposted, "she could log on to my computer and *erase my hard drive.*"

"Does she have any friends here?"

"Who, the possum?" Marty made a face. "Here's a dirty little ethnic secret for you, Mike. Stateside Chinese women are very arrogant—very class conscious. Auntie Chang feels them looking right through her. They won't include her. I took her to the cultural center. She's from Vietnam. Lower caste or something. Ask Mae. She tried playing *mah jongg* with them—but they made even her feel inferior and she was *born* here."

"But, your Aunt Chang? Inferior?"

"Yeah—like a war orphan. Know what I mean?"

"I guess, so. Sure, hey, I'll keep an eye out for her—so be careful flying."

"Great," Marty said, "I just got my wings dry-cleaned—I'm all set."

.. ..

With the help of Mrs. Chang, Hastings loaded up on everything they would need to prepare a Chinese dinner. Hastings hefted the balance of his new food chopper over the nylon cutting board. It felt excellent. A beautiful ideogram was incised into the handle. Undoubtedly it meant luck. Luck or happiness. Most stand-alone Chinese ideograms on key-chains or money clips he would ever ask about always meant luck or happiness. He ran his thumb lightly over the edge of the blade. It was razor sharp. Mrs. Chang had already tucked his kitchen towel around her waist and had distributed all of her special groceries over the few spaces left on Hastings' crowded kitchen draining boards. He showed her the Chinese lettering in the handle of the chopper. She looked at it and quickly translated for him by rocking a baby in her arms. No figuring the Chinese, he thought. She handed him the porcelain Chinese kitchen god and motioned for him to hang it up on a hook. While he did that, she prepped the wok and the rice steamer, washing them in molten soap and water and then rubbing them with oil.

Mrs. Chang moved with lightning speed and efficiency. She seemed very happy as she began to respond to the almost forgotten rhythms of food preparation in this new, unfamiliar world of America. She examined the tea kettle, the slotted spoon the set of wooden spoons, the universal cooking implements, and began to feel more at home in Hastings' kitchen. She looked playfully at Hastings and made as if to play a violin.

"Violin?" he asked her. She shook her head and continued to chop up some Savoy cabbage. Hastings remembered his new phrase book. Maybe she meant music. He found something in the index. "*Zhong-guo gu-dian yin-yue*?" According to the book, it meant 'classical Chinese music'.

Mrs. Chang stopped her chopping and looked at him as if he were crazy. Hastings held the book before her eyes, but she could not read the fine print. He tried again this time, reading a different phrase very slowly from the phrase book, and trying to sound Chinese, he said, "'*Qing yin-yue?*'". Mrs. Chang listened carefully, scraping her Savoy cabbage into a large pile before her. She motioned with the chopper for him to say it again. Hastings repeated, "'*Qing yin-yue, qing yin-yue*'—*light music.*" It really delighted him to watch the old woman try to read his lips. After the third try, her face broke into a large smile. She pronounced the words properly for Hastings and made him repeat several times after her the correct inflection—*qing yin-yue*. "Ah," he said, "you want to hear some music?"

Hastings went into the den and popped a CD into the player and pressed a rocker switch to activate the kitchen speaker. He walked back into the kitchen in time to see Mrs. Chang's hips move ever so slightly to the rhythm of the music he had selected. He looked through his phrase book and ran across the phrase: *Ni-xiang tiao-wu ma*? Mrs. Chang looked at him again as if to say, *whaaaaaaaaaaaa*? He repeated the question and did a little slow shuffle on the kitchen floor, "Would you like to dance? *Ni-xiang tiao-wu ma*?"

Mrs. Chang laughed out loud and said to him, "*Get down and boogie, Babe.*" She had heard the phrase in Saigon, during the American tenure of her city. Nonsense syllables as far as she was concerned, but the phrase never failed to get a laugh at her cigarette stand. She twirled the deadly chopper over her head with bit of flair.

Hastings couldn't believe his ears. "Get down and boogie, Babe? Mrs. Chang, you are *something* else. So, you want to dance? *Ni-xiang tiao-wu ma*?"

"Sorry, GI," she said, turning back to her food preparation, "*Xie-xie dan wo hen mang.*"

Hastings dug into the index of his phrase book, repeating her phrase over-and-over to himself as he looked up its components. *Xie-xie*—thank you—*dan wo hen mang*—I am busy. "Mrs. Chang," he told her, "you *are* something else."

Mrs. Chang looked at Hastings and repeated, "Get down and boogie, Babe," and she laughed out loud. She had prepared a soft dough of rice flour in a bowl and demonstrated how she wanted them rolled into 24 balls. She held up her fingers. Twenty-four.

"Yes, ma'am, Miz Chang."

After Hastings rolled 24 perfect little pastry balls, Mrs. Chang gave him a thumbs up and slid a small bowl of spiced and diced-up pork over to him. She showed him how to make a depression in the rice flour ball with his finger, pushing in a bit of the pork and a bit of chopped scallion and then seal it with a pinch. She instructed Hastings to drop the balls into salted boiling water after he finished each ball and boil for five minutes. "*Wu fen zhong,*" she told him, holding up five fingers. She went back to her cutting board.

Hastings reached for his kitchen timer and set it for five minutes, repeating, "*Wu fen zhong—wu fen zhong.*"

At the end of five minutes Mrs. Chang drew a pint of cold water from the tap and told Hastings to put it in the boiling water. She watched as the boiling subsided. "Good," she said, "more—*duo xie*—more—*wu fen zhong.*"

Hastings furrowed his brow. "*Wu fen zhong—wu fen zhong—*." His face lit up at the remembered words. "Five minutes more—*wu fen zhong.* Got it. Okay, so five minutes more after the second boil?"

Mrs. Chang looked and said, "Hello. Get down and *boogie*, Babe."

Hastings gently observed the simmering pastry balls and noted how a light and splendidly scented oil escaped from them creating a nice sheen on top of the broth. He moved his 24 doughy spheres about with the slotted spoon. "You know, Mrs. Chang—I have a funny feeling that there is more to you than meets the eye."

"Meet the eye," she parodied.

Mrs. Chang had peeled a dozen large prawns and was now slicing carrots on the bias. Another dish filled with crushed ice, held scallions feathered at one end to be used as garnish. She smiled at Hastings' remark, but did not indicate if she understood. "You want *boogie?*" she asked rhetorically. She slipped a pie pan into the oven with some almonds. Hastings had a conventional oven, with handles she could understand, not like Mae Chang's mysterious oven with its pressure-sensitive operating pads that she could never figure. Bravely, she stuck her hand inside the oven to test its temperature.

"Mmmmmm," Hastings said, "toasted almonds."

A new song filled the kitchen. It was Roy Orbison singing *Pretty Woman.* Its sly and seductive rhythm broke the monotony of the bland, new-Age wallpaper tangos and boleros Hastings had at first selected. To his surprise, Mrs. Chang began to hum along with the music as if he were not there. *"Pretty woman—comin' down the street—pretty woman—one I'd like to meet—."* He was delighted. She looked into his pot when the timer rang and took the slotted spoon away from him, lifting up several of the pastry balls to examine them. "Okay, I think, hello," she said.

"They look *hello* to me, too," Hastings said, now humming *Pretty Woman* himself. He brought a teaspoonful of the broth up to his lips and slurped the delicious concoction. Mrs. Chang assembled the wok on the stove and indicated for Hastings to set the kitchen table. He pointed to the dining room. She shook her head, wanting to eat in the smaller, homier room with all its concentration of smells, and with the look and feel of life, much as it was in the tiny living spaces in Vietnam. Later, when the kitchen telephone rang, it startled both Hastings and Mrs. Chang. He had just poured his guest a small glass of plum wine and passed her a sliver of supermarket cheesecake.

Hastings recognized the voice. "Ah, Marty," he said. He looked at Mrs. Chang. She motioned that she did not want to talk to her nephew. "No," Hastings continued, "I saw her earlier today—she seemed fine."

"I call her and call her," Marty said. "No dice. She won't answer the telephone."

"If you want to tell her something, let me know and I'll relay it to her."

"That's great," Marty said. "Let her know that Mae and I are going to take another day. It's silly to come all this way and just rush right back home. Maybe we'll go to the Grand Canyon or over to the ice caves—you know—so tell her, for sure, Monday night. She can have frozen dinners. Mae showed her how to heat them up in the micro. No problem."

Mrs. Chang looked at Hastings and tried to guess what was transpiring.

"No problem, Marty, I'll tell her. Maybe I could take her to dinner—you wouldn't mind?"

"You would *do* that? You're a champ. You know Mike, you don't have ask."

"She's a sweetheart. Maybe a movie."

Marty was delighted. After Hastings hung up, he winked at Mrs. Chang and topped off her plum wine. Using elaborate semiotics, and his wristwatch with its calendar face, he managed to convey that Marty and Mae would be delayed for another day.

Hastings looked at the clock. They'd been cooking for a couple of hours and there was plenty of food left over. He filled two Tupperware containers with pot stickers and stir-fry for Mrs. Chang. While the kitchen was never among his major concerns, they did manage to make it appear a bit more orderly. Containers were still stacked helter-skelter but they were all decently closed. Perishables were tucked away into the refrigerator and an end of the oak kitchen table was cleared off. The deck of Bicycle cards beckoned enticingly. Despite the language barrier, Hastings and Mrs. Chang managed to communicate quite well. Hastings was proud of himself and of her.

"Look," he said to her, "turnabout is fair play—why don't we see if there is a Chinese opera in town." Mrs. Chang smiled sweetly and perplexedly as she watched Hastings flip through the entertainment pages of the LA

Times. A Chinese opera was appearing at the old Chinatown. A Taiwanese troupe. There was a bit of Chinese calligraphy in the ad. He turned it around to show Mrs. Chang.

"Do you want to see this, Mrs. Chang?" he asked her. "Chinese opera, yes?"

Her face brightened perceptibly. "Hello—yes," she said, crinching her shoulders in anticipation of the possibility.

"You're sure?"

"Hello," she said.

"Okay," Hastings said, "it's only seven o'clock."

"Seven o'clock."

"That's right."

"We have plenty of time."

"Plenty," she parroted.

"Right—take your food home and get a jacket."

"Jacket?"

Hastings pointed to a sweater he had tossed over a chair.

Mrs. Chang nodded. "Jacket. *Zippo*."

"Right." He pointed to his wristwatch. He guessed *Zippo* was a word from her past in Saigon. "Come back at 7:15—ready Freddy. Okay?"

"Right. 7:15. Freddy."

"Right, *my way or the highway*. And," he added, "get your pipe with the elephants." He limned puffing on a pipe.

"Right, pipe." She copied him amusingly with her animated expression. "My way—highway."

Hastings pushed back his chair. "You want to *boogie*, Baby?" He opened the back door for Mrs. Chang.

"*Xie-xie*," she laughed and disappeared through the arborvitae toward the back door of her house. "*Boogie*."

Hastings snuffed out the candles in the Mexican folk art candlesticks that he and Frances had picked up in Oaxaca, so many years before. Curlicues of smoke spiraled away toward the dining room. The candlesticks looked very charming on the oak table. Very nice indeed. Mrs. Chang had delicately caressed the three little clay doves on their base with the back of her hand and wistfully communicated to Hastings that they were similar to the folk art of Vietnam and Laos.

.. ..

Whatever Hastings might have thought Chinese opera was, he was not prepared for the reality of it. After skeptically sizing up him and Mrs. Chang, an old woman in the box office sold him two tickets. He had heard on PBS that traditional Chinese opera was a dying cultural phenom. Chinese youth were only interested in heavy metal and rap. There would be no one to pass their ancient cultural legacy to. So, it was their duty to attend.

Hastings could not make heads or tails of the plot. As near as he could tell, the characters seemed to be rigid stereotypes that the audience recognized on sight, based upon their costumes. *Lao Sheng*, was an ancient gentleman with a long beard and a handsome baritone voice. *Xiao Sheng* was a young lover or a student—Hastings was not sure. *Wu Sheng* was a soldier, with whom Mrs. Chang indicated much familiarity. He was in many operas, she indicated to him. Then, there was *Qing Yi*, or Blue Dress, whose role as concubine, mistress, or obedient, faithful and virtuous wife Hastings found very confusing, let alone her ghastly falsetto voice to which he had trouble adapting. Some of the most elegant costumes were worn by *Hua Dan*, or Flower. Other characters seemed to be valiant warriors, dishonest government ministers, ruthless bandits, or loyal servants, not to mention deities and supernatural beings.

Hastings read a bad photocopy of the plot that the ticket-taker handed him. It was rendered in the kind of frustrating English found in the maintenance manuals of expensive electronic equipment from Taiwan. He knew that he would never understand all of the actors' gestures, let alone the songs and the words, but the rhythm; the colors; the mime, the music and virtuoso acrobatics captured his imagination. What the hell, he decided—if Mrs. Chang could sit through *Turandot*, he could certainly make a stab at Chinese opera. Hastings looked at his tiny companion. She leaned forward in her seat, her fingers stroking her chin and repositioning her glasses. She was transfixed and entranced. He would ask her later, how long it had been since she had seen an opera, and he would learn that it had been more than three decades.

"You like?" he asked her.

"Yes," Mrs. Chang nodded, "I like."

... .

Next day, Hastings knocked on the back door of Marty's house. It was just before lunch. Mrs. Chang came to the door, looking refreshed and serenely exquisite, smiling affably.

"Mrs. Chang. You want to go for a ride?" Going for a ride was something one did in Southern California. He made as if he were steering his Honda. "We'll have some lunch somewhere?" Mrs. Chang looked concerned. With her tiny hands, she sculpted a large sphere in the shape of a pumpkin. Hastings knew she was referring to the winter melon they had purchased in Chinatown. They had agreed after the Chinese opera the previous evening, that this was the day they would prepare the winter melon. On the Olympic Games scale, the degree of difficulty was at least a six and besides, it would take some time. Hastings was looking forward to it. "We won't be long," he told her, "—a couple of hours. We can start the melon at—what?—Two o'clock?" He pointed to his wristwatch.

Mrs. Chang rolled her eyes and pointed to the cement block wall that separated them from their rear neighbors. A large rat-like creature ambled along the top of the wall and disappeared into an avocado tree. She shuddered and emitted a thoroughly Americanized, "*Yuuuuck!*"

"I know," Hastings said, "it looks like a wharf rat—but it's a possum. It's okay. You want to get a *sweater?*"

"*Xie xie*—*sweater*—ready Freddy. No sweat GI. *Zippo.*" She disappeared into the house and got a jacket, re-emerging with her house key on a vinyl coil about her wrist, as if she were a latch-key child going to school for the day.

"Let's hit it," Hastings told her. "My way or—"

"—*highway*—." Mrs. Chang warbled, completing his sentence.

Hastings looked properly stunned at the sharp ascent of her learning curve. He turned on the radio and retracted the sunroof of the Honda. In fifteen minutes, they were parked in a turnout at the top of the Santa Monica Mountains, on Mulholland drive. They got out of the car and looked out over the city whose immensity always humbled him. He turned to watch Mrs. Chang.

"It boggles the mind, doesn't it? I mean, the water, the electricity, the roads—*all* of it. The *infrastructure?* Amazing."

Mrs. Chang looked out at the panorama with her arms outstretched and nodded with a pantomimic flair, "*Xie, xie, amazing*—hello." She had no idea what he was musing about.

Hastings regarded her with a fresh eye. This lovely creature, far from her distant homeland had filled him with a warmth and desire he had not felt in a long time. He felt comfortable. Was she just this cuddly orphan whom he wanted so much to please? An adult version of the adorable foreign adoptees relentlessly peddled on television? Twenty bucks a month? What mysteries did her innocent exoticism conceal? He suddenly wanted to hug her as if she were a lost kitten. He wasn't really sure what his feelings were but she made him happy, and he did not want to ruin everything by over-analysis. He wondered how old she was, after all. He was 48. Could she be 55? 65? Discreetly, he slipped his phrase book out of his pocket and thumbed the index looking for the word—*love*. There was no such word between *loud* and *low*.

Mrs. Chang touched his arm and pointed to his phrase book. "What?"

"I was looking for *airport*, Mrs. Chang," he lied. He pointed in the distance to LAX. Even from Mulholland Drive, they could clearly see a jumbo jet in a landing pattern. "Airport," he repeated. He wondered if the Chinese had a word for love. Or was it just a Western notion? *When Knighthood Was In Flower*, and all that. He remembered the recent Chinese film, *Raise the Red Lantern*. There wasn't a whole lot of Western-style love in it that he could remember.

Mrs. Chang looked at the 747. "*Fei-ji-chang*," she said. She made an airplane with her hand and pointed to it. "*Fei-ji*," she said and held up one finger. "One airplane." She landed her finger-airplane on the hood of the Honda with exquisite delicacy of movement. Hastings thought of the Thai finger puppeteers. "*Fei-ji-chang*."

"Airport," Hastings observed.

She nodded. "Airport—*fei-ji-chang*."

The attractive scent of commingled eucalyptus and orange blossoms from backyard orchards bore down upon them from a soft breeze. Intense and fruity. Hastings walked over to a nearby eucalyptus tree and picked a handful of the dagger-shaped leaves. He returned to Mrs. Chang, crushing them in his palm. She breathed deeply of them, oooohing at the unexpected astringency and powerful medicinal scent. She took one of the leaves and put it into a pocket of her sweater. Hastings tossed the rest of them into the light breeze and they watched them as they were borne over the edge of the lookout.

A few minutes later, Hastings drove her along the Santa Monica Freeway and down toward Venice beach to observe the daily sideshow of eccentrics. He parked Mrs. Chang on a bench, while he stepped inside a booth to get them each a cup of creamy clam chowder. When he returned, a huge black man with 'in line' skates, a bongo and bulging muscles was singing a rap song to the bewildered woman. She nodded along with him and pretended to keep time with tentative, clapping hands. Hastings slid next to her and handed her a cup of chowder. She seemed very glad to see him and went daintily at it with a white plastic spoon. Hastings slipped the singer a dollar and he departed.

"Quite a place? What do you think?" Hastings commented.

Getting the drift, Mrs. Chang said, "*Zippo!*"

All around them, a rainbow circus of bizarre street performers, Black, Asian, White, Mexican and Indian, lifted weights, sang, argued, played basketball, and nearly killed each other with their colliding bikes, skateboards and in-line-skates. It was a wonder for her to behold.

"We'll come back again, from time-to-time, if you want to," Hastings told her. "We'll go to the zoo? Maybe Disneyland? What do you think?"

The old woman nodded affirmatively to each of his tantalizing, but puzzling, invitations.

.. ..

Back in the kitchen, Mrs. Chang handed the winter melon to Hastings and made him sit down at the oak table. She handed him a sharp paring knife and reached for his ever-present phrase book with its handy-dandy index. She found what she was looking for and pointed to it with the tip of the knife, indicating that he should do some carving into the melon.

"Carve?" he asked her. "Okay, so let me see what it is." He took the book from her. "*Luck*? You want me to carve *luck* into the melon? I'll need lots of that."

She nodded. "*Yun-qi.*"

"Okay—luck it is. *Yun-qi.* I'll need good luck to make my carving look anything like those." The two ideograms were beautiful but complicated. Mrs. Chang put her thumb and forefinger a tiny slit apart. "Not deep?" He held up his own thumb and forefinger and looked at her through the tiny gap. "Okay." He grabbed a pencil from a cup on the table and began to lay out the ideograms on the melon. Mrs. Chang went back to her chopping block and began to cut up a fryer chicken into small pieces, and then a fresh pork hock, and some ham, starting them on the stove in a stockpot. She soaked dried mushrooms and tangerine peel in warm water to use later.

She stepped over to Hastings and watched him carve 'Good Luck' in Chinese into the melon. "No," she said. She borrowed his knife and made a correction."

"Okay, I see," he said with a smile. "Picky—picky. Thanks."

"*Zippo*." She motioned to the chicken on the stove and held up one finger and made a circle.

"One hour? Simmer? Boil?"

"Yah."

Hastings was just about finished. "One hour? We could play cards?" He pointed the deck of Bicycle cards. The kitchen was warming up and the pleasant scent of the simmering stockpot filled the room. "Okay." He handed the melon to Mrs. Chang. "Okay?"

She touched the letters and sounded out "*Yun-qi*. Good." She took the melon over to the counter and carefully sliced off the top, removing the seeds and stringy portions. She drained the mushrooms and tangerine peel and sliced them very thin. She placed them inside the hollow winter melon along with ginger, lotus seeds, bamboo shoots and water chestnuts. She skimmed the froth off the simmering chicken, delicately discarding it into the upturned lid of the pot that she transferred to the sink. "Okay," she said. "*Okay*."

Hastings had set up several CD's. Some nice Mahler. Richard Strauss waltzes from *Der Rosenkavalier*. A new *Wesendonk* song cycle of Wagner's that had attracted his attention. Some ravishing love songs from the *Merry Widow*. He set them up in alternation. Something heavy—something light. *La Boheme* for orchestra would be good. He had planned to look up from their card game from time-to-time and look right at Mrs. Chang and say—"Listen to *this*—right *here*—". They paused momentarily in their game and she would cock her head, nod wistfully at the beautiful melodies, just as she thought she would—and then go on to win the card game from him. She rose from time-to-time and removed more froth from the simmering pot of chicken with her slotted spoon and return to her seat, pick up her cards again, and smile at him, and tell him—just a half hour more.

"Did you bring your pipe?" he asked her. He looked in his phrase book. "*Yan dou? Yan dou?*"

"*Yah*." Mrs. Chang moved quickly to a cloth carryall and removed her beloved pipe.

Hastings played a hunch. "Was that your husband's pipe?" He tapped her ring finger and pointed to it. Mrs. Chang made a quick nod and looked briefly away from him. "It's very beautiful—darkening like that from the nicotine. Do you ever smoke it?" The question was disingenuous. He knew the answer.

Looking a bit impish again, Mrs. Chang said, "*Shi.*"

Hastings extracted a container of Captain Black pipe tobacco and offered her some. She filled her pipe with it and he did the same. They each lit up and in moments the tantalizing scent of vanilla filled the room. "Captain Black," Hastings said. Maybe it wasn't the best tobacco he told her bewildered face, but he liked the smell of it.

Mrs. Chang repeated the name of it back to him and saluted with her fingertips at her brow. "Captain, sir."

"Now where did you learn, 'sir?'" Hastings dealt some cards for Twenty-One and quickly taught Mrs. Chang how to play. In no time, she was whipping him and he didn't mind. The hour passed rapidly, with Mrs. Chang repeatedly checking the simmering broth, adding a bit of water and doing a bit of tasting. She seemed perfectly at home in his kitchen, Hastings felt—happy as a clam. She puffed silently on her pipe and slammed down cards with lightning speed with a *yah* here and a *yah* there, sweeping cards off the table with the skill of a Reno croupier. The piles of wagered toothpicks moved back and forth between them and the music bathed them in its romantic and sentimental aura of sound.

Checking her watch, Mrs. Chang rose and seasoned the broth with sherry, sugar, salt and white pepper, checking it for correction. "Uhmmmm," she said. "*It good—hao!*" She called Hastings over for a sip. The scent of the steamy broth was way over the top.

"Wow—*Zippo* for sure . . ."

"'Kay," Mrs. Chang said. She set the winter melon into a sturdy bowl and placed the bowl on a dishtowel and then lowered the dish into a large canning kettle with a steamer rack in the bottom. "Okay." She instructed Hastings to pour the hot seasoned chicken broth carefully into the hollow of the winter melon, adding pieces of diced chicken breast that had earlier been set aside. She handed him the top of the melon and pointed inside. Hastings set the melon-top back onto the melon. She then added water to the kettle just to the bottom of the rack where it quickly started to boil and emit steam. "Okay," Mrs. Chang said. She put a tight lid on the kettle. She wiped her hands on a dishtowel and turned to shake Hastings' hands.

"Good job," he said.

"Okay." Mrs. Chang held up two fingers.

"Two hours? Two *hours*?" He looked at his watch. That'll be eight o'clock?

Mrs. Chang made to chop her hand in half. "Two and a half hours? You're kidding?"

She made one last check of the pot, checking for a good head of steam and sat down and fired up her pipe. Hastings looked at the pixie-ish woman. He had no doubt that she was enjoying herself. She reached into her sweater pocket and withdrew the crushed eucalyptus leaf, lifting it to her nose. "Mmmmmm, good," she said. Then, in a very kindly way, she pointed to his wedding band, as if to inquire about his status.

Hastings flipped through his phrase book. There was no word for *death*. Well, no point in ruining a nice vacation phrase book. His book was, after all, for happy tourists, and not for terminal patients in a hospice somewhere. He came upon the word, *diabetic*. That seemed close enough to leukemia. "*Tang-niao-bing*," he said and then he turned the book around so that she could read it. She nodded. Hastings gently drew his forefinger across his throat moving his head slowly from side to side. If Frances were watching, given the circumstances, he thought she just might give her approval to this gentle charade, which depicted her demise. Mrs. Chang reached out and patted his left hand with empathy and understanding. She looked up the word, *photograph*, and turned the book back around, tapping it with her forefinger. The lid of the steaming winter melon kettle rattled merrily. Hastings rose and went into the den, returning with a portrait of his family. He handed it to Mrs. Chang.

"Ahhh," she smiled. Frances looked quite lovely standing with him and his two daughters against a wall of ivy. Four pairs of blue eyes—four blonde heads. It was one of the few photographs she had been happy with. It had been posed in a photo-shoot session on the UCLA campus. The Romanesque archways of Royce Hall vaulted protectively over them like cupped hands—for that brief day at least. The protection had not lasted all that long. Frances died in early autumn. Mrs. Chang placed a graceful palm under her chin and her other hand traced the glass over Frances' face with great interest. "Good." she said. She tapped his daughter Julia. She was a teacher in Orange County, he conveyed to her. She tapped the other daughter, Maree. A librarian, he told her. But what did it matter? There was no way, really, to explain their completely disparate lives to her.

Mrs. Chang excused herself and checked the water under the steamer in the winter melon kettle, replenishing it with a cup of hot water from the tap. She came back to the table.

Hastings motioned to Mrs. Chang's ring finger hoping that she would tell him something of her background. She looked very somber and then held up her arms as if shooting a weapon. A rifle. Hastings tapped his ring finger. "Your husband?" She held up three fingers more. Husband and three children? She nodded, yes. "Omigod," Hastings said. Marty Chang had already briefed him on this information, so it did not come as a real surprise to him. "I'm sorry," he said. He assumed that American forces killed her family. "Americans?"

"No, no—Cong. Viet Cong." Mrs. Chang then pointed under the table.

"My foot?" He closed his eyes. It was only fair that she should ask him. "Yes," he said, "yes—yes. Viet Cong, *too*. Viet Cong. Hue. The Battle of Hue." He opened his eyes and realized that he had been some place far away, beyond a curtain of remembered sound—gunfire and choppers and the anguished screams of his buddies.

Mrs. Chang reached over and touched his hand. Very slowly and enunciating with great care, she managed to say to Hastings, "Thank you—I am very sorry for it." Struggling, she had pulled the words from somewhere.

Hastings shuffled the cards and he smiled. "Mrs. Chang, you don't really have to thank me. *You* got out alive. *I* got out alive." He dealt her some cards. "We were just pawns, I'm telling you. But that's one 'Thank you' I'll treasure for as long as I live." He smiled at her.

Edith Piaf was singing from one of Hastings' CD's. Mrs. Chang quickly placed both of her tiny hands over her heart and closed her eyes, looking up to the ceiling rapturously, as if recalling a delicious moment from somewhere in her French colonial past. Hastings watched her mouth the words to *La Vie en Rose*. He remembered that Saigon had been under French rule for years and that she would surely know how to speak more than a little bit of the language. "*Connaisez-vous*, Piaf, then?" he asked her.

Piaf began to sing *Je Ne Regrette Rien*. Mrs. Chang nodded and then looked away from Hastings. She was embarrassed for him to see her weep. "*Je ne regrette rien*," she said, following along with the bittersweet lyrics of the Piaf song. "I regret *nothing*."

It was a curious remark, Hastings thought. He could almost see her in colonial times, seated at a sidewalk table in front of an elegant Saigon restaurant with a Legionnaire companion. He reached for one of her hands, brought it to his lips, and, in a sentimental gesture, and gave her fingers a gentle kiss. He felt her tremble slightly as if she were a tiny, snared wild thing, unsure of its fate.

When he let go, she rose to monitor the steaming winter melon. "Okay," she said, and flashed ten fingers twice.

"Twenty more minutes? Smells *good*," Hastings told her. He searched in his phrase book. "Mrs. Chang," he asked her, "what is your first name? *Ming*?"

She smiled. "Ahhh. *Ming—Lan*."

"*Lan*," Hastings repeated. It was a graceful sounding and lovely first name and so very much like her. "*Lan*," he repeated. She nodded. "What does it mean? Lan?"

She looked through the phrase book and pointed out to him, *huar*—and then tried to pronounce it—*flower—fleur*. *Lan—Vietnamese name*—not Chinese."

"Happy to meet you, *Lan*," he said. "My name is Mike." He extended his hand for a handshake. Mrs. Chang reached across the table and shook his hand. She seemed a bit subdued. Hastings turned over the score sheet of their card game and printed her name in block letters. "Show me how your name looks in Chinese," he asked her. "*Chinois*," he said in French. "*Lan* en Chinois." Mrs. Chang took the pencil and wrote her name for him in Chinese. "That's beautiful." He tried it himself with her help. He then drew two circles. One for Marty and one for Mae, and connected them with a straight line. Next to Marty's circle, he drew several more circles and connected those to Marty. He tapped one of the circles. Marty's mother, he said, and looked up in his phrase book—*jie-jie*—*older* sister—to *Lan*—*mu-qin*—mother to Marty. Hastings then tapped the other circle connected to Marty—and underneath it he wrote, *mei-mei*—younger sister, *Lan*.

Mrs. Chang covered her eyes and began to weep and shake her head.

"I'm sorry,—what's the matter? Was it something I said?" Hastings was troubled. He backtracked over their conversation. "*Jei-jie*—older sister and—"

Mrs. Chang reached for his pencil and crossed out the circle connecting her to Marty's mother. He was puzzled. She was weeping uncontrollably. Why had she crossed herself out the diagram? "*Not mei-mei*?" he asked her.

"No. *Not mei-mei*." She pounded the table. "Not. *Not*."

Hastings pointed to her chin line. There were the two small moles that confirmed her identity. Marty's mother herself had shown the photographs to him and told him how excited she was. Now, Lan Chang seemed to be saying that she was a fraud and had been brought to the United States under false pretenses. Hastings wanted to tell her that he did not care who she was. She enchanted him and made him feel alive again.

Mrs. Chang tried to brush away the two moles with her fingertips, saying, "No, No." Suddenly, she rose and raced out the door of Hastings' kitchen. He called after her, but it was no use. He knew that he wouldn't see her again that evening. He looked at the kitchen clock. The winter melon was probably done. He tested it with the tip of a small kitchen knife. When he looked at the ideogram for Good Fortune that he had incised into the wall of the melon, to his astonishment it had widened beautifully, due to the expansion of the melon. He was very impressed by the beauty of it. He dialed Mrs. Chang—hoping for the best. As he could have predicted, there was no answer. He looked into the kitchen of Marty's house. It was dark except for a night light in the den.

He served himself a bowl of the winter melon soup with its bits of chicken breast and he scooped out some of the inside of the melon itself. He thought it delicious, but he could only pick at it. He turned off the kitchen lights and sat quietly in the dark at the oak table.

The fun had gone out of the Chinese banquet.

.. ..

Hastings was in a booth in the dining room at the *Iron Horse*, a trendy restaurant and lounge in Beverly Hills. Marty said he would drop by for a chat at seven. Hastings was anxious. He told Marty that he wanted to talk about Mrs. Chang. His neighbor slipped into the booth opposite him. It had been several days since Hastings had seen either Marty or Mae. Their paths didn't often cross on weekdays. Mrs. Chang disappeared for a week after the Changs returned from Scottsdale. When Hastings finally cornered him, Marty told him that his aunt was not feeling well and was pretty much keeping to her room.

After they ordered their drinks, Hastings got right to the point. "Look, Marty," he said. "I think I love your Aunt Chang. I want to marry her. I don't know what she feels for me. I just want to know from you—up front—if I can approach her. Look at it this way—she's not that much older than I am—I could be your uncle."

"Love?"

"Sure. Love is right in there. Right at the top."

Marty shook his head slowly. He sipped his drink. "Whoops. I think we got a problem." He pulled an envelope from his jacket pocket and tossed it to Hastings. "This just came. Look, Mike, you're a lawyer. What do you think?"

Hastings read a short memo from the International Red Cross, suggesting that there may have been a mistake. The real Mrs. Chang had died a year ago. An impostor had taken her place.

"Does Aunt—uhm—Mrs. Chang know about this?" Hastings asked.

"Oh, no—not at all."

"Are you going to tell her?"

"Oh, no. Neither Mae nor I want to do that. What's the point?"

"Why not?"

"For what? Retribution? Look, my mother was happy—she died happy. She thought she got her baby sister out of Vietnam. The way we look at it—hell, she *could* be our aunt. I mean, *c'mon*—we're into a possible DNA thingy here. And, frankly, Mike—Mae and I don't want to get into that."

Hastings took a deep breath and whistled. "That's some kind of shock. So, you mean she doesn't know that you know—and you're *not* going to tell her?"

"Yeah—I think that's it. What am I going to do? Send her back?"

"Legally, I think you'll be okay. You only have to tell INS or the Red Cross—that they were wrong. But, my God—twenty-one thousand bucks for a—"

Marty waved the objection away. "That's over—no biggie. My mom was rich. But my problem now is—what does this do for you? Has this dampened your ardor? Say," he asked, "you two didn't—uhm—*you know*—I mean while we were in Scottsdale?"

"Oh, *please* Marty—remember," Hastings smiled, "I'm a *lawyer*. But you said she's sick? What's the problem?"

"I diagnose," he looked up at the rotating mirror-globe that sprinkled soft reflective discs onto the flocked wallpaper and ceiling, "—uhm—*depression* maybe. She may sense the jig is up. Maybe she feels *guilty*—who knows—and she *should* feel guilty—but, what the hell."

"So, you're *not* going to blow the whistle?"

There was a large silence. "Uhm—*no*," he resumed, "I'll see if I can marry her off." He smiled a big Chinese stockbroker smile at Hastings as if he were trading in pork futures, and recognized a good deal when he saw one. "To tell the truth, she kinda grew on us too—except for that damned elephant pipe of hers—."

"Elephant pipe?" Hastings questioned.

"Oh, some damned thing she brought with her from Saigon. She *smokes* it in the kitchen." Marty tapped the envelope. "We were sorry to get this—you can imagine. You can handle it? Does it change anything for you?"

"I can handle it," Hastings said. He could never turn his back on Lan Chang. What they had each gone through in Vietnam would be with them forever. He lifted his glass. "Cheers." They touched glasses. "I thought you told me you were a stockbroker, Marty."

"Yeah, I know—you are thinking, maybe, marriage broker? Look, buddy, your proposal is a Godsend—really—it is. Out of the blue. You're *sure*? You *want* to marry her?"

"If she'll have me." Hastings crossed his fingers. "Might take a while. I'm committed, but I guess I'll have to charm her."

Marty smiled. "Yeah, that's the tough part." Slowly, he tore the envelope from the Red Cross in half. "Oh, something else."

"What?"

"I suppose I'll have to pay for the wedding?"

"Damn right," Hastings grinned, "the *works*."

"Oh, great. I think I know who the fraud is here—and it's not my aunt."

"Marty—Marty—Marty. Here, you can start with this—it's a pretty cheap engagement lunch—remember *the father* pays for everything." Grinning, he slid the bill for the cocktails over to Marty.

•• •• •• ••

It was Saturday morning. Hastings slipped through the hedge and over to Marty's back door. Marty and Mae had been watching for him, so when he knocked, they were right on the ball. Hastings winked at Marty. "Hi," he said, "is Mrs. Chang home?"

"Hang on," Marty said, "I'll get her—she's in the kitchen." He brought Mrs. Chang to the door. She looked a bit subdued, but very lovely.

"Hi, Mrs. Chang," Hastings said. "How you doing? *Ni-hao ma?*" Mrs. Chang bowed formally to him, not knowing what to expect. Hastings could see Marty and Mae watching and listening from the kitchen. "I haven't seen you for a couple of days. Maybe you would like to go somewhere? A drive? Disneyland? What do you think?" There was a long silence. "My daughter lives in Orange County. We could visit her. What do you say? Disneyland?"

Mae casually came forward from the kitchen, as if she had just overheard Hastings. "My aunt would love to go to Disneyland." Mae put her arms around Mrs. Chang's shoulders and gave her a hug. "*It's a small world, after all . . .*" she chanted.

Mrs. Chang laughed nervously. "Okay, GI. I get sweater. *Disneyland.* Zippo."

"*Zippo*," Hastings parroted. He winked at Marty and Mae. "*Disneyland* it is."

The End

HER OWN
SWEET LOVE

It was so sad. I'd been to the Department of Social and Health Services several times to try to get my state allowance raised. There were so many things I needed for my baby. So many things. They just looked at me there as if I was some kind of deadbeat or welfare fraud. Darlyn, they told me. Get real. We got people out there with problems. You got food stamps. You got nice rooms up on Lauridsen—subsistence housing. What is this, they're asking me? I want more? Damn right I want more. My daughter will soon need to be in head start. And then, K-12. Well, not immediately, she's only nine months old.

She's a smart little devil, she is. I agree to undergo interviews with my child—my daughter, Rosie. An evaluation, they call it. She sits on my lap so sweet, so controlled. All of the evaluators tell me how beautiful she is. How well behaved. And, to tell you the truth, she is. And she favors me a little. Everybody says that. Everybody. Rosie has my cheeks. They all tell me that. And my coloring, too. They try to lift Rosie off my lap and onto theirs, but she don't let them. I really don't like that. I don't like people touching her, really. I guess I'm just possessive. But, I've read about that in so many magazines and columns, like *Dear Abby*, and so on. Don't touch other people's babies. It's a rule now. People should know better. I never touch another baby. *Never.* Before I had my own, maybe, in a market or somewhere, I'd lean over somebody's stroller and give a little pat. But, of course, I've got my Rosie, now, and I don't do that no more to other babies. Who needs that? You always ask first. Always. Even *Dear Abby* says so, you know.

She's there now, on the day bed, fast asleep. I wish her father could see her. He was a bum. Very cruel. I pray Rosie don't have any of his tendencies. He's still hanging out in town, here. In the bars. I can't say I ever loved him. How could you ever love anybody who was cruel to you? Some women can. They are so desperate. Sure, I used to run after him late at night. Begging him to take me back. He was the kind that would insult me at karaoke nights at Smitty's. You're sick, he'd say to me. You sound terrible. You couldn't sing *Jingle Bells* if you had the lyrics pasted to your nose. I don't want you singing up there no more, making a fool of yourself. But, it didn't bother me then, as long as he talked to me. Looked at me. Touched me.

He had his own little band once. He played lead guitar. And he would get me to do his dreadlocks and then dye his hair crimson and then green and then purple. The purple looked best. We never got married. I was too fat, he said. Who'd want to marry a porker? he said. Now what kind of thing is that to say? I told that to my evaluator at DSHS. She asked me if I wanted to go on a weight control program. The state would pay for that, she said. I told her no. I got enough aggravation. I tried to get Rosie's father to marry me and settle down. Well, we lived for a year in a room over a bar. It was bedlam till 2:00 a.m. We'd sleep till ten, eleven, twelve the next day and you never knew who you'd wake up next to—or who'd be on top of you. Everybody *bombed* out of their gourds. That's how I got my tattoos. It's like weird.

He did those to me. My tattoos. He had this artistic streak in him. He was going to save up enough to open a tattoo parlor. Tattoos are very in now. And he had this artistic streak, like I said. He was good at fantasy art and Celtic crosses. He wanted to get into body piercing, too. That's how I got these scars. Look here. And, look here.

Practice on me, you know? That's what I said. Yeah. I let him do that. That's how it was. Rosie's father was like that. Invite everybody over. Let them flop. Send me out to *Seven Eleven* to get pancake mix and syrup. He liked syrup. He could actually drink a bottle of maple syrup. Suck on it all day. All kinds of sweets. He ate sweets till he got sick. His teeth were black and I mean black. Rotten. He screamed in pain when the sweets got in his cavities, but he couldn't stop. Well, he was into dope. He shot up. That's how come the sweets and such. I wouldn't touch that stuff. I told him that he was going to ruin what little life we had left with that crack. Somebody told me his craving for sweets had something to do with mainlining. He shot me up once, forced me into it. I hated it. You know, you lose control that way. I like to have some control over myself. We'd get into fights about that and sometimes he'd disappear for days. I didn't know what to do about it. I couldn't go home again. Had to beg for food around town. A place to crash.

When you start going downhill, the way I did with Rosie's dad, nobody wanted to have nothing to do with you. My mother, my own mother, wouldn't have nothing to do with me. Of course, she had her own men problems and her new guy, Lester, said their trailer wasn't big enough for the two of them and their friends—let alone me and Rosie. He was full of it. Because of him calling the shots, when I got arrested for shoplifting some lingerie, she wouldn't stand by me. Wouldn't go to court. Wouldn't stand by me at all. No way. I didn't really shoplift anything. I don't really know how those panties got into my bag. I don't remember looking at them, touching them—nothing. Why would I buy some silk panties so tiny that I couldn't even get into them—let alone over my calf? I'm not that stupid.

It doesn't even make sense, you know? Then, suddenly, the whole security police was on my case the second I set foot outside the store. Well, the judge, somebody *pro tem*, whatever that is, said I was a real nut case. But, he gave me 90 days suspended sentence and warned me not to frequent *Penney's* for 90 days. He said I was lucky.

A little later I was in *Safeway* with Rosie. I carry her in a denim carrier, facing me—her little head barely sticking up over the top. It's a secure, bosom carrier. I can look into her little face and pat her little bottom, and there she is facing me. It was all of a sudden just like the episode in *Penney's*. I don't even know *what* happened. Suddenly the security people were all over me. I didn't do *nothing*. Somehow, somebody planted a steak on my body. A large cold steak. Shoved it in between my boobs and Rosie. They must have been behind on their arrest quota or something like that. Why on earth would I slide an ice cold steak in between me and my baby Rosie? It don't even make sense. She would scream holy murder if I done something like that. You understand? I don't even like steak, not that I've eaten that much of it. I don't even like it. Why would I steal a damned steak?

So, they look at me like I'm some kind of fool and such—and tell me not to frequent their store either. Well, I got news for you, *they're* the fools. How'm I supposed to get food for my baby? Know what I'm sayin'? I ask you that.

Well, before I know what's happening, all kinds of people are coming up and wanting to look at me and to look at Rosie. I didn't mind showing Rosie to them, if they don't get too close. They're all looking and smiling at her, like isn't she sweet, and standing on their tip-toes to get a peek. I'm a big girl, up to here—five foot ten, you know—tall—so they got to stand on their toes, some of them, to see Rosie. And some of them got this really gross look on their faces. Well, they got their steak back, what are they beefing about? That's when I hear the MEDI-VAC truck show up outside and they escort me out to the truck. My baby may be hurt and need some attention, they tell me, and they escort me out to the MEDI-VAC truck, all red and white and chrome and I recognized Dan, the driver, who went to high school with me—except he graduated.

"Hi, Darlyn," he says to me, "how you doing?" He looks at me up and down. Now, why would a MEDI-VAC driver try to come on to me? He peeks at Rosie. "She is *beautiful*," he said. I held Rosie closer to me. She gets so nervous around strangers.

Dan helps me up into the truck and I hear him getting clarification by radio from somewhere. It was something like being in a movie, with all the people in the parking lot standing around and staring at us. Well, as I remember it, in two minutes we were at the hospital and nurse escorts me and Rosie up to the third floor and the doors close behind us. I still had Rosie snuggled up to my breast to keep her warm. She was very quiet. A doctor that I'd seen somewhere before came into the waiting room.

"Hello, Darlyn," he said to me. "Nice to see you, again." He was so nice. A couple of nurses were popping into the room to say hello, too. It was quite a friendly place. "I understand you're having some kind of problem with the baby," he said. He smelled so clean.

"Well, doctor," I said, "I don't know what that would be—she's just fine."

He peeks at her in her carrier. "Maybe we should just ease her out of there and on to the table, so we can have a look."

Well, frankly I really don't want nothing to do with doctors, if you know what I mean, but it looked like I didn't have much choice.

"Well, you can see for yourself, she is very quiet and well-behaved," I told him.

One of the nurses stepped forward and very gently helped to remove Rosie from her denim carrier, and placed her on the examining table. Doctor placed his stethoscope on Rosie's tiny chest. He winked at me. It was just a formality, he said. I heard one of the nurses whisper to the doctor. I don't know what she asked him, but he answered her very strange.

He whispered, "Dead three weeks—maybe longer—autopsy will tell—." Then he looked at me and he said very gently, "Darlyn, do you have a family here in town?"

Hell no, I got no family, I'm in subsistence housing, I'm on food stamps, Rosie's father is—p*hhhhhttt*! My mother is this whore who sleeps around—trailer trash for godsakes. I shook my head at the doctor. Doctor looked at my arms for tracks. Why would there be tracks on my arms? It's unreal.

"Why, doctor, is there something wrong?" I looked at little Rosie on the examining table. She was so tiny and so still. "Is there something wrong?"

"Darlyn, little Rosie has passed away. I'm afraid there will be some questions we'll have to ask you about all of this."

I saw them cover her body with a blue hospital blanket. Well, I was in shock. I'd been carrying her around with me for *days*. If she was dead, wouldn't I know it? Wouldn't I be the first one to know it? *She was there, hugged right up next to me. Give me some credit for godsakes.* A nurse named Florence came into the room from the nurse's station, right around the corner. She was carrying a doll, a *Cabbage Patch* doll.

Doctor nodded. I heard him say, "That's perfect."

Doctor handed me the doll and he and Florence smiled a lot and told me that I could keep it and drop it right into little Rosie's carrier. They were about the same size. It even felt like little Rosie and looked a little like her, too. Same fat cheeks and squinty eyes. She was very cute.

"Florence, here, is going to find you a nice room to stay in, Darlyn. We're going to get your file. You'll be up here, on the third floor. You can look out over the port and watch the steamers and the ferry come in. And the Coast Guard helicopters. Can you see the San Juan Islands, out there, Darlyn?" He pointed to the glimmering skyline of Victoria on the horizon and to the snow-cone of Mt. Baker that glowed an eerie electric yellow in the setting sun. "We'd like to have you stay here with us for 72 hours. Do you think you'd like that?"

I nodded. Like it? Was he nuts? It was warm. It was clean. Florence, the nurse, was friendly enough and there were probably more just like her at the nurse's station. Like it? I took one more look at little Rosie, but she was gone from the examination table. Somebody had taken her away, I guess—or had they? *Ahhhh.* I looked down into my baby carrier and there she was, looking up at me, just as before. Cute little cabbage-patch face with a crinkly smile.

The doctor nodded at Florence. "Let's go, Darlyn—let's go find you a really nice room. You and your baby must be tired. Real tired, honey."

She was right about that. I was tired and I followed Florence quick enough. After all, she was holding my elbow so nice, so firm. I was grateful she locked the door behind herself when she left my room. People barging in all the time. Very annoying. I really preferred to be alone with my own thoughts.

.. ..

I hated to leave the hospital. It was really quite nice. But, I'm back in my own rooms again, up on Lauridsen street. Everybody was wonderful. Doctor even came up to the third floor on my last day and signed an adoption certificate for my new *Cabbage Patch* baby. What are you going to name her, he asked me? Some question. Rosie, of course. He printed her name in big letters on her certificate and gave it to me.

There she is, now—over on the day bed—taking a little nap. She's so good. When she wakes up we're going down to DSHS try to get some action on pre-school. I have her birth certificate right there on the table.

She's my own sweet love.

The End

THE LAST MOHICAN

Bizarro. From the word go. She walks toward me wearing a brown Smokey the Bear hat—Indian amulets around her neck—grizzly bear claw and Kokopelli icons. That kind of thing. I'm not kidding. A glitzy headband with feathers and small scalloped mirrors. Bling. Many braided horsehair friendship bracelets, woven with beads, and tiny figurines encircle her skinny wrists. She shoves them up her thin arms and they slide down again to raw-boned hands. She obsessively repeats the endless cycle. On top, she's wearing, over a very flat chest, a tie-dyed, Sixties tank top. A long, full, ankle-length skirt, the kind that Indians or gypsies wear, completes her ensemble. And, of course, a decorative tattoo here and there on her fingers and her bare shoulder and who knows where else.

"Hello," she says to me. "I'm The Last Mohican. I am not a man. I am a woman. I repeat. *I am NOT a man.*" She drums her fingers annoyedly on the countertop. "Boss here?" She scans the gallery.

"That's me," I say. Nope. She is not Indian. She's Anglo.

"You wanted to see my clay work. Remember?"

"No." I have a small gallery. God knows what I might have once told her. I draw a blank.

"What do you mean?" she says.

"I mean—simply—I don't remember." I emphasized the 'don't'. She was becoming irksome, but I chuckled. "Refresh me, please."

She produces a small unfinished clay figurine of an Indian mother and child. At least that's what I thought it to be. It was primitive in conception and execution. Undecorated. Unglazed. Unfired. Little red clay loops of indeterminate figuration using the never-dry dime store clay, like *Play-Doh*, the kind that you buy for your grandkids.

"Hmmm," I hedged, "do you have anything else? Anything besides this one piece?"

She looked indignant. "Well, they broke into my place through the windows and broke the tail off one of them."

"They? The tail? Omigosh."

"Exactly."

"And so you don't have any more of them?"

"No. Then they came in and broke the beak off the other one."

I was puzzled. "Do you lock your doors?"

"Of course."

"Why do you suppose *they* are doing that?" I was beginning to capture the style of this Mohican. I could see she had some problemas.

"Because, they can't get in the doors," she sassed. Then she leaned close to me with her Smokey the Bear hat. "And—because they are *assholes*." I didn't flinch. "Honestly—I have to say it, Miss—this figurine doesn't have any sales potential at all—unless I'm missing something. You know, it doesn't look quite finished—or complete." I tried to be gentle. I deal with many artists. "Look around." There are times when I have to be direct. "I'd have to see—you know—a line of them. More of your work. I can't really make a judgment based on just this one piece," I lied. Hopefully, I suggested an alternative. "It's maybe a gift store item? No?"

I crossed my fingers hoping that she would race out of the gallery to one of the nearby gift shops. She doesn't reply. She opened a fringed Sioux medicine pouch and extracted small drawstring bags made of maybe, shiny velveteen. She spreads them all over the counter. She next disperses many, many cheapo dangling earrings and bracelets of the Native American tourist persuasion. She plows through her medicine bag and looks for something else. She grasps a comb. A large comb with a wooden handle. She removes her Smokey the Bear hat as well as her beaded headband and begins to comb out her long hair over my countertop. There are no customers at the moment. I'm entranced by her flagrant violations of the rules of etiquette, but remain cool. She again rakes through her medicine pouch and fiddles with many bags of stuff and junk. Nervous and jittery she sets more little velvet bags about the counter and then rearranges them the way a con man would rearrange shells in a shell game. I watch, unable to figure it.

"Well, what do you think?" she brightly queries.

"About?"

"Do you think it's ready to set up?"

I hesitate. "Uhm, what does 'set up' mean exactly?"

"Where do you want me to *put* it? Set it up over there?"

"The figurine, or—?" Apparently she'd ignored everything I said.

"Well, you said you wanted to see it when I was finished with it."

"You know, you look vaguely familiar. Was that last summer?"

"So what? This is now and here it is." She starts to re-comb her hair, shaking it out as she does so. Her behavior was so disjointed, I thought I might have a real loony-tune character on my hands.

"Well, it's very abstract, no? You're not going to—uhm—glaze it—or decorate it or something?"

"Of course not." She looks forbiddingly at me and raises her voice. "It's *naturallllllllll!*"

"Okay, now, what do you mean, again—set it up?" I leaned forward.

"*Set it up*—over there." She makes a wide sweep of the gallery space with her skinny arm. "Set it up means, *sell it!*"

"Oh, sell it?" My annoyance level is rising.

Suddenly she raises her voice and says, "*It's NOT for sale.*"

"Oh, it's not for sale?"

"It's *mine.*"

"Sure," I tell her, "—you know the Coffee House Gallery is a good place to show something like this. Around the corner. They have a lot of clay things over there. They might like to have a look at it. Marcie, over there, the owner, she's really into clay work." Marcie would kill me if she could hear me. I glanced again at the pathetic, childish figurine.

The Mohican blanched. "It's not for *sale.*" She raises her voice ominously. She looks rapidly through all the belongings she has spread on my counter top and levels her gaze at me. *"I'm missing an earring."*

She gives me a chilling, suspicious look. She is very strange. An anorexic six-footer. Doped up? Fried brain? "I don't have your earring." She continues to attire herself in shawls and scarves, retrieved from her pouch, tying the opposing corners into loose square knots, eyes fixed on her image in a non-existent mirror, pursing her lips, moving her face side-to-side. She then continues to rearrange the small draw-stringed velvet bags. I watch.

She opens a blue velvet bag. "I smoke *Camels*, now." She takes out a cigarette, places it in her lips—and reaches for a butane lighter with the picture of a wolf head on it.

"No smoking in the gallery," I say to her. "I'm really sorry."

"I wasn't *going to.*" She fixes me with a stare.

She opens her purse again and after much searching, finds a small container of folded paper. She unfolds it carefully and breathes deeply into it. Flutters her eyelids ecstatically. What? Chemical? Dope? Perfume? She picks up a deep purple petunia she had fingered from my flower box on the way into the gallery and inhales deeply from its fragrance and throws it at me. I notice an Aquarian ornament on her hat. I pick up the bruised flower and twirl it between my fingers, pondering my next move. I really feel that my forehead needs to be iced. I grope for my next comment.

"February your birth month?" I was an Aquarian, too.

"Yes. February 6th, 1969. The year of the first lunar landing."

"Oh." Figures, I thought.

She finishes her adornment. "Well, Trisha told me that she was going to put the chemise in here. The one with the green bow."

"Chemise? In there? Is that like a slip or something?"

She ignored me. "She said she'd put it in here." She looks around.

"Yes ma'am? *Trisha*?" Do I know her? I'm puzzled.

She raised her voice again. "In this bag here—."

"Okayyyy—in the bag?"

"Yes in the bag. And if she *didn't* and she's trying to do anything *else* with it, she's going to be in *big trouble!*"

Whoa, I say to myself. At what point do we call 9-1-1? Is this woman okay on her own? Tough. Skinny. Lots of bruises, I noticed. Sort of pretty. Where was she headed? How do these people get by? She put on her headband and her Smokey hat and then loaded up her large medicine pouch with all the little bags of goodies. Lastly, she picked up her mysterious figurine and drifted out—her scarves and shawls shimmering away behind her—thong sandals whooshing along the parquet floor, The Last Mohican.

"I'm outta here," she says puckishly over her shoulder. She lit her *Camel* cigarette just inside the entrance to the gallery, challenging the NO SMOKING sign—like a naughty child.

The End

ONE OF A KIND

I had to go to Sucia Island. It's just a mere three miles north of the tip of Orcas Island. It's the last chip of the archipelago that belongs to the U.S.—right on the 48th parallel off the coast of Washington State. Anything beyond it—North of it—except for one little island named, Patos, belongs to Canada. It's pretty cool for the very adventurous birdwatcher, snorkeler and occasional rock and ammonite hunter. Well, I had to go there to pursue my field studies. Sucia is unique in that it has so many ammonites and argonauts and petrified squids and chitons and mollusks and paper mollusks and purple-green whelks that have all that margination and ornamentation on them. Beautiful scallops, too, of the genus Pecten. Pecten scallops. Ammonites, they're from the Mesozoic period. Beautiful fossilized mollusks with very elaborate coiled and chambered shells. Well, the Cretaceous period is really the third stage of the Mesozoic era—oh—80 to 200 million years ago. Cretaceous means chalk, you know, and all these things are turned to limestone—fossilized limestone. Chalk. Chalky. The place is a field-scientist's delight. A lot of the things found there are from the Cretaceous and Jurassic and Triassic periods, you know, and that's why I just went into cold sweats and that's why I wanted to get over there and that's why I want to write a paper on it and why I've been studying that whole period—the Cretaceous.

And so, I went to *PayLess* drugstore and got me a thirty-five dollar, two-man rubber raft, you know, the kind you blow up with a foot bellows? And so I just hopped in it and lit out for Sucia from the north end of Orcas Island, by that little jetty there, and I found an old broomstick and an old mop floating around in a tidepool and I used them for paddles. Well, about one third of the way over there, it was getting dark and the wind had come up. It was freezing and the wind was whipping up five, seven foot seas, and then, wouldn't you know, a couple of huge seals, big and black, breached the water right next to my rubber raft—well neoprene, really—and they'd probably just come up from a ten-minute dive and wondered who in the hell you are and they'd open these huge gaping mouths—and those huge spooky, rolling eyeballs—and let out a horrendous hoarse cough and, hell, all I could think of was that they were carnivores and they were so close and how could I know what they'd do? Overturn my boat? There could be sharks nearby—sharks love seals, after all—or even worse, maybe orcas—you know—killer whales—they love seals as well—I was very nervous and worried. If an orca gets close and decides to fool around—well that *PayLess* raft has got to look like some form of marine life, no? A mammal? I could imagine myself down there looking up at my rubber raft and thinking I myself might look just like a tasty seal or dolphin or whatever. The charts show that the water there is 150 foot deep, and so what do I know? Spooky. And, so I was scared for the first time in years and scared good. Oh, I can swim, but in that cold water, what? You last for fifteen minutes at that temperature—the water was 40 degrees. Suddenly, the wind began to hit me broadside and it began to tip my dinghy, which is pretty flimsy you know. I could have been flipped entirely over in a second if I didn't hold it down somehow. You know me—so, I'm pretty big—right? I just spread myself out on it.

Well, this guy who saw me push off from Orcas Island, from that little landing near the jetty—I learned all about this later—he thought I was crazy—and he watched me the whole time from a spotting telescope in his living room and he was sure I was in trouble and so he called the Coast Guard. Well, it was getting to be a little bit touch and go. No kidding, I rowed for all I was worth with those two sticks, that mop and that broomstick, and I did everything I could to keep that dinghy flat against the water but the swells were just about impossible to work against and I kept turning around in circles and I began to worry that my flimsy inflatable raft from *PayLess* simply couldn't be seen in those wave troughs. Believe me I did get a little bit nervous because I knew then, that if I didn't, you know, *prevail*, then the wind would have taken me past the island of Sucia, and that would be the last point before I was really in the Strait of Georgia, big time, and then the current and the wind would have taken me right up to Alaska. Nobody would have seen me frozen, dead—lifeless. There's a terrific, strong current there in that Strait of Georgia; you simply have no idea.

So, thank God for that guy who thought I was crazy and who watched me the whole way, even though I felt that I conquered the current, and the waves, and so on—on my own—well, I *guess*. But everyone gets a share of the credit—you know what I'm saying? For saving me.

After a while a chopper showed up and dropped a couple of Navy SEALS or frogmen in wet suits—I don't know what they were—and they guided me ashore and, since I had made it almost there, all by myself, I sure didn't need any help from them at that time, but I hated for them to waste their skill and energy and so I let them do what they had to do, you know—just gave myself up to it. After all, I'd been taking care of myself for a number of years. So, like I said, since I didn't really want them to know why I was going to Sucia, I just sort of gave myself in to them. Well, I clambered up on the rocks and just sat there absolutely exhausted and freezing cold. The SEALS—they told me to try to walk to the other side of the island of Sucia—that should warm me up, they said. I think they were annoyed that I had put them at risk for what?—they're thinking. I couldn't believe it—that was another *two miles*.

Well, I did it, for sure. The SEALS told me that there was a little jetty dock over there and a Coast Guard vessel would try to tie up there and pick us up, the helicopter was off on some other mission or something, and couldn't be spared any longer. We did hike on over there, pushing on past the little cabin that passes for a house on that island and headed for the quay and, like *voila*, there was the CG boat and, omigod, there were eight or ten Coast Guard guys and would you believe it?—a news cameraman from KING-TV. I was so pissed and embarrassed that everybody from Oyster Cove would see me on the evening news, all I could do was hide my face.

Well, needless to say, that was the end of my blow-up dinghy from *PayLess*. Punctured. Scraped. Shredded on the rocks—thirty-five bucks all shot to hell. Just like my right leg, It got all scraped to pieces on the barnacles and what's left of it is probably now in the shipping lanes of the Georgia Strait, like I said, one of the most powerful currents in the world, so help me. So the Coast Guard took me to Bellingham of all places, instead of back to Orcas Island, and they let me out with my water-logged backpack, as if I were just a hitchhiker they had picked up on the road somewhere, and I just slept overnight in the park there, freezing my ass off, and at ten the next morning I took the Greyhound back to Oyster Cove.

Well, I like to travel free and travel light and travel fast, and bring home a lot of fossils and do my studies with them and I was going to fill up my dinghy with them and give one to Ed and one to Bill and maybe Mary, and a couple to the college and even one to you, you know, if you want one, and you know, they're worth some money, and they have them in that gallery in Port Townsend, one-hundred bucks a pop for a really good looking, well-formed one. They're from the Jurassic and Triassic, like I say, periods. From what I saw, they were sure there in quantity—just like what I viewed on some slides up at the college about that fossil-heaven location on Sucia Island, and I'm definitely going back next month before somebody else gets out there and aces me out. I told you, remember? The weekend sailors and rock hounds get there as soon as winter is over and they look for the ammonites and argonauts, etcetera, that are stirred up by rough tides and ruin it for all of us us serious fossil hunters.

The fossils? Well—200-300 million years old. Mineralized, nacreous shells. Nacreous and prismatic. Nacre just secreted from their mantles, and turned, well—like opalescent. Those tourists just break the iron bands of those ammonites, and break up the covalence after the winter storms and high tide. The only other place you can get 350 million-year-old ammonites is in Coeur d'Alene Idaho—well, around here. I can't remember the names of the rivers there, I forget. You know the glacier pushed all that stuff down there to sea level—and it just rose and fell according to the movement of the tectonic plates under this area. Those plates would just push them up 1000 feet, just like the cliffs at Sekiu. Oh, yeah. Fossil clams and fossilized leaves. And those tourists just get them and pick them over and you know it's a really rough winter—and a rough winter and high tides will *wreck* them, and crack and break them up, and you have to be careful with them, because the iron oxide in them breaks down when it's exposed to oxygen and you got to get them in glycol and dip them in acrylic and so on to keep the oxygen off of them. They'll break right up. *Wreck* 'em.

Oh, sure, I was going to put two hundred, maybe three hundred pounds worth of ammonites in the dinghy. Don't laugh. Well, hell, it's was a two-man dingy and I only weigh 245 pounds so there was plenty of space left in it—it doesn't matter if I bought the damn thing in a drugstore—what the hell. I'm a big dude ya know—here, feel my arm.

Well, I can't do much about it right now, I guess. I sure don't have another thirty-five bucks. I'm going to get my flu shot next week and then I'm going to go out in the woods up to The Point. Look for agates, with what we call creamy egg yolks in them, variegated chalcedony—you've seen those—and you find them in the woods pushed up from the volcanic basalt just like geodes and just pushed right up when the tectonic plate activity occurs and pushes them to the surface—but you got to know what you're looking for. Over at Ellensburg, and the Columbia River Gorge, it's all that ancient basalt and the mineralization process—it's all been completed eons ago and the covalence of atoms, you know, a one-for-one, atom-for-atom substitution of organic material for iron and so on, and, if you know what you're doing, then you can pick these areas over and if you know where to look, for example, around volcanic vents and places where calcite forms and in the valleys and stream beds, you know about that—and you can pan there for garnets and topaz and rubies and, even up here, at Kalaloch, and at Ruby Beach, where they used to actually find rubies. *Really.* You can go over to where the eagle's nest is there, at the end of that trail, and go on down to the tide pools—but there are three real treacherous switch backs, where, if you fall, the tide will come and get you and haul your ass out to sea, big time, unless you are with a buddy, and you can slip and hit your head on the rocks there, and if you get down there safely, be careful because all of the rocks at low tide are covered with that black algae and it's slick and dangerous and I don't think you'd want to take your wife, like I said.

The Jansen creek area has had some slides and there are a lot of cannon balls up there, too, your sedimentary rock with a center that forms around some fossil shell or a piece of petrified rock, or something, you don't know until you break them open and, when you break these cannon balls open, it's always a terrific surprise about what you'll find in there. Yep, they're mostly clay—well—and silica—with iron bonding crystals in there too. I guess I'll have to write my Ph.D. thesis on this project—ha ha—they love to read those papers and what the hell, I can write a paper, can't I? I know I don't even have my BS yet, but I could write a Ph.D. thesis on fossils as good as any on file at UW.

I'm going up there where the whales come in real close and roll in the gravel to scrape off the barnacles. That's really something to see. The gray whales are migrating right now, and so I'm going up there to just see all that whale action. Real exciting. Most of the people don't know about that. There is another beautiful place up there in the field where I want to study the tidepools—they're so rich and there's coral, red, purple and green and yellow. If you know where Wadah Island is? At low tide—hell—you can just walk right out there but you have to be careful and watch out that you don't get stranded out there when the tide rolls back in. That's probably why they named it Wadah Island, right? People get trapped out there—tide comes on in—they look up and say: *Wadah*! Just kidding. But there are gorgeous mussels, and Pecten scallops and conches and whelks out there. And cormorants must be nesting nearby; they just dive and fool around, totally unafraid of humans since they don't see so many. They're not *habituated*, you know? It's something to see I got to tell you. Those cormorants.

Well, up in the mountains, I'm going to look for fossils and agate and carnelian and so on—petrified rock—and what I do is stash my finds behind certain trees and cover them with brush, so nobody can find them and they aren't noticeable and then, later, I come back and pick them up and haul them out in my back pack. I mark the location of the trees on my US Forest Service Stream and Hiking Charts. No problem. I guess I'll do that until the weather stabilizes and I did get that flu shot, you know, and I got asthma—and the kind of collecting I do, I mean—listen to my breath—my chest—it's bad for me, but I can't stay indoors, no way. I got to get out; otherwise, you're not alive. Hopin' to toughen up—lose weight out there hiking. Right?

So I'll go back to Sucia Island and, in fact, I didn't mention that I got a phone call from my buddy and he's got a Boston whaler—it's a ten-footer and you can't sink one of those, you know, so we'll throw it into the back of his pickup truck and take his two dogs and we'll take the ferry to Orcas Island and just sneak back on over to Sucia Island—spend a couple of days—as soon as the weather clears. It's not privately owned, I don't think, but I'm not going to worry about that—maybe the government owns it.

But, I'll have to decide when the weather is right and I can't wait this time. I'll get my ammonites and argonaut shells and—but what I'm really looking for—and please, don't think I'm *crazy*, I'm looking for a counter-clockwise spiral whelk from the Cretaceous period. That would be a *real* find and that would be some big dough. Like finding a five-leaf clover. Hell, I could live all next year on what I'd make if I found a counter-clockwise spiral whelk, you know—and there are *epistobranchs* and *prozobranchs*? Well an *episto* is what they mostly are and I'll probably get dizzy just following the spirals trying to find one going the other way. Wouldn't it be something?—a fossilized whelk, *Buccinum undatum*, about three inches long? A spiral-shelled gastropod. And then, if I can *ever* find one going the other way. Well, wow.

You really wonder don't you, what makes a gastropod decide to go into a left spiral as opposed to a right spiral? It's probably like, you know, 'handedness' in Homo sapiens—I don't know—but if I find one, it'll be like finding one of a kind. A lottery ticket is probably easier, one chance in ninety-three million. Ha ha.

Oh, and *please*—whatever you do, don't tell *anybody* where I go to look for ammonites and Mesozoic mollusks. *Please*. That's why I called you. I just thought that since you were so interested, you might be thinking of going over there yourself—you or your wife, except, I notice that she has a bad foot and you might want to be careful. It's—you know—my secret spot and I don't want anybody to know about it.

Well, I've really go to go now, I've got to go to Swain's to get me a blue ground tarp for my sleeping bag. I'll talk to you later.

The End

PARALLEL LINES

Police Report Feb 7 Friday West End:
Dante Hajdu Kaldero (1) Obtain evaluation; No contact
with victim, pay restitution; $500 fine. (2) Resisting arrest;
180 days in jail, $250 fine; (3) Possession of firearms with
no valid license; 30 days jail, 28 suspended. (4) Use of
vicious attack dog; 180 days jail; $500 fine. (5) Attend anger
management class.

It's an impossible situation, this thing that happened to me. My neighbor, he's a Nazi airhead, you know what I mean? Dirty Jews, and so on. That's all they talk about—those skinheads over there. They bait me. Dirty Jews and niggers. Hey, Dante, this garbage asks me, you a dirty Jew? He laughs. No, as a matter of fact, I'm not. My parents were Romanian Gypsies. Roma. Run out of Europe by those Nazi lice. What do they know about oppression? If I had my way, I'd blow them all to kingdom come. He told me my big Gypsy nose and my Van Dyke beard reminded him of a Jew he knew once. I'll be godamned. I'll Jew him, that racist punk. Here they talk like that. *The heart of America*. Can you believe it? It makes the hair on the back of my neck stand right up. Trying to tell me the Holocaust didn't happen. Do they think I'm a godamned idiot?

My golden retriever was 18 years old. He died six months ago. He was my buddy. He was like my kid. I loved him, you know. I can't talk about it. Not really. I got a daughter in New York. Haven't talked to her in years. No letters—nothing. No phone calls. Nothing. She's trash. She's history.

Got me a new Rottweiler that was psychologically damaged or something. Legally, the breeder couldn't sell her. But I got her for a few bucks on the side. No papers. She's doing good now and I think she's going to make it. I keep her with me in the house. She don't tolerate strangers. We get along good. She's smart. Smart as hell. You gotta go through her to get to me.

I hate godamned cats. They get in my garden and they poop all over everything and ruin my garden. Digging. Digging. Everywhere. You know what I did? You want to hear this? It was *something*. I trapped two of them godamned things one night. The neighbor's cats on the other side. Not the Nazis. And I took those two cats to the woods and I blew them away—right in the cage. They didn't have a chance. That's what I think of cats. The neighbors come skulking around looking for the bastards. I didn't tell them a godamned thing. Why should I?

Yeah, so they come around looking for their cats all pious and moony, as if I didn't tell them a hundred times to keep their cats off my property. And, I don't say nothing. I got me my new dog. Next time, I'm going to try poison. Then their cats can go home and die on their own godamned property. There were some poisonings in my neighborhood last year. Pets. I'm not saying I had anything to do with it.

This Nazi neighbor and his buddies dug a trench for me with this backhoe he rented—and so I owed him—and I told him that sometime I'd do an oil portrait of him. I paint, It's a hobby. What the fuck. Anyway, he dug this trench a ways along my property line—so I could divert the creek into my garden. You know? An irrigation canal? I can't afford county water rates to water my garden. There's a pool there where I lined it with black plastic and I can haul water to my crops with a bucket. I don't need the godamned county water. I'm on a fixed income for godsakes. Well, as long as he had the backhoe—as long as he was *there*—he said sure, no problem, little Jew Dante—and how I hate him and that troop of Nazis that live in his house, and I can hear their amplifiers all day and all night playing some loud and offensive crap. Blaring amplifiers. White rap music with all that filthy-racist, skinhead talk. They come over last week and want me to donate to some godamned Holocaust denial pamphlet. I told them to get lost. I thought there were laws for that crap. Their shack is very close to my place—piles of beer cans—pizza cartons—blowing all over onto my property—know what I mean? We each have five acres, but for some dumb reason, our houses are right next to each other—practically right on the godamned property line and they drive me nuts. I don't have no privacy you know. Why the hell we aren't in the middle of our respective properties, I don't know. Get my drift?

Then, there's that bitch across the street. She was visiting over next door and she was looking across at my new irrigation ditch. Oh, yeah, she's buddies with that broad that's got all those cats. She hollers at me, is it a proper ditch? Did I get a permit for it? Fucking rat-a-tat nosey. I figure something is fishy with her. I told her it was none of her godamned business—if she wants to know—go on down to the city hall and find out if I got a permit. The creek doesn't get a permit from me when it decides to flood my property in the winter. What the hell is her problem—do I have a proper permit?

So now, I go over to this Nazi to give him his portrait—and so I took a while to do it—it's art—and you know you got to be up for it—not like with a gun to your head—something like that. It's art, you know. I worked from a photograph he gave me. It was a good job. Looked good. Well, I took the finished canvas over to that Nazi punk, and he says to me that there's something we got to talk about. Discuss. Like *what?* He says my new dog barks and whines every time I go away. Well, that's bullshit. My dog does *not* bark when I'm away. That's bullshit, I told him, and then this Nazi thug has the godamned nerve to tell me that he might want me to paint a picture of his wife. Go piss up a string, I said to myself. Hey, I'm not stupid; I didn't say that to him. I tell you one thing, I'm not going to paint no portrait of his godamned Nazi skinhead wife with her big boobs sticking out of her filthy tank top. They're riff-raff. They're bikers. Godammed bikers with drunks and skinheads congregating there—a flophouse in the sticks. Renters. Jesus!

Only one thing worse than fucking cats and that's the godamned gophers. Hundreds of them. Huge mounds everywhere. I'm trying something new. I piss in the gopher holes. I read about that in an alternative farmer's almanac. It's supposed to work. Polack peasants invented it. They do that over there. No, they didn't invent pissing, for crissakes! They don't have no rat poison—none of that stuff like we have. And piss is free, after all. So, I mark a gopher hole with a white stick so's I can find it in the dark, and I drink a late beer, and just after the weather report, at 11:20 p.m., I go out in the moonlight and look for my white marker stick, and I piss right down into the gopher hole. Next night I do another one. And, it's supposed to work. You'd think it'd work, wouldn't you? I'll let you know.

One night, a biker spots me in the moonlight. Nails me. What the hell's going on? he hollers over at me. What the hell do you *think's* going on? I said to him. I'm pissing into a godamned gopher hole. I told my dog to come on. My mutt comes on all right, but he stops and he pisses on the white stick, too. The biker, he takes one look at my Rottweiler and he gives me thumbs up in the moonlight. I don't know what the hell his problem is. I'm suspicious of him being out there in the night. What the hell is that moonbeam racist up to? Put in the night staring over to my place. The moon is blinding white. You could read a book by it. I look for cats out there, but I don't see any. They say you could see the spacecraft Endeavour, or Mir, or Spacelab or whatever the hell it is up there—with the naked eye if you know where to look. I'm out here looking and I don't see nothin'.

The cats wreck my peas-on-a-string. I trained a whole bed of green peas. Trained them up string ties. The sugar peas. They destroy everything, cats do. That string's not cheap. They destroy it every time. But I'll tell you one thing—I'll trap them too. And blow their brains out in the woods just like I did the others. What the hell do I care? What the hell else am I supposed to do?

Like I said, I have a daughter in New York. She's trash. Just like her mother. I don't want nothin' to do with her. I had this disgusting wife who all she wanted was more stuff. Buy me this. Buy me that. What happens to women? They start out so pretty, you know. So slim. So nice. Then, something goes wrong in their heads—and like they just want more stuff—more *things*.

I was just a graphic artist. How much could I give her, for godsakes, on my salary? A graphic artist for 40 years? Drawing elegant merchandise I never had no hope of owning myself. You know? Nose to the grindstone. Drawing advertising copy. And then, once they get what they want, they put on the pounds. My wife turned into a godamned tub. She never stopped talking. Never stopped eating. I didn't even want to look at her anymore. Gimme this. Gimme that. I finally divorced her, and gave her half the house, and all the *stuff*, and I told her—good riddance—get lost—and get yourself somebody with some dough who can look you in the face, you greedy bitch. I don't want no *stuff*.

I come here to this end-of-the world Peninsula to get away from all the crazies in the metropolitan areas. And what have I got now? Now what have I *got*? I got $750 a month social security and aggravation. That's what I got.

I live very frugal and do my garden to supplement my social security and it ain't much. I keep that freezer of mine full. You know you can eat sugar peas right off the vine? Squash, turnips. My own apples. You know what I mean? From time-to-time, I do a portrait. A few bucks under the table, no taxes, no 1099 Form. Yeah, North Light gallery in the village. They give me a call, and I do a commission portrait. You know, from a photograph. If I have to take the photograph myself, it's thirty-five bucks more. Inflation takes every penny. I can't hide nothin' away for later. And the gallery gets a cut, too.

Cats in my garden. Godammed cats. The other day, a pot-bellied pig from Vietnam. Rooting in my carrots. Would you ever guess that our legacy from the Vietnam War, *all that grief*, would be a bunch of Vietnamese pot-bellied pigs walking around the sidewalks of America on leashes?

Rooting up American gardens? As far as I'm concerned, *they* won the war, not us. Sending their godamned gook pigs over here. I was going to blow that little black porker away with my rifle. Oh, I have the right to do it. It's on my property. This is my five acres, here, ya know. We still *do* have a Constitution, don't we?

Pigs. People keep them for pets. They're filthy. Who in the hell would want to keep a pig for a pet? And sitting on the sofa beside them, at that? Watching television. It's disgusting, it really is. They take them into their houses like a dog. Can you imagine? It's that bitch across the road. I went over and I gave her a piece of my mind, believe me. I was really pissed. Her pig will never be back over here on my property again. Believe me.

So, here I am with my portrait of this Nazi punk in my hand, presenting it to him in the name of neighborliness, and all that, right? And he tells me that shit about he wants me to do a portrait of his FemiNazi wife with her bleached hair with the black roots. They're pigs and they don't care how they look.

I'm an artist for chrissakes. After this crap about my dog bugging them with his barking, he's got the nerve to blackmail me into doing a picture of that dirty-blond bitch. We'll just have to have an understanding about your dog, he said. Oh, I get it. The understanding is that I'm supposed to do him a free portrait. Then I'll bet he won't *hear* my dog barking anymore. A tree falls in the forest . . . oh yeah . . .

So, you know what I did? I told him I only do commission referrals from the gallery, at gallery prices, and I told him which gallery to call. If he figures he's going to get something free out of me, he's got another think coming.

I called the gallery this afternoon and told them that if anybody answering the description of those Nazi punks comes in there to ask them about my work, then *up* the godamned price to $425 godamned dollars—and that's *without* a frame. I'm not painting his godamned wife in her dirty tank top with her big boobs hanging out. No way. She can go see Andy Warhol. Fuck 'em.

So, here it is. I got a telephone call from the County Building and Inspection Division. Some bureaucrat—a guy named Peterson. Somebody, he says, told him that I had illegally diverted the godamned creek onto my property and he's coming out to photograph it and discuss it. Couldn't reason with him. Wouldn't listen. Environmental health is the issue, he says. Septic systems. Salmon spawning habitat. Hell, there hasn't been a salmon in this creek for twenty-five years. Everybody knows that. The Indians net all the salmon down at the mouth of the creek where it enters the Strait—some old treaty rights. If the government wants to do something, why doesn't it take off after the Indians? No salmon is going to get past them from the Strait up this stream. It's another case of Big Brother hassling the little guy. Ya know what I'm sayin'? Government always meddling. Would they rather have me up at the Safeway with a sign around my neck saying: **HOMELESS—WILLING TO WORK FOR FOOD?** And I know who blew the whistle on me. You better believe I do. It's that bitch across the highway with the pigs.

I saw her today walking her pig on a leash over to my neighbor's. I could see her through my Venetian blinds, and I could see the both of them on the front porch, looking and pointing over at the creek-diversion. I was going to set out my cabbages and winter broccoli today. But I can't do it now. I'm so upset. I'm going to have to go over there and let them know how I feel. They shouldn't be allowed to disrupt my life like this. It's getting dark early now. I'll try to eat something and go over there after chow. I'm really going to let her have it.

She won't forget about me in a hurry—I'll tell you that.

The End

POOK

So, like I said, this guy comes in with a tote bag and a young woman who I took to be his wife. Oh—and there was a baby in a stroller. The guy looks a bit, well—tough—to say the least. He's an Indian. A Makah. They have a reservation up on the Peninsula. Lots of them are mixes, who look more like Sicilian numbers runners than real full-blooded Indians. Most of the ones I know are, in fact, half-Indian-half Mexican. This guy, swarthy and handsome had a broken nose, with scar tissue going from the bridge of it up to his inner eye. Lots of curly black hair, but more on the neck and sides than on the top, if you know what I mean. Like a mullet. He said he had some Indian art to show me. So, I said, to myself, what the hell.

Like, I need some money, man, he said. I've got this mask I'm carving. It's—well, I'll sell it to you.

I tried to find out what his game was, because a white guy had come in my gallery a couple of weeks ago with two pretty big masks and very good ones at that. But I was sure they were hot. He said he'd sell them to me for three-hundred-fifty bucks each. I said no dice. They were nice but the deal smelled. Then he came back later and said I could have them both for two hundred bucks. I asked him who made them and were they signed by the artist? He said sure they were signed. He'd give me a receipt. Or, a bill of sale. I told him I could give him a bill of sale for my wastebasket, too, if he wanted one—but it wouldn't mean much.

Well, I called Marl at home. We keep an office there where she does the accounts. Lucky. It allowed me to stall for a while and dump the decision on her. That would let me off the hook and both our faces would be saved. It's just business, I told him. Nothing personal. I buy from local artists. I do consignments. The idea seemed to make him happy. I'd call her. He said he needed 'medicine' for his kid. Well, this guy, he was a white guy, just over from Canada, he said. He looked shiftier than hell. I didn't buy this sick kid business for a second. The oldest trick in street sales. I thought I was pretty good at getting a fix on people. Well, luckily, Marl wasn't all for it anyway. Cash flow problems and all that. I whispered into the telephone. I told her I wasn't real sure about the masks being legit. In a town this size, if you stumble once you're in trouble. I wasn't interested. I could see the headlines—LOCAL GALLERY OWNER ARRESTED FOR RECEIVING STOLEN PROPERTY. I hung up and told the guy, no dice, but thanks anyway, and I told him about the pawnshop down the street. It had a bunch of Indian stuff in it. Some good. Some bad.

So, he repeats that he just came over from Canada that morning and needed the medicine real bad for his kid. Well, I was sorry but what could I do? He came back in a half-an-hour and said I could have them both masks for seventy-five bucks. He pulled them out of a big brown grocery bag and I examined them again. Sorry, I said. I was sure tempted, but sat on my hands. Thanks, Buddy. Maybe next time. I haven't got the money. Well, Jesus, he comes back *again* in and tells me I'm a sucker not to take them and he'd give me one last chance: No reasonable offer would be refused. Boy, I could taste the deal. I wanted some Indian masks up on the walls in the worst way. Tourists love them. I could hear the pitter-patter of little tourist feet getting off the ferryboat, headed my way, and asking for Indian stuff. I looked at them again, but I knew damn well that they were stolen.

Later, after work, I crossed the street to go to my car and happened to look in the pawn shop window. Sure enough there were the two masks that my Canadian friend had tried to sell me. I figured I'd call later to find out how much they were. I bet the markup was five hundred percent. Little did I realize that I'd soon get another chance at some other masks.

So, as I said, this Indian from the reservation up on the Peninsula said he could let me have a small cedar mask he'd just carved and painted for ten bucks. I asked him if it was his. He looks pretty formidable and he says you better believe it. I don't fool around with nothing hot, he says, or anything like that, man. I say, oh, of course not, swell, but, I'm asking myself, why is he willing to sell his masks so cheap? I figured it was just another very ordinary mask by one of the local tribes. Ten bucks is not a lot of money, exactly. All of the other Indian *artistes* I know sell their masks in Seattle, Portland and Carmel for four to seven hundred bucks, cash. That's why I didn't have any in my gallery. You need a lot of dough up front to have any of the good stuff—Indian folk art. Indians don't like to work on commission. Everything cash. So, he says he needs the money and besides he has to make a name for himself before he can charge big bucks and besides again, he says, he likes me. I take time with him and sound encouraging and treat him with respect. *Fear* was more like it, but he doesn't know that. I'm looking at that scar on his cheek. Fear and respect are pretty close relatives, as he probably knew. He said that in the summer he was going to carve masks down at *The Landing* for Michael in his crafts store. Tourists trooping past from the ferry. Him—local color. Sounded okay to me. I looked at his wife. She had tattoos on her hands and a look so icy cold it could have killed a yeast culture. No problem. She would have made a great study for a mask herself. Or worn one, maybe. Then her dislike of the white man couldn't be seen.

Anyway, so I bought the little mask for ten bucks and hung it up on my gallery wall. It was a bonding gesture. Everybody likes it and I put a tag on it, 'NFS', which means 'not for sale'. It was the first Indian mask in my new gallery, and I wanted to keep it as a memento. The Indian said it would protect my gallery and bring it good luck. Sounded like a deal. I asked him to sign it and he did. It was hard to read but I caught the name. It was Luke. Luke Delta.

Well, boom. In he comes again. No kid or wife this time. I was out on the sidewalk seeing Marl to her car. She had come down to the gallery for something or other and she was saying goodbye and telling me I ought not to feed the pigeons that hung around on the sidewalk in front of the gallery. They were addicted to my KFC crumbs and the occasional French fries I used to toss out for them. This was about a month later. So, Luke, he sees me out there and he says, I want to talk about some more art to you, man, if you got a minute. I thought Marl would be interested too and I asked her. I don't make too many major expenditures unless Marl gives the okay. She is my accountant and runs the business side and knows where the bucks are going.

Well, she says, sure, and we walk back into the gallery and Luke takes six or seven little drums and a warrior mask from his tote bag. We enthused over them and I complimented Luke on his craftsmanship. They weren't really the best I've seen by a long shot and believe me I'm no expert. The art work just wasn't all that slick. Definitely not. But, for what they were, I guess they were okay. Luke definitely needed practice in recording Makah imagery for posterity and for the white people. There was stippling and stuff on the wings of the thunderbirds that looked wrong from a design standpoint. It crossed my mind that Luke might have been smoking something strange when he carved them. If he carved them. I just felt that the whole presentation could have been a lot better, but what the hell, the tourists don't care about that. I'd shrink-wrap them in plastic and type a little description sticker and they'd be ready for impulse purchases. At least they weren't hot. And they weren't so hot either, but, what the heck. A lot of little white tourist kids would be happy in the stifling back seats of a lot of station wagons, banging on those little drums. And, meanwhile, Luke is learning his craft and I'm picking up on what Indian art is all about and so—I'm fine with it.

As Marl and I were turning the masks this way and that, admiring them, Luke suddenly got all heated up about the hides used to make the drums, so help me. He got rhapsodic. Hey, man, he says, that's deer skin. Some dude hit the thing with his pickup—and you know, man, people don't even stop to see if it's—like—*dead*—you know? Road kill. I mean, like what's wrong with them dudes, you know? So, Jeeeez, I jumped off the truck where I was there with my cousin. He had a truck. I run over to the deer, man, and I held it in my arms—you know what I'm sayin?' It was still warm, you know, man? *Alive.* Then we just took it back to the rez, man, and you know? I just put it out of its misery. Luke made a horrible cutting motion across his throat. And then, man, I cut all those pieces out for my drums and cured them on the wall of my woodshed. See the nail holes—right there? He pointed to the edging.

After his impassioned outburst, the scar on Luke's face was quite red. I was holding one of the drums. I think it had the image of *The Windblower* on it. I hadn't thought once about it ever being real deerskin. Just like I don't think about pork chops being real. I just eat them.

Trying to distance myself from the gory event, I said to Luke, well, this all happened like last winter? I nodded up and down, hopefully. No, man, he says, this happened two weeks ago. I dropped the drum I was holding. It might be alive with coli form bacteria or something equally dreaded. How, I asked him, did it get so stiff and cured in two weeks? I thought about the tattooed human-skin lampshades of Nazi Germany. Man, c'mon, I put them out in the sun. They're air cured. How could anybody be so stupid? Know what I mean? I winced. I mean, to hit a deer, man, and then not follow it and kill it? That's gotta be ugly. His face and eyes got very fierce. Right, Luke, I said. Think it was a white dude that hit it? I found myself unconsciously shifting to his lingo, a bad habit of mine. Think it was a white dude? Man, he says, it was on the rez. I told you that, man. Oh, yeah, you said that, I said.

Thinking to change the subject, I asked Luke to tell me and Marl what the different images painted on the drums meant. The Indian symbolism varies markedly from tribe to tribe. I needed to make up gallery labels for everything. For later. For sales. The tourists want to know what everything is. So he recites the names: *Windblower*; the *Warrior and the Killer Whale*; the *Thunderbird and the Whale*; the *Cougar and the Crow*, and so on. I had the uncomfortable sensation that he was winging some of the names because he kept looking at the ceiling as if they were printed up there. The main mask he says, is called—uh—the *Friendly Warrior*. I feel that we are drifting toward safer territory. Marl examines the masks and listens with great interest.

Friendly Warrior had lots of ornamentation and was very intriguing. Vermilion, green and black. And a wig. Man, Luke, says, look at the cedar-bark hair. It's *fantastic*, man. My little sister, she cut it from her cedar bark dress. She said, man, if you want it. It's yours. She probably respects Luke, too. It's not every sister who'd cut up her prized ceremonial dress for her brother's masks. She says to me, he says, you worked hard on the mask and you should have some cedar-bark hair for it—so go on ahead—cut my dress up. He smashed some cedar-bark hair onto the mask and arranged it in a fierce and horrific fashion. And look, he says, I've got some bangs for it too. He dropped to his knees to rummage through his tote bag. I said that's okay, Luke, I've got the picture. I was afraid he was going to pull out more body parts of the damned road kill deer.

He set the cedar bangs aside and picked up one of the drums then, and showed me and Marl how they worked and he did the little DUM dum dum dum, DUM dum dum dum that we all learned as kids. I guess all of the Indians have the same rhythmic bent or else we've all seen the same Indian movies. It was quite a sales pitch. I was glad no one came in just then. One thing I had learned about the Indians in my neck of the woods was that they didn't use the color green in their artwork. So I said, uhm, Luke, I thought only the Bella Bella Indians used green paint. He looked malevolently at me. Man, he says, so what—I use green paint. That was that.

I quickly tried to write down all the names of the totems for the labels I was going to make when I saw a white carved mask about as big as a grapefruit. It was painted all over with a white matte finish. Marl was quite interested in it and examined it intently. Running the office at home, she'd never really interfaced with the local Indians before and was very empathetic and generous-spirited about Luke. She began moving the things we were going to buy from him into a pile, like winning poker chips. Luke's eyes were getting bigger and bigger as it looked like we were going to buy out his stash.

Man, he says, like we need *diapers for the kid, yeah, diapers.* Real bad.
I'll give you a deal on all this stuff, man. Looks good, Luke, I said, I think
you're going to be able to buy a lot of diapers. Marl had moved five drums
and the *Friendly Warrior* to her side of the counter and I was getting excited,
over-zealous and sure—okay—greedy for more.

What about that white mask, Luke? I asked him, what's its story? Well,
man, I gotta get diapers. *Huggies.* That mask? That's, like, *Pook,* man.
Here's the legend, man. I wrote the word *Pook* on my notepad. I would
learn later that the correct name was *Pook-miss.* He went on. There's this
warrior whale-hunter dude, man, he goes to sea to catch him a whale,
yeah. He snags one and then the whale hauls him down, right? Right into
the water and drowns him. Yeah. His buddies and the village all, whaddya
call it? He looked stumped. Grieve? I offered? Yeah, man, that's it—they
grieve—that's it. They all grieve for him, right? They can't find his body,
you know what I mean? They dive and dive and everything. I nod. No
body. Yeah. What then? Well, goddam, in two weeks, his buddies find this
corpse washed up on the shore and they run over to check it out. You know
what I mean? Yes. Then what? Well, man, just as they got to it, they saw
that it was all white. Chalky white. No blood. Yeah. His ebony eyes were
on fire. So they send this kid back to the village to tell the others. Just then
the spirit went back into *Pook-miss.* He gets off the sand and he starts to
walk towards them. And they are real scared. Wouldn't you be? And this
ghost says real spooky: *pook—pook—pook.* Luke begins to walk around the
gallery in his plaid shirt with his thumbs stuck in his armpits, his elbows
out like chicken wings, his scar bulging to the bursting point and his chin
thrust to the ceiling, hollering: *pook—pook—pook.* Well, Marl and I look
at each other, getting edgy. Whew. So, man—like his spirit come back but
his voice didn't—. He looks at the mask and strokes the lips. That's why
his lips are pursed. All the *Pook* masks have pursed lips. He hands the mask
to Marl.

What then, Luke? I ask him. He's irritable now. Well, that's the whole
point. I just explained it, man. He points to the mask. That's why his
mouth is shaped like an 'O' shape, man,—he's saying—*pook—pook.*

Hey, I'm hip. I had no problem with that. Marl runs her thumb along
the cheeks of the mask and strokes the *pooky* lips with her fingers. I wrote
down all of the legend too—real fast—on a scrap of invoice—in chicken
scratches—just like you see it here. Marl tells Luke that we'll buy that
mask too. The *Pook* mask. But Luke says he's gotta *finish* it first. Yup. No
warning buzzer went off. I nodded supportively. He needed to paint the

mouth and eyes black and red and finish up the horsehair on the skull. God knows what else. So, if we could just pay him first—oh yeah—he'd finish it later and bring it back to me in the afternoon. How late were we open? That'd be fine I said. He'd buy some paste wax, too. I don't have no paste wax, man, he said. I'll get some and I'll come back and I'll wax all those drums and I'll finish the *Pook*. I had just totaled up and written the check. It was for two-hundred-sixty-five dollars. Not exactly chicken feed, but I didn't have to hock the gallery. He looks at the check, turning it over and over, as if we were trying to rip *him* off. Like, man, do you have to give me a check? I ain't got no identification. Somebody stole it from me on the bus, man—yeah—on the way here. I need cash real bad and my kid, he needs them *Huggies*. You know what I'm saying? And I'll come by later, yeah—before you close. I *trust* you, man, he says to me, and I'm giving you a *real* deal. They're selling those drums at the rez, man, for ninety-five bucks each. And you got yourself a bargain. He knew he had me cold when he told me that *he* trusted *me*. Centuries of wrongs against Native Americans were suddenly righted. He raked Marl and me with a sly but magnificent smile and zipped up my *Pook* into his tote bag. He got Marl to drive him to the bank with a new check made out to cash. She handed him his money in a little white bank envelope. He then he conned her into driving him to yet another destination. He'd get the *Huggies* later, he said. The other place turned out to be a location next to the waterfront bars. Later, man, he told her. Later.

Needless to say, I never saw the *Pook* mask again—or the wax. It's been over a month. I'm going to go down to Michael's before the tourist season is over to see if Luke is there. Sitting on the floor, a dangerous romantic, his blood-red scar throbbing, in a circle of admiring tourists, as he carved an ersatz canoe paddle, or maybe another *Pook* mask. Maybe my mask—the one I bought and paid for—is up on the wall down there at Michael's. Or, maybe it's at the hock shop. I wondered how many times Luke had sold the *Pook* mask since I'd seen him last.

Well, there is one way out of the mess. I'll just jack up the prices of the drums I bought from him to make up for my loss.

You know what I mean, man? *Pook—pook—pook.*
Yeah!

The End

THE RAIN HAT

-1-

The door of *Mac's Book Nook* blew open again. Caught by the wind, it slammed against the brick planter containing an evergreen juniper, the only vestige of plant life left downtown. The tourists had photographed the public planters and hanging baskets, with their tiny Niagaras of pendulous blossoms, for the last time before winter set in. Dried by the constant wind from the waterfront, the baskets were filled now with nothing more than desiccated sphagnum moss. They bonged forlornly against the light standards to which they were affixed. And then, right on schedule, the day after Thanksgiving, the city work crews stripped the planters and stored the wire containers for next year. North Bay was closing up for the winter.

Mac was on a ladder swapping out a framed poster of summer water-skiers on Lake Sutherland for a more seemly poster of grinning Halloween pumpkins and Indian corn. It was a seasonal ritual. He timed it to coincide with the autumnal equinox—the date of which he dutifully noted on the chalkboard behind his cash register. His customers always read the notices. They knew when Albert Einstein's birthday was; they celebrated Guy Fox Day and dutifully noted the day Sacco and Vanzetti were executed—and they could be reminded of other, more or less fascinating, historical and social milestones. It was that kind of bookstore. Chalky reminders everywhere. There were used books, new books, greeting cards, and magazines. For music, there was a shelf of New Age CDs—auditory experiences of all kinds—harps and crickets, flutes and crashing waves, the scree of gulls and raptors with Celtic accompaniment—as well as a large collection of magical white-noise CDs. Outside, near the door, was a vintage orange crate filled with ancient hardbound books for a quarter each and moldering, fog-moistened pocketbooks for a nickel. That was the *Book Nook*.

Inside, there was local art for sale high up on the walls where it was impractical to place bookshelves. Mac took in wall hangings on consignment by local weavers and a watercolor painting here and there. A warm and friendly gathering place smelled of cinnamon and cloves from his potpourri cooker. Motes of book dust hung motionless in shafts of weak, white sunlight from the front window. Today was a slow day. It was the opening day of the county fair. The town was deserted. The last of maroon and gold autumn leaves swooped toward the choppy Strait, Victoria in the distance, collecting in drifts in the gutters.

Mac had something to add to the bulletin board, but it had escaped him for the moment. He leaned on the top of the ladder holding his chalk in hand and tried to remember. His notices were tailored to his slightly leftist reading public, and to the habitual browsers sitting on their haunches in the in the book stack corners who never bought anything, as well as the regulars who just popped in to buy the paper and check the blackboard. Those who knew about Sacco-Vanzetti nodded knowingly and invoked the names of Julius and Ethel Rosenberg. Those who did not might look them up in the one-volume *Columbia Desk Encyclopedia* where Mac had placed colored markers to match the color of the chalk he used on the blackboard.

Mac turned toward the entrance to see a tall, blond, and very skinny hiker with a backpack a mile high. It was a seventy-five pounder. Easily. He stood quietly, looking around.

His eyes were tired and rimmed in dark sockets. He seemed thin for his height. Undernourished. A hiker's diet of granola and water, probably. His camper's clothing looked slept in and his stressed face was a map of Olympic hiking trails and campgrounds. He would ask for a trail map. Mac was sure of it. Not a bad guess considering the number of European and American hiking enthusiasts who frequented the area in the summer. There were always four or five in the store exchanging information in several languages and fractured English. But it seemed more than a little late in the season for hiking. The mountain trails had been closed to the public for a couple of weeks. Mac smiled at him—this last robin to go south for the winter.

"Mind if I set this somewhere?" the hiker asked.

"Sure," Mac said, "right there by the door." The overloaded backpack was ready to dispatch a teetering rack of risqué greeting cards to the floor. The kind of cards not found at Hallmark.

"I like to check the stores when I come to town."

"Great. Look around. We have some good stuff. You're a reader?"

"Well," he said hesitantly, "when I can." He moved toward the stacks and then turned and looked back toward the wall hangings. "I miss looking at beautiful things. I noticed your weavings—those wall hangings, up there," he motioned. He savored some arty posters, and then blinking, eliminated them as objects of interest. He continued to scrutinize the weavings.

"You're from out of town?" Mac looked down at him from the ladder.

"Yeah. Right." He removed a khaki cap.

"If you're camping, I've got a bunch of local trail maps. For the Olympics. Government maps. Right over there." Mac pointed from the ladder to a nearby rack.

The hiker reached up to touch a tapestry. He was concentrating hard. Mac watched him. "That's okay," he said absently. "I'm all set with maps. Thanks."

Mac fussed with the Halloween pumpkin poster. He had guessed wrong about the hiker. Who'd know? "So—you're traveling, I guess?"

"Yeah. Well, I've crossed the United States by foot."

Intrigued, Mac came down a couple of steps on the ladder. "By foot?" He looked again at the lean, almost wasted body.

The hiker examined a wall hanging more closely. It was titled: 'Cloud Fortress'. The artist had incorporated four-inch cactus thorns into the weave. A label informed that the thorns were gathered in the Anza-Borrego Desert of Southern California. The sculpture was a showstopper. Without looking up, he responded, "Yep, walked from Connecticut."

Mac said, "Connecticut?"

"Yeah."

"So, where are you headed now?"

"I live out on the coast. In the Hoh. The rain forest—toward La Push. On the reservation there." He didn't look at Mac.

"You're Indian, then?" Mac took note of his blond ponytail.

"No," he responded, "I'm a caretaker."

A lot of Mac's success as a retailer had to do with communicating. It was the bartender syndrome. He pressed on. "A caretaker?" he inquired, affixing the pumpkin poster in place with pushpins. "Like for an older person or something?"

"No," he said. "They hired me. The Indians. I look after their long house. I'm a caretaker."

"Oh, sure," Mac said. "I know a caretaker here in town. The state pays him to take care of a blind guy that lives here. He cooks for him and does his laundry and all that."

"No," he replied, "that's a care-*giver*. You know—the long house. They have dances there. Indian dances. They meditate. Chant. Things like that. Cultural things. Like a big day room, in a way."

Mac nodded. "So, you walked across the US?"

"Yes."

"Alone?" Mac was incredulous and curious.

The hiker moved to the entrance of the bookstore and glanced outside. "No," he said wistfully, "with my dog and my friend." A large and very lean dog watched the entrance from curbside for a glimpse of his master. It whined for him through the glass.

"Girlfriend?" Mac was prepared to be surprised that a woman might want to undertake such a journey.

"No. My friend. My friend and my dog. Just the three of us. He might do a book, my friend. A book of our trip. He's a photographer." He fingered a thorn embedded in the tapestry.

"Terrific. Meet a lot of people? See a lot of great things?"

"Oh, yeah." His voice was soft and whispery and he seemed tired and burnt out—Mac couldn't put his finger on it. "People were terrific everywhere," he continued. "It was quite an experience."

"How long did it take?"

"A year."

"A year? Whew. So now—you live out there at La Push? That big rez out on the coast? I've never been out there myself."

"Yes." He moved to a table and flipped absently through a book on the sale table. He seemed to want to chat.

Mac was persistent and curious. "But, how can you live on the reservation if you're not Indian? I mean, all the maps say trespassing is forbidden and all that."

"Non-tribal members can live there—with permission—they've sort of adopted us."

"You mean the tribe?"

"Yeah. Sort of."

"Adopted you?"

"Yeah. Well, it's way out there. You know, isolated. But, they're cool with us. We live in the long house and caretake it. Nobody bothers us. They're teaching me how to weave."

Mac thought that all of the Sixties dropouts, revolutionaries and flower children were wearing pinstriped suits these days. Day traders. It was a surprise to him. What was this bird? A New Age mystic? *Nu Age*? "That's great," he probed. "So they're teaching you to weave and—dye. That's good. So, okay, now, I'm guessin'—you're actually en route to someplace else, or, is this it?"

He smiled wanly. "No, this is it. *The Land of Oz*. It's green everywhere up here. Emerald City. Utopia. The Olympic Peninsula. We've been looking all over the US for just the right place. This is it. This is what we've been looking for." Mac sensed they were a gay couple.

"So, then, you're going to live out there in the long-house and now—how will you take care of—I mean—you know, my experience with the Indians has been that they mostly hate us white guys. Have you had to cope with that yet?"

He nodded and measured his words just a whisper above conversational. "Yes—as a matter of fact, there has been some hostility to our being there—they don't like gays, but the elders prevail—so to speak—they're mostly tolerant—they're cool. Lucky for us—when the elders say something, you know—*decide* something—well, it's the law. So the others—who *don't* like us—just let us alone."

"Because—?"

"We're a couple. Committed."

It didn't bother him to say that. That he was gay. Mac had no problem with it. "And you just sort of stay in the long-house? You don't get antsy? Isolated?"

"Well not really. But, yeah, we just hang around the long house. It's made of logs. Actually, it's pretty comfortable. We're splitting firewood for it—for them, you know? My friend keeps a journal, and we meditate—do Yoga—take care of the grounds. We pay our way."

"Sounds good. So—you'll kind of spearhead a craft-renaissance with traditional weaving projects and things like that?"

He nodded. "Well, it's turning out to be something like that. The thing is, the younger generation Indians—what with boozing and doping—right?—They don't want to learn any crafts—nothing of the old ways. They've left the rez. I'm going to get the elders to show me

'The Way'—the techniques—everything. I'll learn and document what they teach me—and all of that—and then I'll teach—*I'll* be that next generation—you know what I'm talking about?"

Mac said, "Terrific." He was impressed.

The hiker warmed up a little. "Well, look. I was a hairdresser in Connecticut. I had to get out of that—back there—stress. So now, I cut hair here. It's ironic, I guess. Whites don't like to cut Indian hair. But, I do it. I like to do it. It's something I can do for them. So, in a way, we trade. Some of those old ladies come out to the long house. I shampoo them and style them. They're very happy about that." He checked the entrance again. The dog caught his eyes and riveted to attention. He turned back to Mac.

"So, what have you woven, so far? Anything? Any baskets?" Mac asked.

"Well, I've just about finished a double-lined, cedar-bark rain hat. It's the traditional kind used by the northwest cultures. You know? Quileute, Makah—even Bella Bella's over on the island." He jerked a thumb toward Vancouver Island. He was pleased by Mac's interest. Mac moved over to the cash register. A couple of customers came in looked around and left. Mac was glad of it. "Do you want to see it?"

It was right up Mac's alley. He'd done some reading on northwest tribal art. He was a generalist. He knew a little about rain hats. They were collector's items on the Peninsula. "Absolutely," he responded.

The young man dug deep into a pocket of his backpack and extracted something wrapped in a tie-dyed, mostly indigo-blue cloth. He unrolled it on the counter and revealed a terrifically well made rain-hat. The edges were not quite tied off yet, but it was absolutely authentic in every respect. Mac had seen them before. This one was very fine. And beautifully made—with meticulous attention to detail. He looked at the young man's long slim fingers trained in the hair-grooming profession. Sure, he told himself, the rainhat was made the way a hairdresser might have made it. Lacing, braiding—weaving. It was perfect.

"Look," the hiker said, "it's made of split cedar bark. Inner bark. Not the outer stuff. You soak it for days and then take something sharp, like a knife or shell and strip it into these skinny strips and weave it into this cone shape here. Now this one is not quite finished. I've still got to go another inch or so. I've learned a lot of stuff from those old women. Things like—well—you've got to dig like exactly 15 feet from the center of the cedar trunk to get a certain kind of root for a basket. I mean they know all that." He seemed to be warming up a bit to Mac and to his subject. "And look," he said, "It's got two potlatch rings. I wove them in—for the sake of a design. You know I've never *been* to a potlatch—but—." He smiled and shrugged.

Mac noticed. He was intrigued by the artisanship and commented, "I used to wonder, looking at pictures of these hats, how they could keep anybody dry—let alone a clam-digger or a whale-hunter, you know, in a rain storm." Gently, he picked up the headgear. "But, it's actually two hats—isn't it? Double-woven? A hat within a hat?"

The hiker was pleased. "Yeah—that's it. And she taught me how to do it. Ida Redfern, mostly."

"You know," Mac said, "it looks like a museum quality piece to me—each strand of cedar is perfect. I can't imagine anyone—Indian or anybody, making a rain-hat this fine. I've never seen one this fine. Think of the hours. And you collected the cedar, too?"

"Well, thanks. Yes, I did—dyed the potlach rings with berry."

"Does it fit? Could you try it on?"

"Sure." He slips it on. He looks dopey, of course, with his sallow complexion, camping attire, long blond ponytail and wispy Fu Manchu mustache. But it fits perfectly.

Mac was curious. "Are you actually going to wear this? I mean, is it for sale, or exhibit, or barter, or what?"

"Oh, no. I'll wear it. You bet. The rainy season is just starting."

Mac laughed. "Well, I hope none of the loggers from Forks sees you hitch-hiking with that on." Forks, a neighboring logging community, had demonstrated intolerance toward exotic outsiders.

"Yeah. You're right. It's bad enough with my backpack. I go through Forks real fast and don't draw attention to myself."

Mac looked at his long blond hair and earrings and wondered how he avoided being noticed. His blue backpack had a large peace symbol painted on it with the words PEACE QUEST forming half-circles over the top and bottom of it.

More customers popped in to get out of the fall winds and read the green chalkboard. Mac retrieved his ladder, folded it and placed it against the wall in an alcove. He indicated that it was time for a commercial interruption. "Well," he invited the weaver, "be sure to drop by and keep me posted on what you're doing and how you're getting along. Who knows, maybe someday, I'll be able to buy a basket or something from you." He pointed to the wall exhibit. "Maybe hang it up there on commission—sell it for you."

The hiker rolled the rain-hat neatly up inside the blue cloth. "Thanks," he said. "I'd like that—you've got some great stuff in here. When I get to town to buy supplies—I'll drop by. You know," he said, sighing a little at the irrevocable path in life he had set for himself, "—touch of civilization. You got a Zen section in here?"

"Yeah, sure. Whole shelf."

"Great—I don't have any money right now. Maybe next trip in. Thanks." He took a business card from the brass holder next to the cash register.

Mac thought the hiker enjoyed their little talk. All that reach-out-and-touch-someone business. But, he didn't get his name, then, as he should have. He could have passed his name around to some of the galleries in town. They were always looking for new exhibitors. He went on about his business.

The hiker looped the straps of his backpack around the shoulders of his quilted jacket, creating the pleasant zip-whisp-whisp noise of nylon against nylon.

"Okay, so long," he said.

Mac nodded.

The hiker oomphed out the entrance with his heavy burden. His wriggling dog stayed put, waiting for the hand-signal to heel. Mac imagined that they slept together for warmth. He had a mental picture of them in the long house.

-2-

A couple of months later, Mac received a telephone call. It was in the afternoon. A man's voice addressed him by name.

"Hi, Mr. Tanner?" he said. "Do you remember me? It's Russ." Mac thought he said: Russ. The connection was not good.

"Not exactly," I said. "Give me a clue."

"Well," he explained, "I'm the hiker who was in your bookstore recently with the rain hat—the Quileute rain hat."

Mac remembered. "Sure," I said, "could you speak up?"

"Yep. I've got a problem. For personal reasons, sir, I have to return to Connecticut."

Mac told him he was sorry to hear that. Russ' voice dropped to a whisper again and he couldn't readily hear it. Maybe he needed twenty bucks.

"Well—you know—my mother has cancer. I've got to go take care of her—and there isn't much choice. I'm just in a phone booth here—can you hear me okay, Mr. Tanner?"

"Yes—I'm sorry to hear that—go ahead." He made change for a newspaper and handed it to a customer.

"Oh, sure, thanks. I'm really sorry—and I hate to ask you—but I was wondering—do you remember that rain hat you admired? The one I tried on for you?"

"Sure, terrific—yeah—I remember"

"Well, I've *got* to sell it. I've got to get money to get back to Connecticut."

Those requests always bothered Mac. He'd always tried to help starving artists when he could. He got several requests a month from starving artists to hang a watercolor or show some art. He was a soft touch. He tried to buy some things outright when he could. Hang them on the walls. Try to sell them. Take them in trade for books. Independent bookstores were folding all over the place, thanks to *amazon.com* and *barnesandnoble.com*. Cash was tight. Cash flow was the thing. And difficult to tinker with on short notice. "How much do you need for it?" Mac asked him.

"I need five-hundred dollars. I'm not asking for charity, sir. You remember, you said it was a good hat. Museum quality." He shouted into the telephone. "I remember you said that."

Mac knew he couldn't pop for five-hundred bucks wholesale and then price it to make a profit. And then, Jesus, was it a con? Fake baskets? Stolen rain-hats? Counterfeit canoe paddles and drumheads painted by closet white hobbyists were a growth industry on the Peninsula. Ersatz native art. Gallery owners were taken in regularly by white hustlers with Indian front men. Dealing with them was a roll of the dice. There was a lot of that. After all, the hiker's rain hat, good as it was, was not even authentic in the sense that an Indian wove it. Provenance is everything to the savvy tourist. So many little decisions to ponder. Mac reluctantly decided against it.

"Russ, you know that's a bit out of my range. I'm sorry to tell you that, buddy. I know it's disappointing." Mac felt reasonably certain that the hiker didn't have much more in assets than his knapsack and his dog. His dejection was apparent.

"Look," Mac offered, "next time you're in town drop by, I'll give you twenty bucks, if that'll help you out any." Mac thought of something else. "Okay, now listen, I'm going to give you the name of the owner of the *Spirit Caller Gallery*. She's a friend of mine. She really values the real McCoy. You know what I mean? She only buys the best and she pays top dollar. But I just want to warn you that she might have trouble selling a rain hat woven by a blonde, blue-eyed white guy—just so's you know. She's honest, Russ, and she won't knowingly misrepresent any Indian art. She works out of her house by appointment only. Hang in there—and keep trying until you can get her. Her name is Jan. You can mention my name to her. Okay? Will you do that?" He cradled the telephone and idly fingered some nearby books. "I really don't think you can get top dollar knowing that—but give it a try. See what she says."

The hiker's response crackled through layers of static and disappointment. "Sure," Mac thought he heard him say. He gave him Jan's telephone number, told him he was sorry about his mother and wished him luck. He knew he wouldn't call.

Mac was embarrassed that he had swallowed the hiker's entire story about learning the Indian culture and weaving hats and baskets. He'd believed it all. Right up until he had to put up or shut up. It was easy to believe when there was nothing involved. No money. No commitment. The hiker could be for real. Or he could be a con artist. The most Mac could lose now was twenty bucks. He was ashamed of his suspicions. But, after all—over the telephone. What could he do? Five hundred bucks? Jaysus! He cradled the telephone and shook his head. Jan would know how to handle it. She was a pro. And, besides, she owed him one. From way back.

-3-

A week later, there it was, in all the papers. Mac was on one knee, loading up the orange crate in front of the store with used books, when his eye lit on the article. It was on the front page. A hi-balling logging truck speeding on Hwy 101, just out of Forks, had killed a hiker and his dog. The hiker had apparently been traveling east, with the traffic, instead of against it. The accident was unavoidable. The truck driver said so. He had swerved on black ice to miss them. It looked as if they had moved off the shoulder to pass an obstruction and carelessly drifted too far into the traffic lane. He told investigators that the hiker had a very large backpack that extended over the top of his head. He seemed to be bending forward to adjust the heavy load. He didn't know what hit him. The trucker knew that for sure. It was so sad, he said. It wasn't his fault. The hiker didn't even know what hit him. The driver was not held.

Mac moved inside the store, out of the wind, and scanned the newspaper article again. He checked the hiker's name. It was Russ. Russ something or other. He rose slowly and went inside his shop. According to a member of the tribal council, the long-house where he had been staying had burned to the ground. He was returning to California to spend the winter with his family. Not to Connecticut to nurse his terminally cancerous mother, as he'd told Mac. But, the kid was dead now. It hardly mattered which of his stories was a lie. Maybe they both were.

Mac looked at the chalk board. There were the usual tidal and moon bits; the meteor shower bit—the celebrity birthday bit. The schtick-of-the-day bit. The witty bits. The pungent aphorisms and the 'This Day In History' bit.

Mac looked at all of the announcements and then erased the board clean. He thought about the hiker's dog and he kicked the counter as hard as he could. It was terrible about the dog, too. He remembered how lean it looked, and how he had wondered if it were malnourished, too, its bloody footpads scraped raw on the black ice of remote rural highways. A loyal, adoring pet with his master, caromed into eternity by a logging truck.

It was a pretty sad affair. Mac put another pinch of dried herbs and cinnamon bark in the potpourri cooker. He lifted his eyes to the grimacing Halloween pumpkin in the poster on the wall above the book stacks.

There was no answer there.

The End

THE SEAGULL

With his cruel bow he laid full low
The harmless Albatross
Samuel Taylor Coleridge

A raking offshore breeze whiffed of iodine. It was cold, with the taste of salt, and the sniff of decaying seaweed and grasses. Half a rotting whale carcass deliquesced into the tide line. A sign from the Coastal Commission pounded into the sand read:

WARNING:
DO NOT TOUCH

Green-glass net floats from Japan were randomly strewn about the surf by wind and sputtering tides. Another sign:

WARNING:
Private Reservation Property
Collection of Glass Floats is Forbidden

The sound of the shorebirds below was tossed, like windy flotsam, to the top of the cliff. I stripped to my skivvies and got into my wet suit. I began to warm up immediately. I hefted my wind-surf board off the back of the pickup and hauled it down to Point of Arches—and then back up again for the sail, and my fishing gear.

It was then that I noticed the fledgling gull. It came at me with a clattering beak and piercing squawks, spooking a flock of snipe which were grubbing along the water's edge. Its mother tried to entice it away. She swooped low over me, perturbed and anxious to separate us. The tide was moving rapidly in from three sea stacks which were about 50 yards out from the high-tide line and the water was now too deep for me to return the chick to its rookery and get myself back. It must have fallen from its nest on one of the stacks and waddled ashore during low tide. I dropped my

gear and walked over to the bird, cornering it against a rocky outcropping.
I decided that the best thing to do was to set it up the cliff face behind me
where the mother could feed it and watch over it. I looked back up the cliff.
There were plenty of footholds and some protective madrona overhang.
Perfect. It was no big deal.

When I picked up the bird and started to climb, I was very surprised,
not only by its weight, but by its unexpectedly high body temperature. It
felt very alive. Pinfeathers and barely emergent flight feathers erupted from
its fat, healthy body. It was strong and very aggressive. It bit the back of
my hand with a powerful beak, like needle-nose pliers, really, and refused
to let go. I swore and reflexively, almost threw the gull to the beach below.
I pried its beak off my hand and quickly released it to the safety of a rocky
shelf about 25 feet up the side of the cliff. The distraught mother wheeled
and cried at me to get away from her chick. I obliged by descending at
full tilt and when I looked at her again, she had tuned me out and was
regurgitating a meal into her chick's yawning beak.

I went slightly north, around the crescent of this inlet, to a location
where I'd always had good luck with rockfish, and cast out, using as bait
some frozen herring I'd picked up at Swain's. I could quite easily see the
mother gull and her chick interacting on the cliff and I, her hero-protector,
felt self-satisfied. It was early evening yet and the illumination from the
late afternoon sun was excellent. I snagged a couple of sculpin in fairly
short order and leaned against the rocky abutment, smoking and thinking
and checking out those two birds. On one of her trips, fretting over this
safe, but otherwise unwelcome location for her chick, the mother floated
over to me and, hanging stationary on a zephyr, fixed me with a cold stare
before disappearing to search for another meal for her voracious offspring.
I suspected that she blamed me for the fix she was in and I could well
understand her concern. Very few birds in my experience ever survived the
trauma of nest dislocation.

When I next looked in the direction of the fledgling, I saw a wedge
of deer bolt along the edge of the surf and vanish like mist into the forest
which played tag here and there with the water's edge. Advancing wavelets
immediately erased all evidence of their hoof prints behind them and I
wondered that I had seen them at all. At some point I noticed that the
hyperactive fledgling had somehow fallen from this new perch on the cliff
where I'd placed it. It flapped about for a few pitiable moments before it
was spotted and stalked by a red fox which I'd earlier seen foraging on the
beach for small crustaceans.

I dropped my fishing rig immediately and raced over to the foot of the cliff. The fox retreated when I came into view, but I was too late. The young gull had apparently broken its neck in the fall and it now lay lifeless upon the rocks. By this time, the mother bird had returned with another gullet-full of sea life and took in the situation at a glance. There I was again, somehow implicated. She dove at me repeatedly, in exasperation at this new plight of her offspring. I didn't have the guts to bury the just-dead chick, nearly as large as a pullet, in a hole in the sand—bury it cold, deep, wet and alone. If I had known then what was to transpire, however, I would have hidden the corpse from its tormented mother who, sheering above us, plaintively beseeched it to rise with her into the heavens. To bury the chick at all seemed, somehow, an unholy thing to do; it had been so recently throbbing with life. Maybe it would be better to remove myself from the loop, an interfering human animal, and to consign the fledgling to the food chain. I knew the fox was probably still watching. And other animals, perhaps. Ravens. Hungry. All waiting. Coyotes in the bear grass. Watching. I looked at the pink-and-grey translucent skin of the lifeless creature at my feet and pondered how nature could ever transform such a helpless, clumsy sheath of pinfeathers, filled with regurgitated fish, into a sleek, mean flying machine. Getting from—A to B—was certainly one of the mysteries of existence.

I went back to my fishing gear and prepared to cast out again. Soon enough, the bold fox, unafraid of me across the crescent of lagoon which separated us, warily reemerged from the edge of the forest and claimed its sizable trophy—a magnificent windfall—for itself and its kits. I felt terrible. I'd hunted and fished for years with Max and couldn't remember when I'd felt so bad about an animal in the wild.

I returned to my fishing and cast out a fairly sizable piece of herring. It hit the water with a neat splash, but before it could sink, the mother gull, which had been monitoring me, dropped from nowhere like a peregrine falcon, as if she had been watching and waiting, to snag some possession away from me—tit for tat. She immediately swooped skyward, taking the bait and the hook with her. It was pretty obvious that she had the hook imbedded in her throat. I released the lock on my reel and allowed her some slack, hoping somehow, to avoid the damage to her gullet that would be caused by my retracting the line.

The bird turned and looked at me in complete surprise. I wasn't sure what to do. She was a living kite. I thought perhaps that if I gently reeled her in I could capture her and remove the hook. The loosely billowing fishing line described a gentle but hazardous connection between me and the bird. Frantic, but with no other choice, I slowly reeled her toward me and listened to her now terrible cries of distress as she tried, in a frenzy, to disgorge the hook and bait. Her irrational panic alarmed me and, as she drew near, I was afraid that she might fall into the rough water and drown. I was absolutely sure that this bird was the mother of the chick I had previously saved, and I desperately wanted to help her. Dozens of squabbling, tufted puffins and common mores, feeding their own young, seemed indifferent to her plight. As she approached, I stumbled on the slippery rocks. My right arm was numb with pain from finessing my heavy surfing rod. Nervous and agitated, I dropped it into the water churning below me, but at the last instant, I somehow managed to grab the line with my hand and to get my knife out of its holster. I quickly cut the fishing line and the bird was now free and able to wheel about.

She flew toward me then, supported on a fairly strong offshore breeze, and once again seemed to look me straight in the eye with about twenty-five feet of that thirty-pound test line hanging from her beak. After a moment she flew above my head and disappeared over the top of the cliff behind me.

It was all over in a couple of minutes. I was devastated. Depressed. I packed up all my windsurfing gear and hauled for home. I wouldn't windsurf tonight.

.. ..

"Lewis, honey—Jackie and Little Max are coming by tomorrow on their way to the Greyhound—she says she wants to drop something off for you before she goes to Seattle." She held the telephone away from her mouth, lit a cigarette, and, with her little finger, picked something from the tip of her tongue. "You going to be here?"

"What time?"

"What time?" she relayed to Jackie.

"She says around eleven. Bus leaves at 11:45."

"Sure." Lewis tossed the TV Guide to the top of the coffee table.

After Dee Ann hung up she came to sit beside Lewis on the sofa. She took his collar in her fingertips and smoothed out some wash-and-wear wrinkles and brushed away some Cheeto crumbs from the front of his shirt. He didn't like it when she tidied him up as if he were a little boy. He was in a black mood and he seemed to have no control over it.

"That's the end of a chapter, Lewis. Jackie going to Seattle. Starting over. We're going to have to start over too, honey." Lewis knew that Dee Ann would be giving him a pep talk. He could sense it. She always pulled the theme out of thin air, cobbled what she needed from someone else's life experience, some self-help column, and adapted it to suit their own needs. "Lewis, honey," she began, "I know how you feel about that seagull, but believe me when I tell you it was nothing personal—if you know what I mean—when you said it looked at you in a funny way like it was accusing you.

"But the thing here is, Lewis, you got to put that behind you—and you got to put the death of Max behind you—we both have to—and you got to go out and get a job. Now, listen, why don't you go on down to that hiring hall at the port. Get an application to join their longshoreman's union, like you said, if that's what it takes. Or, honey, hang around there and find out what it does take. You know how to do that—talk it up with the guys down there. Union pay is good pay, Lewis. They got benefits, honey. Medical. We got another aircraft carrier coming in here to scrap—it's in the paper—you saw that—that'd be six-months work—that new yacht outfitter coming in here—we don't care if we do have to wait for a while until it's our turn to get into the union. I can still do perms down at Dottie's. You can do anything, Lewis, while you're waiting. You don't care. The thing is, you have to be ready and you have to be upbeat and you have to have a real positive attitude so that when opportunity presents itself—you'll be ready for it." She sat back and gazed up to the ceiling figuring how she could refine her message further. Jan, at her work, said that she had a real knack for talking up problems.

Her voice, and the now familiar message, sounded sing-songy. Lewis thought it could be set to music. Lewis didn't answer immediately. He'd heard this pep talk a thousand times. "My head is killing me." He massaged his temples.

"Look, honey, I know it has something to do with those damned seagulls."

"Two beautiful birds, Dee Ann."

"Lewis, c'mon, already. Seagulls are rats with wings. Rats with wings. They hang out at the garbage dump over by the airport. There's millions of them. I mean it's not like they are eagles, Lewis. Or even albatrosses. Albatrosses—they mate for life, Lewis. Elegant. Spend years at sea. Do you know what I'm talking about?"

"But look how she suffered. I saw it in her face. I swear I did. She thought I killed her chick and then—what happened after."

"Lewis, you know that if you just went out and tried to get a job, you wouldn't let your mind play tricks on you this way." Lewis got up and popped a beer. "I mean, honey, it's a trick your mind is playing on you. Animals do not *think* like that. If they did, we'd all be in trouble. And Lewis, trust me—you can't read anything in the face of a seagull-like the face of Jesus in a tortilla for god sakes. Seagulls are rats with wings—I'm telling you."

"That's b.s.," Lewis said, in a dark monotone. "Everybody knows *pigeons* are rats with wings." He slumped back onto the sofa.

"It's seagulls—Lewis—seagulls—ask anybody."

"Get some batteries, Dee Ann, while you're out. AAA batteries. The batteries are damn dead in this here damn remote." Lewis tossed the remote to the top of the coffee table.

.. ..

From time to time, when I park my pickup truck at the top of the bluff at Point of Arches or when I stand at the cliffs overlooking Shi Shi Beach or Ruby Beach, and I look past the sea-stacks at the horizon stretching away from me, I am as primitive man, wondering what's over the edge of that horizon line. And beyond that and beyond that. Not all the maps in the world can take away the wonder of discovery and the promise of the unexpected which come to me when I look upon that thin straight line. Is it true that, at sea-level, the distance between you and the horizon line is only 60 miles? Or is it 90 miles? I've forgotten. But I know where to look it up and I might do that.

I have an urge deep inside me to sail my board over to the edge of that line. It's a powerful urge. Powerful and instinctual. Windsurfing does that to you. The effect is hypnotic. That's the best way I can express it. The thrill of getting out of the sight of land on my board, with only me and my sail, is part of it, too. Dangerous and stupid. The potential danger of it—that feeling of terror in the pit of your stomach—that's a big part of the attraction. How close can you get to the edge of that edge before you fall off? There are times when I really think I do have two selves since Max died. Myself, the one that Dee Ann is married to, and another self who I know is there, somewhere, but a self I cannot see, invisible, but a presence, like the wind, pushing me—pushing me tirelessly. Nagging. Mysterious.

I have only to incline my sail into it. Catch its power. Everyone is two people, Max used to say. And I used to laugh at that. But Max might be right. Max always knew about those things.

So, yes, I do have this dream. Since Max's death. I can't shake it. I have this dream that I'm headed for that horizon. Trying to race ahead of this other self who is knifing through the water just behind me. I'm trying like hell to outrace him. Or—outrace it. Whatever it is. Maybe it's Max. Maybe it's our dad. Maybe it's me—that other self that I think about. My alter ego? As he gains on me—and we are out of sight of land, way, way out there and I screw up somehow, shearing-in my sail, so that it doesn't anymore—catch the wind anymore—to pull me along anymore—but instead fouls my sail and dumps me, in a massive wipeout, into black, inky water filled with what I'm sure are horrific, grasping, unimaginable aquatic monsters and, for the first time, I'm afraid, and my board is out of reach and I flounder toward it gasping for air and the water is like ice and that's when I wake up and pull myself together in the dark of our bedroom with Dee Ann beside me breathing quietly and dreaming her own sad dreams. I drop back down upon my pillow, dank with night sweat, and the game starts all over again, that dream race—that wind race—and it's just getting so I can't handle it anymore—can't ignore it—and it won't go away and each night, I pray that I might wake from that dream and start my life over again as somebody else. Another self. To get it right.

.. ..

Her voice was stressed. "Lewis, if you want a salad, you are going to have to make it yourself—I'm running late." Dee Ann looked around the kitchen door jamb to where Lewis was sitting on the sofa. The shades were pulled. CNN was on. The audio was off. "You still got that headache?"

"Uhm."

"Margie said that they are going to open a WAL*MART over there across from K-MART. You know, Lewis, you could get a job there in the garden department or the paint department. You could be a WAL*MART associate. June's brother is A.M. in the paint department in the Boise K-MART and he's got nothing you don't have in spades, Lewis."

"A.M.?"

"Assistant Manager, Lewis. Here, you want to taste this?" She offered him a teaspoonful of spaghetti sauce. He waved it away. "I got the chunky style, Lewis—mushrooms and garlic. Remember we liked that last time?"

The rejection didn't bother her. "You know, Lewis, when you get a job—a regular job—your headaches are going to go away just like that." She snapped her fingers. "You never had a headache when you worked at the shake mill—I would've remembered." Lewis shrugged. "Are you still having those dreams, sugar?" He nodded. She put the spoonful of spaghetti sauce into her own mouth and returned to the kitchen.

"Lewis, you hear what I said?" The suffocating scent of spaghetti sauce wafted in from the stovetop. "If you don't want a salad, hon, please make one for me and I'll eat it after I come home." Dee Ann's bowling league met every Friday for beers and laughs. "But put some Saran over it and put it in the fridge and don't put any ranch dressing on it—it wilts the lettuce. Oh damn—flies getting in here." She batted her hand. "I did four perms today, Lewis," she hollered at him. "Four. I'll put on my own ranch dressing when I get home." Lewis winced. "And just leave the spaghetti on the stove—but cover it—it's too hot for the fridge."

Lewis picked his bathrobe off the floor where the dog had been sleeping on it. "C'mon, boy" he told him. It was warm from the dog's body. Lewis pulled the terry-cloth belt from the robe and wrapped it around his forehead and twisted it tightly. His migraine was going into overdrive.

"You know, Lewis, this town is dying. We could easily move into Port Angeles—hook up our trailer in Cedar Cove Park and get the jump on all those WAL*MART wannabes." Dee Ann's voice crackled from the other room like heat lightning. She snapped her fingers, thinking aloud, "What do they call them, again? *Associates*. Well anyway, there won't be a trailer slot available in the whole damned county once they start construction." Lewis didn't answer. His temples were throbbing. "Attention, Wal*Mart shoppers," she chortled. If he had a gun he would have shot himself. "I look okay?" She came around the corner, smoothing her jeans. "They're new, Lewis. Like them? I don't honestly know how I can go bowling after doing four perms—it is so hard holding up your arms like that for hours, Lewis, doing rollers—pin curls—the smell of that perm solution?" She didn't look that tired, Lewis thought. She adjusted her bra straps and looked down at him. "Lewis, honey, you going to be able to eat some? Look, don't worry about the salad. I don't even want a salad—not after today—really. Jan brought in some broccoli florets and some dip," she lied. Lewis looked up at her. "Oh, God, look at those eyes. So dark and troubled." She flipped a quick look at the clock. "And Dr. Karsch, he won't give you any more of those pills? They didn't work anyway, did they, hon?"

Lewis shook his head and tightened the terry-cloth binding around his skull until his eyes were drawn together.

"Lewis, that looks awful—it always leaves those marks in your forehead like you've been tortured or somethin', honey. Lewis, you want me to stay home? I could give you a cold bath—ice cubes?" She breathed in his ear. "Whatever you want." She looked at the kitchen clock over his shoulder and reached for her bag.

Lewis shook his head and closed his eyes. He felt her quick kiss and he heard the front door of the trailer rattle to an inconclusive close behind her—like the lid on a trash can. The balance of the trailer on its cement block pinions shifted slightly as she moved onto the steps. Lewis could feel that. When he felt like it, he'd have to shim up the trailer again. Dee Ann would have to stand inside and rock the trailer and he'd watch underneath to see where to insert a cedar wedge. A glass of beer, or a cup of coffee on the kitchen table, like the bubble in a carpenter's level, told the whole story about that trailer. It was the last thing he and his brother, Max, had done together. Pain, like hot rivets, hammered into his skull. He covered his eyes with his arm looking for blackness and relief. Max had manned the hydraulic jack and Lewis had inserted the shims. It was a piece of work. A real piece. He and his brother laughed like lunatics during the installation. Hot. Sweaty. Dee Ann had to come out of the trailer and squat down to see what was so funny. Two grimy moles under the trailer, laughing at some silliness from their childhood. A glass of water on the pink Formica kitchen table was down a half-inch on the north side. Dee Ann wouldn't let them out from under the trailer until the water in that glass was level.

Lewis remembered there was this trick house when he and Max were kids. It was somewhere between the Tillamook cheese factory in Oregon, and Gilroy, the Garlic Capital of the World, in California. The House of Illusions. You walked along from room to room in this old house after paying your twenty-five cents—threadbare carpets tacked to the floor, saucers and teacups glued on to tables with two shortened legs—and your body thinking it was walking up an incline or sideways and your muscles pulling on the back of your leg exactly the same as if you were walking up a hill or at a slant. But it was all illusion. A fake. Lewis felt nauseous when he got out of that house and Max and his father ridiculed him for it. He'd been fooled by smoke and mirrors and made a fool of. Max was a rock. Said he had a gyroscope in his head. Kept him upright. He was like their father. Nothing fooled Max.

And now, this sad trailer. Like a box of Old Fashioned Quaker Oats. Cylindrical. Shifting crazily with each footfall and each step, creating a mysterious, echoey resonance when they walked from room to room as if they lived, maybe, inside an oil drum or inside another house of illusions. Boom. Bah boom. Bah boom.

.. ..

There was a time. before he got married, that Lewis and his brother had quarreled. It was friendly rivalry, really. Max had asked him how he could ever marry a girl named Dee Ann Traci, who dotted the 'i' in her middle name with a cutesy little circle. He told Lewis that he had a plastic Safeway bag filled with love letters from Dee Ann if he wanted to read them. Lewis figured Max was lying just to get his goat. On the other hand, Max had slept with every girl in the west end. They were attracted to him like iron filings to a magnet. He had an open, sunny face and an easy masculine grace that both men and women found irresistible. The personality kid. Lewis tempered his worship of his brother with a certain amount of healthy skepticism. Max always offered his seasoned observations on every girl Lewis had ever dated or who even brushed up against him in the taverns and singles bars. Lewis just wished that Max would shut up and let him do his own cruising and make his own mistakes with women. Max always bequeathed him his leftovers. Chippies. Bar flies. His very jaded conquests. They'd hoped that they were getting another Max. They weren't. They'd never get another Max. They got him. Lewis. The other brother.

There would be no more memories of Max. Lewis would have to make do with what he had. Windsurfing and concerts at the Gorge; getting sunburned in the open air amphitheatre, over there, listening to Tom Petty and the Heartbreakers. Listening to Mark O'Conner playing Ashokan Farewell; listening to Max noodle away on his blues harmonica and joking with Dee Ann. Joking with her and winking at her so cool, but neither of them ever letting on they had slept together. Sooner or later, Max married Jackie, who he'd met in the billiards' playoffs at Loomis' Tavern. And now, here she was moving away to Seattle, taking Little Max with her. Life goes on, Max always said—you never in this world, can step into the same river twice. What? Lewis, asked him, where in the hell did you hear that? And Max would laugh. So, here they were. Dee Ann and her two miscarriages, barring a miracle, assured Lewis that there would never be a Little Max or a Little Lewis for them. So far, there were no miracles on the horizon.

Max was killed on the job. It was a freak accident. He was a chaser for Bennington. Before Bennington bought a log processor all the trimming was done by muscle. A cedar log Max was stripping rolled unexpectedly, ripping away his leg and part of his hip. He died a horrible and protracted death on the forest floor surrounded by a thick carpet of trillium and golden, odiferous skunk cabbage. Wrapped in a Carhart shroud. His cries echoing through the clear-cut. One of his beefy logger buddies wept when he told Lewis that Max looked so peaceful there, among those flowers; that he looked as if he'd already been laid out in the funeral parlor. Lewis went there himself. Alone. And he took in the site, looking skyward and tracking the fall of that old-growth cedar, long gone already to the mill, and converted to two-by-fours, and he arced his arm several times to get the hang of the fall of the giant tree, tracked where it had lain, and he paced out its length and followed along it to the patch of trillium, which had no reason to lament Max's death by shriveling up, and he could smell the skunk cabbage, just like Max's buddy had said, a putrid odor like rotting flesh. In that other world, on the dark side of death, Lewis surmised, funerary urns were filled with skunk cabbage.

Lewis sat down on the stump of the tree that had killed Max. Morels would soon enough pop up through the spongy vegetation. He looked about and figured that if Max had to go, maybe this was the perfect place. A forest floor a thousand years old, a thousand feet deep, exposed now, to the dazzle of harsh daylight. A clear-cut. Tiny blue wildflowers poking through the shag. It took forty minutes for the rescue helicopter to get to him. Somebody forgot to pack the smoke flares. Most likely it was Max, himself. Happy go lucky. Immortal. Lewis pulled the seedling out of his pack and unwrapped it, spreading the roots gently. He made a slit in the soft aromatic soil near where Max had been crushed and inserted the little cedar. Amazing Grace. How sweet thou art. In 100-years, it too would be turned into Adirondack chairs and picnic tables. A cedar for Max.

"He didn't suffer, Lewis," Jackie had told him. "He didn't suffer and nothing's going to bring him back again and you got to buck up."

Lewis looked blankly at her. Of course he suffered. He guessed she was in denial about that. She didn't want to imagine Max's screams of agony, there in that forest, and so she made up protective clichés. He didn't suffer, Lewis. Let's get on with it. Lewis would not forget and Lewis would not deny. Jackie repeated all those things as if they were memorized shtick and as if those were the exact same things that others had said to her, in ritualized kindness, at the funeral parlor. Everybody knew what had happened. They all came to the funeral. Nodding their heads. Shaking their heads. Looking grim. Who'd be next? It's lucky, Lewis, you are a twin. Twin brothers. It's like having a backup, buddy. Sicko Ben Hillyard said that. Whispered it to him—a sincere, sad and sickly smile on his beer-bloated face. So Lewis was a backup now, with no backup.

Afterward, Little Max reached out for him and called him daddy—he looked so like his twin. Lewis held little Max on his hip as if he were his own and hugged him hard and wondered at how much he looked like Big Max and, therefore, like himself. Gimme a hug, little buddy, he said and I'll catch up with you later. Would he be alive to see him grow into manhood? He was glad Jackie went to live in Seattle with Little Max. There were no stands of timber over there in Seattle waiting to be logged—waiting to roll on you when you weren't looking. What would Little Max remember about this day? Little kids don't know from twins. What a gas.

It was shortly after Max died that lumber had gone all to pot on the Peninsula. Shake mills began closing right and left. California passed a dozen laws forbidding shake roofs on homes in the foothills. For many years, the Golden State was the biggest customer for shakes. The downturn in business was swift and catastrophic. The Peninsula withered. Lewis was, for the first time, an unemployed forest products worker. A statistic with a fancy name.

Jackie knocked on the door to the trailer just before she left town. Dee Ann let her in.

"Go easy," Dee Ann whispered to her, "he's really bummed out." She tapped her temple with a long acrylic finger nail and took the baby from Jackie's arms. "Headache."

Jackie handed Lewis the shirt Max was wearing when he was killed. She had carefully washed and folded it. Max's red logging suspenders were coiled neatly on top. It looked as if she were presenting him a flag at a military funeral.

"Max would have wanted you to have these," she said. She started to bawl. "And Little Max, too." She turned to Dee Ann and took the baby back asking him, "Wouldn't he, sugar?" She looked back at Lewis. "You know, Lewis—just so's you know—Max really loved you." Little Max looked owlishly at the proceedings. Jackie glanced at her Timex. Her mother tapped the horn of the Bronco. "Well," she said nervously, "bus'll be leaving from Gordy's in ten minutes."

"We'll write," Dee Ann whispered to her. "Y'all call us and give us your new address right away."

Lewis gave Jackie and Little Max a hug.

.. ..

Lewis' Mistral Energizer XR board was a very good choice for him. He and Max had scoped it out. It had cost a little more up front, but it had great speed, handling, and the weight was right at 15.1 pounds. The width and volume forward made it tolerant of mistakes in weight distribution and it worked perfectly on all the jibes they could think of, especially the carving step jibe, the pivot and the carving pivot. It was a great board for nasty Cape Flattery ocean chops and swells, and the cape was a perfect place to practice water starts after a wipeout. Lewis could keep his Energizer on the water when the other race boards around him were taking off like Catalina flying fish. He was glad he'd got it. It was his last major purchase before the Olympic Premium Shake Mill folded for good. No regrets. Max gave it his approval. They had both learned windsurfing on Max's convertible wave board. There is probably no place on the West Coast that's better for sailing a convertible board than Cape Flattery. The winds are highly variable, 10-35 knots, and you can sail nearly any imaginable condition in any seventy-two hour period. Lewis was ready for an upgrade and the Energizer board fit the bill.

Lewis had earlier checked the Weather Channel report for the north Pacific high, which circulates air clockwise and strikes the coast from the northwest, a powerful system affecting most of the weather in the U.S. All systems were go.

.. ..

Saturday night on the sofa. Floor lamps off. CNN flickering. Larry King weekend. Dee Ann had just left. Two nights in a row, now. What's going on? Jan picked her up. Bowling league finals, Dee Ann told him. Something like that. Sure you won't come, Lewis? You sure? We gotta go, Jan nudged her. We'll be late. So long, Lewis. Jan smiled at him. Dee Ann leaned over and gave him an air kiss.

The telephone rang. Lewis gently shooed the dog off his feet and limped in to the kitchen table, his head bound again in the terrycloth belting. He picked up the telephone.

"Hello?"

"Hi, honey, it's me."

"Hi." He tried to sound upbeat.

"How you feeling, Lewis?"

"Great." He twisted the binding tighter around his head.

"Oh, that's super, honey. Now listen—we're still waiting for our lanes. I been sitting here and talking to Reverend Petersen—you know, the Church of Christ league?" Her voice had a habit of rising at the end of her sentences, as if she were asking a question. As if she were raised in Canada, just across the Straits.

"Right," Lewis said.

"Honey, Reverend Petersen, he says that he believes that you have depression—says that you are depressed?" Lewis hears her turn away from the phone and the background noise of the Evergreen Lanes is very loud and intrusive. The sound of strikes and of raucous laughter and good-natured cussing almost smothered her voice. He hears her ask Reverend Petersen if that isn't right, what she had said. "Yes, Lewis. He says you've probably got clinical depression, honey—that's different from regular depression—and he says that you should seek professional counseling and he would like to talk to you sometime soon. He hasn't seen you since he married us?"

Lewis tried to hold in his anger. He whispered into the telephone, placing his cheek onto the cold pink Formica table. "Dee Ann, I've told you never to talk about me or us in public again in any way and you just don't get it. That stuff's personal. Do you think I want all those godammed bozos down there to know anything about me or my headaches? Jesus."

"But, Lewis, Reverend Petersen, he says that your problem is—you think too hard—too much—he says you should lighten up, honey. He says that—"

"Oh, for Christ's sake."

"Lewis, I'm just trying—"

"Jesus, why don't you just write out our whole life story, including your miscarriages, scribble it right out on the score sheet and project it on the overhead so the whole go dammed bowling alley can read about us? Dee Ann, how many beers you had?"

"Well, I don't know. Two?"

"You been gone thirty minutes and you already had two beers? Are you chuggalugging, Dee Ann?"

"Lewis—"

"*You* might want to think about counseling."

She lowered her voice. "And, Lewis, you might just want to take three deep breaths. I know you didn't mean that and you know you didn't mean that."

"I'm sorry—but please don't talk about me in the bowling alley and in the checkout line at JiffyMart. You know what that little blonde clerk said to me the other day? Up at Road Runner's? That Judy? She said to me she hears they are going to start a program up at the college to train displaced timber workers to be either plumbers or guards out at the prison and I, like really, ought to fuckin' look into it. Now, why in the hell do you suppose she said that to me, Dee Ann? Did I just happen to look like I wanted to be a plumber as I counted out my food stamps? What do I have to do, Dee Ann, to find a market you haven't been into talking about us?"

"Okay, honey-okay-okay-look, our lanes are freed up now—look—what do you want me to do? You want me to come on home?" Her voice faded as she turned away from the phone to talk to someone. "Say whaaat, now, Lewis?"

"Oh, hell no. Have some fun. Bowl your heart out. You deserve it. We just have to discuss this, Dee Ann. I might go for a sail, there's some time left, yet. Two hours of sun."

"Oh, honey, that's great. Maybe tonight you'll see that green flash. Sky looks clear. Know what I mean?"

"Maybe." Lewis was sorry he'd told her about the green flash.

"Just like you told me, Lewis. It might be a sign. You watch for that."

"Right, Dee Ann." Maybe he would see the green flash. The Holy Grail for nature watchers. Lord knows he'd tried often enough. All you need is an unobstructed horizon line and clear air. Light refraction on a cosmic scale. Just when the last crescent edge of the sun vanishes at sunset—that flash of green.

"And Lewis? Reverend Petersen wants you to listen and see if the sun hisses when it hits the water—isn't that a stitch?"

"Sure is, Dee Ann—you can just tell Reverend Petersen that's a *stitch* all right." He could hear Petersen snickering in the background. Lewis blew Dee Ann a kiss and hung up the phone.

The kitchen table wiggled annoyingly beneath his cradled head. The cedar shims were crumbling. The whole trailer—his life—a house of cards. Teetering. Slanted. Ready to slide off the foundation.

.. ..

Lewis felt a subtle shift in his windsurfing plans for the evening. Usually, he'd wear his long-legged wet suit with short sleeves. Perfect for June through September. At least down at the Gorge. But this time, for no hard reason that he could think of, he suited up in his dry suit—a full steamer. The low humidity and clear skies on the coast made it cool at night and he didn't need a wipeout in 40-degree water.

By the time he got loaded up and out to the launch site at the headland, there was about an hour's worth of sunlight left. He plowed through a carpet of ferns, salal and huckleberry. Cormorants and pigeon guillemots darted about anticipating nightfall. He glanced at the sea stacks eroded into fantastic shapes by boiling surf—ghostly sea bathers urging him to join them for a swim. The water was wonderfully bracing and somehow just being in it made him feel better. He paddled out to a point just beyond the surf and made a water start.

The sun was a coppery red. A shimmering, spellbinding disk. It perched on the edge of the horizon, and beckoned to him irresistibly. The sky itself was afire. He was mesmerized by the beauty of it and close to sensory overload. His exhilaration knew no bounds. The slap of the ocean, and the movements of the chops and swells, transferred directly from the bottom of his board to his bare feet. The sensation was that of running and he was intoxicated by it. His toes moved back and forth on the rubber grips, looking for the perfect balance. His muscles flexed comfortably as he gripped the rail and he leaned into the back draft as if it were a supportive palm. He heeled in the sail to achieve maximum wind power and he was soon a mere whisper from becoming airborne.

The wind was behind him, now, and he directly harnessed its powerful energy, hurtling through the water toward his goal, the enormous, pulsating disk of that setting sun, which seemed the very essence of his consciousness. He observed anxiously that it was now beginning to slip over the edge of this new universe in which he found himself, and descending rapidly into a molten sea, spangled with broken shafts of ruby laser light, too bright, nearly, to look at. Max. Dee Ann. The trailer. All of that. Vanished.

Lewis wanted to catch up with that disk as if he were in some kind of cosmic relay race. Max had told him that they could carry the baton for only a while and then, maybe, with a bit of luck and perfect timing, they might hope to pass the baton to someone else coming up behind them. And that was what seemed to be happening—that recurrent dream of his—a virtual reality—come to life, somehow, taking him inside that dream, and yet external to it, observing its particulars—but powerless to change anything—a passive player unable to control any aspect of it.

Suddenly, out of nowhere it seemed, a large gull, white against the crackling red sunset and against the disk of the rapidly falling sun, floated directly in front of him, engaging him to look at it. Lewis clasped the handrail even harder and stared back, puzzled by the gull's startling single-mindedness until, after a moment, he noticed that it had a length of fishing line trailing from its mouth. Lewis let out a squall of recognition and quickly executed a maneuver with his monofilm main panel to frighten her away from him, but she easily eluded everything he threw at her—fancy pivots and acrobatic jumps. What could she want of him? Lewis thought of her chick, flopping uselessly with a broken neck at the foot of the cliff. The gull swooped low, staring eye-to-eye in an accusatory manner, keeping pace with him, playing the prevailing westerly, hovering upon it, nearly stationary, as if she were in a wind tunnel.

Lewis clawed at the air in a futile effort to snag the wind-whipped fishing line protruding from her beak. Artfully, she stayed just out of contact as if to lure him into abandoning his board, in one daring and risky overreach, and then to fall into the sea and drown. Lewis shouted hoarsely at the gull to get lost—to leave him alone—and, after a time, apparently more tired of her grim, taunting game than any of his threats, she disappeared.

Darkness descended then like a theater curtain. The play of the water which had always seemed so inviting now struck fear in Lewis. He felt terror. Panic. Emptiness. He looked over his shoulder and he saw that he was now out of sight of land, but he couldn't comprehend how he'd traveled so far. He'd lost all sense of time. Even Tatoosh Island and its lighthouse, like a drunken cupcake, with a birthday candle on it, had been extinguished, immolated in the sea behind him. Lewis also had the sense that something was gaining on him. He didn't know what it was, but he could feel its presence. He looked again over his shoulder into the void. Blood-red sky and water—one color. Nothing.

He turned back. He was on a roll now and he had a profound sense of mission—an even keener desire to peer over the edge of the horizon line—just over the edge of it—to see right into that red and awesome disappearing disk—moth to candle flame.

For a few moments Lewis experienced a heady feeling—a heightened awareness of both his solitude and his puniness on a vast and empty sea. A spiritual event that he couldn't really define. It was followed by a momentary thrill of utter aloneness that prickled his skin. He immediately passed through an invisible portal and entered a kind of emotional paradise—a drugless high—a transcendence. The experience was overpowering. He wanted Max to be there to explain it all to him. Max, his twin. His other. His alter ego. He wanted Max to pull him into eternity after him, even as he'd led the way for him, by two minutes, through the birth canal, and into their sad and haunted lives.

The sun dropped rapidly and, in the blink of an eye, Lewis knew he'd never be fast enough to overtake it. He felt and heard the whisper of the wind against his wet suit and felt the rhythm of the roiling whitecaps as they connected with the underside of his board. He heard himself holler out the name of his brother but there was no answer to his cry. He looked again over his shoulder. It was completely dark now and there was little to see. He watched the last slim crescent of the sun disappear. It was just then that an explosion of green hit his retina for a fraction of a second—the green flash. It was immediately swamped by the stronger red spectrum of the setting sun. But he caught it. That haunting glimpse of emerald. No more than that. All systems go. Off to see the Wizard. Emerald City.

Lewis wasn't sure when he understood that he was finally on his own. Solitary. Disembodied. Far from landscape. Remote from memory. He'd undergone a catharsis and a massive, crippling fatigue began to set in. He didn't know how long he'd be able to hold on to the boom of his sail. But he knew one thing for sure. He wouldn't need Max to explain anything to him anymore. He had no dread. His soul was quiet. As he headed out to sea, he fathomed at last, that it was Death which had been haunting him in the miserable nights since Max had died. He was in a relay race with Death. And he'd have to pass his baton to the grim, wet-suited reaper, trolling around out there somewhere behind him in the dark—breathing down his neck—nipping just at his heels—close to overtaking him.

The angry gull, hovering in the dark periphery of his vision, cried sharply, reappeared and dropped low over Lewis for one last, red-eyed assessment of his misery before evaporating over his shoulder into the haunted night sky that enveloped them both.

Her mission completed, the gull headed back toward the mainland without him.

The End

TATTOOS

I

The gallery had only been open a few weeks. It was a converted restaurant with several nice rooms and pleasing broken views so that customers weren't aware of clerks and owners. If they wanted to whisper about this or that painting, they could whisper. And maybe snicker at the prices. There was a dog-leg turn and an arched doorway, and a bend here and a turn there and friendly little alcoves where small-town lovers could meet for hurried confidences.

The old steam-table and salad-bar grotto with its fancy copper hood had been retained by the remodelers and it now housed a perfect mini-office with a typewriter, desk and a potpourri-cooker to make the gallery smell like cinnamon and cloves. There were times when the owner felt as if he ought to slice roast beef in it just for the old-timers who remembered the place as a restaurant before its abandonment many years earlier.

Partridge looked around. He was satisfied. The old building had finally been rehabilitated. His wife had decorated everything in a discreet grey to show off the art. Trak lighting added the crowning professional touch. The lower dining room was made into a frame shop. It was separated from the main gallery room by a six-panel mahogany screen carved in China early in the century. The frame shop had all the latest equipment. Oval mat cutters, glass cutters, straight mat cutters, joiners, vacuum presses, glass. Molding lengths in various colors and patterns reached to the ceiling in neat soldierly rows, and hundreds of sample frame corners covered the walls.

Lina ran the frame shop. Miraculously, Partridge had found her in the want ads. He watched over the watercolors, drawings and fine art prints which hung on the gallery walls and, when anything needed to be framed he discreetly paged Lina up to the main desk for introductions and consultation.

That first month Lina concentrated on framing as many fine art posters as possible. The walls had to be covered with prints—a large deli-case of low-end art. She framed over a hundred of them during those first exciting new-business weeks. The shop hadn't yet had any requests for custom framing from walk-ins. Partridge was nervous about it. That first order loomed forbiddingly, like nearby Mt. Olympus. Would the public ever discover the gallery? He hoped it would. And while he dreaded the moment, he knew it would come. He'd never had a frame shop before, nor any other kind of retail business. Everything about the gallery was a classic application of how-to-start-your-own-business. Right out of a book at the library. It was a humbling experience. Not just the thousands of dollars spent but a dozen other variables as well. Fortunately, Lina was a quick study. She knew she could handle the frame shop. Not to worry, she told him. And she honed her skills on the new equipment, cutting fancy mats and frames and waiting for that first custom frame order.

Lina was an artist. She lived out of town in heavy timber country. She lived in a place called the Rat Hole at the end of Paradise Valley Road. It was an enclave of run-down houses barely adequate to ward off onslaughts of nature, torrential rains, summer heat, and blizzards. The Rat Hole was home to alienated Vietnam veterans and logging industry dropouts. They were all secretive about their lifestyles. Nobody asked questions. There was even a commune of gay loggers who wore cocktail dresses, long beads and logging boots after hours. They were tough. Nobody lifted an eyebrow, at least in criticism. In time, AIDS accomplished what the community didn't dare. The commune dispersed. The Rat Hole was quite a bit out in the country. It took Lina almost thirty minutes to get to the gallery in her old Mazda wagon—in the summer. In the winter, she told Partridge, who knows? There'd be snow. Lots of it. Sometimes the Rat Hole was snowed in. Would that be a problem? Partridge liked Lina and the way she came across. Besides he was desperate. The Peninsula wasn't exactly a hot-bed of unemployed picture framers. He was lucky to get her. He'd worry about the snow later. His hunch about Lina was correct. She was fast, accurate, uncomplaining and loved the work. And she was a prolific artist as well, with a good following in the small red-neck, blue-collar, mill town.

If there was one sour note, it was Lina's marriage. It had gone from bad to worse. Partridge watched a certain heavy sadness settle over her. He realized the job at the frame shop meant a bit more than relief from domestic unpleasantness. It meant escape into a world of beautiful French mats and veneers and artworks. In due course Lina would kiss off her failed-Yuppie husband whose secret pot plantation deep in the mountains left him with a lifetime narcosis and an aversion to work. In a few short years he'd gone from a sharp engineer to uncaring bum with no desire for work. Lina stuck by him for four, eight, twelve years. But the marriage drifted and then foundered.

Lina's husband, Mr. Whelky, was a recurring motif in many of her watercolors. With his red hair, red beard, red moustache, camouflage flak-jacket and always a salmon, held high over his head. Lina could chart the collapse of their marriage by his presence or absence in her paintings. She was a prolific artist and painted many of her dreams. Fey dreams. Day dreams. With Mr. Whelky lounging against doorjambs, peeking through windows, standing in streams, peering behind Douglas firs, all the while holding a fifty-pound Chinook salmon aloft. Critics would later call her work 'idiosyncratic'. Meaning, Partridge guessed, that she didn't paint conventional still-lifes of flowers and things like that. Well, the brooding Mr. Whelky began to do a quick fade from her paintings and was replaced by other recurring images of dogs, buffaloes and the like. Lina was a painstaking perfectionist who had a powerful sense of design and a commitment to detail which drew gasps from her admirers. In one watercolor, she painted spool-after-spool of embroidery thread so realistically that one wanted to reach out and touch them. Lina had a large portfolio of photographs of her paintings stashed under one of the framing tables. If the subject of her art ever came up, she'd bring it out and display them and, on occasion, make a sale. Partridge was interested in seeing her get a break and frequently would urge her to show her work.

As he knew it would, the day Partridge feared finally arrived. In walked a customer with a wooden carrying case. He seemed average in height and from what Partridge could tell was a little over fifty. There were bags, creased into heavy crescents beneath his eyes. He was either not well or burning his candle at both ends. Partridge suspected the latter. He smelled strongly of cigarettes and booze. Probably whiskey. Since it was ten o'clock, Partridge was surprised. His clothing was pretty much Peninsula standard. Nondescript pants and a flannel shirt, but buttoned at the cuffs and at the throat. Partridge briefly thought it odd. It was July and sweltering. But, he'd early learned not to rush to judgment. Chamber of Commerce scuttlebutt had it that there were seventeen millionaires on the Peninsula. Most of them, it was reported, dressed like undistinguished ranch hands. One of his goals was to sell a million dollars worth of art to each one.

"Hi there," he asked brusquely, "you do framing?" His navy-blue eyes smiled.

"Yes, sir," Partridge responded.

"Great, I need some framing done." Partridge called Lina to the front desk on the squawk box, hoping his voice sounded upscale and elegant. "Do you know the work of Bennett?" the customer asked.

"Bennett?" Partridge responded.

"Elton Bennett." The customer looked annoyed.

Partridge was new to business. New to retail. New to the world of galleries. But he was a quick learner. He knew all the impressionists and most of the locals who were currently exhibiting in town. And he was thoroughly boned up on all of the Rauschenbergs, and O'Keeffes and Pollacks of the world. True, there were many, many more. He'd never know them all.

"Well—," he hedged, "not exactly."

"You run an art gallery on the Peninsula and you don't know who Elton Bennett is?" He seemed politely incredulous.

Partridge felt his authority and expertise go down the toilet. There had been a lot of one-up customers lately pulling yet another obscure artist out of a bag. Fortunately, Lina arrived at the desk. Partridge asked her, "Lina, do we know Elton Bennett—artist?" She shook her head. "Well," Partridge continued, trying to salvage something of the encounter, "I've only been in this game a few months, but I'm quick." He smiled. "Who's Elton Bennett?" The customer frowned. "He's the most famous artist who ever lived up here. He died in a plane crash. 1979? Yeah, 1979 or so. In Samoa or somewhere like that. C'mon," he prodded, "you're kidding me. You know who I'm talking about."

"'Fraid not," Partridge said.

"Okay. Well, it really doesn't make any difference to me. But you might want to brush up on him. He's big up here. Anyhow, I've got four or five Bennetts I want re-framed. I'm just up here for a week from L.A. My father died. They belong to him. My mother is in a home up there." He points up to Lauridsen Boulevard with his thumb. "But, that's neither here nor there. The main thing is I don't have a lot of time. Let me have you do just two of them and if I like what you do, I'll bring down the rest."

Partridge was excited to get started and he and Lina exchanged Meaningful Glances. Their first custom frame job. He learned early in the game that it was useful to use the customer's name frequently. It made a good impression. It was in the book, *How To Start Your Own Gallery*.

"My name's Dodge," he says, "Bill Dodge."

"Mr. Dodge, nice to meet you," Partridge said, "and this is Lina, my framer. Come on down to the shop and let's see what we can do for you. And we'll learn all about the Bennetts."

Dodge smiles and looks around appreciatively. "Didn't this used to be a restaurant?"

"Right," Partridge agrees, "the old Harrington restaurant. You've—eaten here?"

"Spent a lot of time in the bar—which was—uhmmm—over there, right?"

"Right," Partridge says, "we've sealed up the wall. You've got a good memory. I've heard it was once the 'in' place in town."

Dodge snorted. "The only place." He placed his wooden carrying case on the work table and extracted several interesting looking prints. A lighthouse; the Olympic Mountains; a clipper ship. They were definitely original in style and composition. "These are what I'm talking about," Dodge explained. "This artist used to sell these all over the peninsula for—ohhhh, fifteen bucks apiece. He believed in affordable art. He was a big favorite. Look at the lighthouse. It's a wonderful piece." Lina smiled in appreciation and watched with bright interested eyes. "They're silk-screens. If you couldn't afford one of his prints, he'd give it to you—or charge you a dollar. They guy worked in one of the mills around here. It's quite a story. They're silkscreen prints. I'll bring you an article on him. There's one at my father's house. I just ran across it. I'll bring it down. But yep, silk-screen prints. Every one an original. Look here, you can tell how many screens he used by counting the colors here on the border. The registration is a little off. But each one a certified original—different by that much." He held up his fingers, making a space so thin tissue paper couldn't slip through it.

Lina and Partridge nodded. "But," Dodge continued, "these weren't taken care of. They're abused. My dad didn't think anything about them. He made up some of the frames in the garage with his router and some wood strips from Hartnagel's. He just stapled them in place. He had no idea how valuable they'd become."

"They're signed, too," Partridge adds.

You want to know who signed them?" Dodge continued. "His daughter. And his wife. He didn't believe in signing anything. He thought it was pretentious. Everybody should be able to own one of his prints, he said. Dealers could get more money for them if they were signed. He knew that. But he wouldn't do it. People wanted them signed. He wouldn't do it. That's his wife's signature there. You can tell. After the plane crash, the price of the Bennetts skyrocketed. Now a good print is worth anywhere from a thousand to two thousand dollars."

Taking it all in, Partridge whistled through his teeth. On the job training, he called it. He looked at the prints. They were pretty well damaged on the borders where they had been stapled and then ripped and rusted where the points went through to the board.

Dodge smiled at them both. "I don't care that they're damaged. I wanted them framed first class. They're sentimental, right?" His voice was rich and gravelly and he seemed embarrassed by his revelation. "And I want to give one away—you know, for favors. People been taking care of the house. Like that."

Partridge left Lina with Dodge to work out the details of the matting and framing. He noted it took about an hour. He heard them laugh and they seemed to be getting along famously. Maybe the first frame order wouldn't be the terror he thought it would. Later, Dodge came up to the desk and slapped down a VISA card and paid for the whole order up front. Partridge was very pleased about that. He asked if Lina had proved helpful.

"She's sharp," Dodge says. "Very helpful. She had some very good ideas."

"She's an artist," Partridge added. "It really helps in the framing business. I don't know what I'd do without her. She's that good."

Dodge wanted to go, but he asked politely, "What does she paint?"

"Watercolors and acrylics. She's really good. Very different." Partridge spoke as if he were revealing a confidence. "You got a minute?" he asked. "Come on down. You can flip through her book. I'd really like you to see some of her work." He loved to push her art. It was original and interesting.

Dodge shrugged his shoulders and followed Partridge back down to the frame shop. Lina brought forth her portfolio and flipped through a few of the pages with Dodge and Partridge. At first reluctant, Dodge, quickly showed real interest. And then seemed rather impressed. Then, really impressed. Partridge left them together and went back to his desk to wait on a client.

Dodge popped up later. "You're right," he said. He was smiling. "They're good. Really good. Very fine work. Tiny lines and detailing. I'm impressed. I bought one. She's going to deliver it to me later. I'll be back for the framed stuff and bring in some more. Looks good. I'm going to Japan for a quick trip. I'll be back in August. Just hold everything here for me. Any trouble with that arrangement?" Where he had at first seemed quite brusque, Dodge mellowed out nicely.

"Terrific," Partridge said. They shook hands. What luck. The first custom frame order. Payment up front and a promise of more. He couldn't wait to tell his wife. "Off to Japan, then? Terrific. Great place. A little vacation?" Partridge knew he was pumping, but he was curious. Was he one of the seventeen millionaires just waiting for his gallery to open?

"Business," he said. He wouldn't nibble. "I've got to get going. My mother is up at the care center. She has some—problems. I come up from L.A. to check her out as often as I can." He paused. "Oh, and what is your framer's name again? Lorna?"

"Lina," Partridge corrected.

"Ah, yes—Lina—Lina. I didn't see a ring. Is she—uhm—by any chance married?"

Partridge didn't want to disclose personal information to this stranger. "Well—looks like, maybe—she's—." He wiggled his little finger and thumb in a motion that suggested that maybe she was available.

"Well, you know, she said something that made me think she might be uhhhhh—well, she's very nice. Please thank her again for me."

"Sure", Partridge assured him. "Sorry about your mother and—sayonara."

The crescents under Dodge's eyes wrinkled and doubled. "Ah, you speak Japanese?"

"Naw, that's it. Have a good trip, sir. See you in August?"

Okay, then." Dodge turned and left the gallery.

Partridge thought about him. A curious guy, Dodge. What was it about him? The beard? The dark circles under the eyes? The air of education and affluence? The odor of booze and the quick trip to Japan? He wanted to learn more. He could wait. He didn't want to be obvious, but Dodge left no opening for further probing. The gallery was proving to be more entertaining than he had dared hope.

Lina came up from the frame shop. She was smiling. She held a folded check and gave it a little kiss. Dodge had bought one of her more expensive paintings. Five-hundred dollars worth. Lina's dream of leaving Mr. Whelky to become a self-supporting artist was a step closer. Fantasies of a small house with a studio danced in her head. "He loved my stuff," she said, "and he's going to buy another one."

The plot thickens, Partridge thought.

II

The weeks came and went. Custom frame orders came and went. The frame shop and the gallery were doing fine. People had discovered the shop. The art community had discovered the gallery. Partridge enjoyed the process winnowing through paintings and slides submitted by artists for consignment. The gallery had become a bit of a showplace for the small town and summer tourists by the hundreds trooped through it, sniffing the cinnamoned air, buying art pottery and watercolors and fine art posters.

It was August. There was a lull between marching bands on the street outside the gallery during the Arts in Action Street Fair. Partridge sat at his desk humming *Colonel Bogey's March* and holding a sixteen-pocket sheet of fiber art slides up to the trak lights. They looked good and he made a note to call the artist. Suddenly, there was Dodge before him. He looked a bit rattled. He greeted Partridge.

"I didn't realize I'd be back during a street fair." He looked through the window at the activity outside. "Too much for me. I've been up all night. Just in from Japan. Jet lag." He was carrying a portfolio of what were obviously more prints. "If Lina is in, let's go down and look at these others—my Bennetts."

Partridge pulled Dodge's completed frame order out of nearby rack. Dodge looked at them appreciatively, but he seemed anxious to see Lina. "They're great, just great. She did a terrific job. Just the way I wanted them to look."

Down in the frame shop, Lina and Dodge greeted one another. Lina was very close to leaving Mr. Whelky and seemed to project new sexy vibes. It was difficult for Partridge to figure it exactly. But there was something different about her. She'd been running around with another artist. A guy named Duncan. He did watercolors, too. It was totally platonic. They went to exhibits and so on. But they didn't sleep together. Not even Mr. Whelky would have suspected anything. Fishing, art classes, lunches. That was about it. She'd told Partridge that she was so starved for love that she'd have thrown Duncan in the bushes, ripped his clothes off and raped him if he'd shown any inclination for her at all. But he didn't and she remained chaste and demure. Meanwhile, word was out. She was going to leave Whelky as soon as she had somewhere to stay. Anywhere would do.

Dodge greeted her and effused about her work. It was obvious that he was sending out vibes too. He spread out his new Bennetts and they examined them together. They worked another hour over the matting and framing details after Partridge returned to the gallery. When Dodge was finished he came up and continued to laud Lina. "She's really terrific. I'm going to have her go ahead with those new prints and, with your permission, I'm going to have a limited edition print mailed here to you. I saw it in Alaska on a stopover flight." He was obviously a man used to having his own way. Partridge was pleased to cooperate. He loaned Dodge his telephone and Dodge placed a credit card call to a gallery in Anchorage and ordered the print. "Thanks, that's great. I'll have it sent right to you. Lina can frame it. Let her do anything she wants with it. I trust her completely. She'll know just what to do with it. It's an expensive print. A Haida Indian motif. Really terrific." Partridge noticed the strong odor of alcohol on his breath once more, and observed that he seemed to be sweltering in the heat with a wool Pendleton buttoned to his throat and both cuffs rolled down and buttoned. "She tells me she's going to get divorced," he commented.

Partridge didn't want to get into it again. But he agreed that it did seem likely. Lina was a talker. There was no guessing how much she'd told Dodge, but he didn't want to add anything to it.

"She told me she needs a place to stay. I offered her my father's place."

Partridge was shocked. "You're kidding?"

"No. We're going to work something out. I need somebody to house sit while I'm in L.A. The neighbors have been watching the place for me, but this way she can have some independence and a place to paint and—hey, everybody wins." He stole a quick look at the parade through the front window of the gallery.

Partridge suddenly realized that he was, as they say, out of the loop. Lina had her own life to lead. He wasn't her father. Maybe Dodge could drop into that slot. He was 20 years older than she. Partridge knew he had to say something. "That's very generous. Terrific. She's a great person. Very responsible. It's perfect." What else was there to say? He felt he'd just given Lina away in marriage.

"Okay, I'll be back in three weeks. I've got to fly to Switzerland on business, but I'm going to stop over here and get it set up and check on my mother at the center. Let me pay you for those other four Bennetts."

Partridge was happy for the windfall. It was another pre-paid framing order for several hundred dollars. Dodge flipped out his VISA. The amount was no problem. He barely looked at the bottom line. "Yep, she'll do a good job." He signed the ticket. "Oh, and one more thing—I really don't want all of these Bennetts. I'm going to take one to L.A. Gonna give one away to some neighborhood girl who's been doing me a favor—and let Lina take any one she wants for herself. You tell her. It's a present. No problem. And the rest I think I'll leave them here and let you sell them on consignment. What do you think?"

Partridge didn't want any more art on consignment. It was more trouble than it was worth. He hated the idea. The Bennetts didn't look all that saleable to him. The imagery was old-fashioned. Of course, the new matting and framing jazzed them up a bit. He felt trapped. Dodge was coming on a bit strong. Aggressive. Partridge was still learning how to say no and hadn't developed his defense mechanisms yet. As a retailer, he had much to learn. He weakened and accepted the excess Bennetts as if Dodge were doing him a favor. He wrote him up a gallery agreement for 90 days.

"That's great. Don't worry, you'll sell them. They'll go like hotcakes. Guaranteed."

Partridge shrugged. "Terrific," he replied weakly. "Okay, we'll see what happens." How could he refuse? The VISA receipt for several hundred dollars still lay in view on the counter. He looked at the *hotcakes* leaning against the counter and he imagined he could see butter congealing on their surface.

Dodge looked on the walls. There were several of Lina's paintings there. Dodge scrutinized them. "I'd like to buy another one of hers. I can't get over the really amazing detail. She's good. She's really good."

He fanned himself with an advertising card he picked up from a nearby holder. "I'll call you and let you know which one I decide on." His face looked stressed. He was hot and his eyes puffy. "Okay, I'm off to the care center. I'll see you in three weeks."

Lina peeked around the corner. A batch of tourists had moved into the gallery. She hissed at Partridge. He walked over to her. "I don't believe it," he said. "What did you feed him? He's going to buy *another* painting? I can't believe it? He doesn't even know which one. He's going to call me later." Lina smiled a goofy smile and hunched her shoulders with palms up. She started to speak. Partridge interrupted her. "Don't tell me. You're going to move into his house." She nodded with the same goofy smile. "Did you tell him about your dogs?"

"Sure," she replied. "Sure."

"All three of them?" She had just picked up another dog from the Humane Society.

"Of course. He likes dogs."

"Oh, my god. Lina, you don't even know this guy. What is this? What if Mr. Whelky finds out you've moved out on him into the lap of some old geezer you don't know anything about. He'll come over and blow both of you away." Partridge was warming to his theme.

"Don't worry," she says, "he'd never do anything like that. That's ridiculous."

"You're crazy, Lina. There are thousands of women cowering in 'safe' houses all over the peninsula who said the same thing. I'm telling you—you don't know anything about him. He reeks of whiskey. That's just one thing." Some tourists needed attention. Partridge lowered his voice for the sake of appearance.

Lina looked at him real silly. "And that's not all. He's not going to charge me any rent."

"Jesus," Partridge said, "you weren't born yesterday. There's no such thing as free rent—wake up, Lina and smell the cinnamon."

"Don't worry," she says, "I'll be all right."

"And look, he wants to give you one of the *Bennetts*—can you believe it? Look at them."

A woman with blue hair noticed the Bennetts leaning against the wall. "Excuse, me," she asks. "Those *are* Bennetts aren't they?"

"Yes, Ma'am, but they're not for sale, they belong to a client. Aren't they interesting?" She nodded and moved away. "What is going on, already? He's giving you Elton Bennetts and he's buying Lina Whelky's. I don't get it. Just invite me to the wedding."

A week later, UPS delivered the print from Alaska. Partridge and Lina examined it. It was beautiful. Spawning salmon. A limited edition print by Marvin Oliver. He was a prominent northwestern Indian artist. There was great potential for a knockout frame job with a nice price tag attached. Later that morning, the postman delivered a letter for Lina. It was from Dodge and it was postmarked Geneva. Partridge delivered it to her in the frame shop with some sassy remark and returned to the gallery. A few minutes later Lina comes up with an incredulous expression on her face.

"I don't know if I should let you read this," she says, "but I've got to tell *somebody*—". As he reads the letter she does this voice over "I don't believe it—I absolutely don't believe it."

Partridge reads the key phrases aloud: ' . . . very few people realize that I have had a lifelong obsession with oriental over-all body tattoos. It has long been my desire to have my full-body tattoos rendered onto canvas so that I can hang them up and admire them when I choose to. I feel after knowing you only for this short time, that you are a very sympathetic person whom I can trust, as well as someone who might feel challenged by the intricacy of the work. Your wonderful paintings suggest, certainly, that you are capable of doing the work. You can do it in any style you wish. I won't dictate that to you. My only desire is that you do not use my face in any format whatsoever. I am very well-known in the international community in my specialty and I wish for reasons of my own to keep this a private matter between you and me. I am willing to pay you well (you can set the price) for one set of a full-body rendering on canvas or other medium and you can execute as many more as you wish for your own purposes—for sale, or exhibit, etc., as long as I am not identified. See what you think. I'll be back in town in a week for three days before I have to go back to L.A. Let me know then what you think of my plan and your method of proceeding with it.'

Partridge shook his head. "I told you there was something funny about this guy and you wouldn't listen. What are you going to do?"

Lina rolled her eyes. "What do you think I'm going to do? I'm going to *do* it. I can't turn down a commission like that. I need all the money I can get. I've got to file for divorce. My car needs work. What do you mean, what am I going to do?"

"Oh, boy. Okay, do it already. Just remember I warned you. All you need is for Whelky to come over some day bitching at you about the divorce and see you painting Dodge's tattoos." Partridge realized he hadn't thought the project through the way Lina obviously had. "By the way, how are you going to accomplish this little number? Is he going to sit around with his biceps flexed for you in the north light of your studio?"

Lina looked unperturbed. "Photograph him, of course."

"*Photograph* him?"

"Sure. What else?" She laughs. "What's the big deal?"

"*All* over? Lina, this guy has all-over body tattoos."

"So, what's the problem? So I'll photograph him *all over*." Partridge feigns exasperation. The whole thing was unreal. "Okay—I don't believe any of this. Just tell me one thing. When he comes in here next week, I don't know *anything*, right? I already think of him as a dirty old man and nothing is going to change my opinion. But I'm going to keep a straight face. And I know *nothing*."

"About the tattoos. *Right*. I need that job."

"And you need this job, too. So get back to work."

Lina walks off. "No problem, no problem."

III

The week whizzed by. They got a lot of work done, but Dodge was never very far from their thoughts. Partridge fretted about Lina's well-being and worried about Mr. Whelky and his reaction to Lina's pending desertion of him. He suddenly felt over-involved in her concerns. But it was too late to turn back now, he was hooked. The whole tattoo business had him stumped. Intrigued but stumped. Where would it lead?

Before he had time to worry about that, the phone rang. It was Dodge. He wanted Lina to pick him up at the airport and then he was going to show her the house and take her to dinner. She was flying high and raced through the remainder of her workday. At five o'clock, she sped off to the airport. He could have spared himself any anxiety about their 'date'. He already knew down deep what the outcome would be. He just had to wait until morning to receive confirmation of it. He was right. Lina was ecstatic over the prospects of the bungalow. It would suit her needs perfectly. She could have her dogs and a studio in one of the extra bedrooms for as long as she wanted to stay. She'd keep up the yard and house and in return, Mr. Dodge, as she called him, would fly up every couple of months from California and they would have dinner and well, talk. He'd sleep in his own bedroom, of course, and check on his mother up at the care center and in a couple of days he'd be on his way back to California. It was too perfect. One look at Lina's face said it all.

It was obvious that she was wowed by Dodge. He was a masterful, moneyed older guy who knew how to manipulate. It wouldn't have been incorrect to characterize him as a classic charismatic sociopath so beloved by radio call-in psychologists. The business with the full-body tattoos simply added another fascinating dimension. Lina had shown a penchant for the off-beat in her paintings and in her sense of humor. Partridge was certain that the whiff of Dodge's exoticism positively electrified her. And, luckily for him, she liked to tell all. He leaped in to fill in some of the blanks.

"Did you find out what he does?"

"Sure. He's a professor at UCLA." She seemed surprised at the question.

"Of what?"

"Uhmmm. Population or something. The science of demographics. He didn't go into it that much."

"Didn't you ask him? You should ask him."

Lina waved that away. "You know what we did?"

"I'm afraid to ask."

"He broiled us filet mignon and we had cheesecake. He fixed everything himself."

"Oh, boy. Then he poured you some Madeira?"

"I don't drink. What's Madeira?"

"Lucky for you."

"And, it's all set up. I can move in anytime I want to." She formed her lips into a smile that said, I told you so.

"Hmmmmmpf," Partridge grunted. "Looks like he's the one that's doing the movin' in. But, forget that. What about the main thing here? The commission or whatever—the painting? Did he bring that up again? The stuff in the letter? Or is he going to rip you off?"

"Of course." She was stringing him out, to tease him.

"Oh my god—and? And?"

"I'm going over tonight to photograph him."

"Jesus. You're so—nonchalant. This guy could be an ax murderer. How do you know his mother even exists?"

" . . . before he leaves." Lina ignored his remarks.

"Leaves?"

"For California."

"Oh." Partridge sounded resigned. Apparently he couldn't change her mind. She seemed determined to go ahead.

"He'll be in this afternoon to pick up his art. Tonight, I'm going to my house and get some things. I've already told Mr. Whelky I'm leaving."

"And . . . ?" Partridge shuddered.

"He didn't say anything."

"Great. Wait until he finds out about this mess."

"Why do you keep saying that? Everything's going to be just fine."

"And why do you keep saying *that*?" Partridge fussed. "If you were my daughter, I'd lock you in your room." Lina smiled her little goofy smile and went down to the frame shop.

A couple of hours later Dodge showed up. He seemed very much different from the last time. More alert. There was still the alcohol on his breath and the buttoned up Pendleton shirt. But his hair was combed and he seemed more rested and even a bit jovial. He scanned the walls for Lina's paintings and referred to her in a most possessive fashion. Partridge had sort of thought that Lina belonged to him. She was his employee. Now this stranger whom they barely knew was referring to her as if she were his special property. His—Partridge couldn't even say it—his woman.

"Hi, there," he growled pleasantly at Partridge. "Great day. I had to wait three hours at SeaTac go get the flight over. But it worked out great. Got in last night right at 5:30. Perfect."

"That's great," Partridge responded. He was still a small business proprietor and he tried to maintain the client-customer relationship—even though Dodge seemed more like Lina's first date. "Well, you're back." He knew that Dodge wondered how much he knew.

"Yes. Yes. I'm back. A couple of days here and then back to Japan."

"Sounds like—fun." Partridge knew he was in trouble conversationally from the word go. He couldn't think of anything to keep it rolling. All he could think about were Lina and the tattoos. He tried to imagine what Dodge would look like stripped naked in the gallery with nothing on but his tattoos. He could stick a price tag on him. What were the tattoos? Moms and daggers? Japanese prostitutes? Swirling masses of blue and green and carmine tendrils? He looked at Dodge's eyes. They were deep navy. The bags beneath them made him look peculiarly forlorn and burnt out. As if he stayed up a lifetime of midnights toiling over population trends or studying books of tattoo designs by candlelight.

"I can't decide which one of Lina's paintings I like best. I'll think about it. I heard she's going to have a show here in town."

"That's right," Partridge said. "At the Woodbox—it's just up the street—around the corner." He saw his commission going down the drain. But he smiled. He wondered if he had said anything at all that could have given Dodge the idea that he and Lina had discussed his tattoos. There was no sign. Dodge handed him a wooden carrying case. It was nicely made and could be useful to carry prints.

"You might like to have this. I have no more use for it. Toss it out if you don't want it." Partridge thanked him. "Well, I guess I'll go down and talk to Lina. We still have a couple more things to discuss. That big print from Anchorage—I'd like to take that one back to L.A."

He excused himself and went down to the frame shop as if he was the owner of North Light Gallery and Partridge were the client. Partridge carried the cast-off wooden case back to his office. It had an address on it. It was addressed to Dodge and beside his name were the letters: PHD. So, Partridge thought. He's a full professor. Interesting. A fully tattooed PHD. Doctor of Tattoos. He smiled. What was he getting so upset about? He had his own life. His own wife. Lina had nobody. Dodge had nobody. Or did he? Well, a few more polite questions here and there would set his fears to rest. He had no justification to feel proprietary about Lina. Get over it, he thought.

An hour later repeated the scenario three weeks earlier. Dodge pays up front for a big order, makes plans to have Lina frame a collection of rare Japanese stamps using silk shantung mats, shadowboxes and Japanese Hokito hand-rubbed lacquered frames. It would be beautiful he assured Partridge. He'd be back later to pick everything up. Meanwhile, he was off to Japan in a day or two. He was working on a book he said. With some other professionals in his specialty, he said. "And that is—?" Partridge queried.

Dodge figured it was time to offer a bit more of himself. They edged towards the front door of the gallery. "I'm a demographer. Demographics."

"Terrific," Partridge said. "And you teach at UCLA?"

"Right. That's right. UCLA."

"Oh, so—like population trends and like—that?"

"Yeah, that's right. You know—right—righto—population trends and—birthrate, migration—yes—all of that."

"Sounds really interesting," Partridge lied.

"Yes, it's—uhm—well you know—life's work—sort of boring—and well, it's—it's very complicated. As soon as I can wrap up this book I'm writing in Japan, then, well—." He clearly didn't want to discuss it.

"Oh, sure—" Partridge commented. "Sounds like a challenge—good summertime reading I'll bet," he joked. Dodge passed on the intended hilarity. "Well, then, I hope you have a great trip. Then, if I don't see you—if you don't have time to drop by again—well—have a great trip." Partridge edged him towards the door. He felt like Lina's father forcing her boyfriend to say goodnight. Mercifully it was over and customers began coming in again. Lina left an hour early so she could go to Mr. Whelky's house and pick up some things. She told Partridge that Dodge was going to prepare prime rib for dinner and invite over an old friend. A woman. Someone he knew in the neighborhood years ago. Before he went to grad school and learned all about population control and tattoos. After she leaves, he told her, they could start the photo session. He was going to set up her up with his father's 35MM camera, drop his pants and turn her loose. Afterwards she could have the camera. Candy to a baby. Oh, yeah.

IV

The following morning, Partridge raced through the motions of opening the gallery. He flipped up the ultra-violet sun shades in the front display window and he flipped on the lights in the main gallery room and he flipped on the coffee maker and he waited impatiently for Lina to arrive. He drummed his fingers on the smooth grey countertop in anticipation of her report on the photo session. When she did arrive, she said good morning and tried to head on down through the alcove to the frame shop as if she didn't want to be bothered so early. There was no one in the gallery yet, so Partridge called out for her to come back.

"Yeah?" she asked.

"Lina, what happened? Jesus, don't just leave me hanging like this. You're still alive?" She shrugged her shoulders in the impossible way that had become characteristic of her and said, "Of course. You were expecting, maybe a serial murderer?" There was a faint smile on her lips. A secret, untold, whirled about inside her.

"Welllll?"

"Well, what? I took the photos. They'll be developed and so—I'll paint the pictures and—what else?"

"So, after dinner, you muscled your guest out the door and—"

"No, we didn't muscle anybody—she just left and then we took the pictures. So, what's the big deal?" She shrugged again."

Partridge gave up. "Okay, super—." He was through for the time being.

Dodge flew off to California or Berlin or Bern or Durban or Tokyo or wherever a day or two afterward. All his affairs were taken care of. He feted Lina with exotic cuisine prepared at his house. Each day she came to work with baron of beef sandwiches that a logger might envy and descriptions of haute cuisine desserts that Dodge had prepared. And then he left.

Things settled down at the gallery once again. Lina had sent the film of Dodge off to a custom processor in Seattle where they were enlarged to 16x20 and in a couple of weeks she got them back. This time, it was her turn to be excited and she pulled Partridge down into the frame shop and pulled out the finished enlargements. They were fantastic. Beyond belief. Lina and Partridge outdid one another in recklessly silly observations about what they saw. There were the usual pirate ships and many square feet worth of swirling phantasmagoric line drawings in vivid color. The photos were good. Far better than computer scans could ever be. There'd be no need for a retakes. Lina was relieved. It was not a new camera and the whole thing was a turkey shoot. She kept saying 'wow' and look at this and look at that. There were Japanese samurai warriors and their women and swords and sabres and dragons and monsters and tall ships under sail and the names of women and bracelets and wristlets and anklets and down at Dodge's left ankle, on the inside, written sinuously across the ankle-bone was a long and complicated mathematical formula. There was no bare skin below the neck line.

The mathematical formula, Lina, explained, had made Dodge as famous in his 'specialty', demographics as Einstein's E=MC2. It was widely used and taught in universities. She didn't know much more about it except that he would sometimes sneak a look at it during a seminar or meeting. He'd just cross his ankle over his knee and surreptitiously push down his sock and glance at his formula. It was tattooed so as to be read upside down.

Lina sorted through each aspect of Dodge's anatomy. His armpits. His groin. His thighs. His calves, elbows, kneecaps and biceps. It was amazing that a man would bother to do that to himself. Maybe crazy. Finally, Lina, with a flair that P.T. Barnum might have envied, saved the last for best. She revealed the by now—not so very private parts of Mr. William Dodge, PhD., Demographer. She slapped the photo down. There they were. Partridge looked in amazement at the tattooed splendor of his phallus. Lina looked in amusement.

"I don't believe it," Partridge muttered. He covered his eyes and placed his elbows on the carpet-covered worktable. "Unbelievable. But, there it is—or, there they are."

Lina smiled. She was kind of proud of her accomplishment. She shrugged. "Yup."

"Lina. There it is every fifteen-year-old boy's erotic fantasy and all you've got to say is 'yup'?"

"Well, what do you want me to say?"

"Well, I don't know, but Jesus, all that tattooing on his privates. It must have hurt, no?"

Lina smiled again. "I guess. That's what he said."

"Well, I hope you're charging him a fortune."

"You bet," she replied. "Plenty. And, I can take my time. He doesn't care how long it takes. And he says I can exhibit anything I want as long as I don't identify him." Partridge looks again at the pictures and slides them around on the framing table. "Well—he's sure got a case of industrial strength ego or exhibitionism, but his face isn't in any of these pictures. Who'd recognize him? Of course, his uh—things—would be a little hard to forget."

Lina giggled. "You got that right."

Partridge looked at her carefully. Had they been fooling around? He figured yes. But it was really not his business. He and Lina indulged themselves in the huge private joke of Dodge's tattoos and showed off the pictures to all of their gallery intimates. Hadn't the old boy told them they could? Well, not to feel guilty, they reasoned. Whoever came down to the gallery got the grand tour. The members of the Art League, special friends, and that sort of thing. The word spread and people, who would never at all have come in, somehow found their way into the frame shop.

From time-to-time Partridge would hear a certain readily identifiable squeal of shock coming from below and he knew that Lina had shown yet another unwary female the body art of Mr. William Dodge and then—in a final coup of heavy-handed theatricalism, toss out the bewildering crotch shot of the tattooed penis with wicked erotic art swirling up from there to his pectorals. And, as was plain to see, he was shaved as slick as a whistle. The demographer was completely charted. Oh, there was a spot here and there that a skilled tattoo artist could squeeze in a little something. Partridge shook his head at the thought of Dodge sweltering through all those summers in the temperate zones of the world buttoned to his neck and wrists, while his academic companions strolled about in seersucker and shirtsleeves.

How they must have wondered to see Dodge booted and spurred and puffing about St. Mark's Square or Johannesburg or the Ginza.

Lina was scheduled for a group show at the gallery along with some other artists and she framed one of the nude views of Dodge and stuck a price tag on it. It was a 'photographic' entry, she reasoned. Partridge was not too pleased about it and Mrs. Partridge was indignant. But he backed down. A tiny hint of big city sophistication wouldn't hurt the little logging community. It was, after all, a fairly decorous nude buttocks-eye-view of the old boy, posed looking over his headless torso with his hand placed artily on his hip. A sort of beaux arts, student model pose. It was a show stopper, of course, and if anyone wanted to see 'more', Lina would pull out the other photos in the privacy of the frame room and tell the story once again amid discreet shrieks and whispers of surprise. Even Partridge's three ancient aunts from California were given the 'treatment'. They were highly amused. A tattooed penis was quite possibly not the biggest thing on their lifetime shock list, but a penis tattooed with a full length python with scales and fangs quite possibly was. That and maybe World War I and World War II combined tatted on his buttocks.

V

As time wore on, Lina and Partridge had run out of people to show the pictures to and the novelty kind of wore off. Things moved ahead on many fronts. Lina moved out from Mr. Whelky and left him to stew in the summer sun in his Paradise Valley cabin. She filed for divorce, made some new friends and moved to town and into Mr. Dodge's house. She installed her three dogs within and kept the place clean and mowed. And she occasionally entertained there from her assortment of artsy types. Mr. Dodge would call occasionally about this or that minute framing matter and just to talk. It seemed as if the gallery and the frame shop were a lot on his mind. He finally set himself up for Thanksgiving. He told Lina that he'd fly up and fix the whole ball of wax. Gravy, mashed potatoes, turkey, cranberry—the works and he'd expect her to pick him up at the airport as she had before. All of this was pretty heady stuff for a forty-year-old woman who'd been neglected for a dozen years. Lina found herself flying pretty high.

A bit later Lina set up her one-woman show at the Woodbox Gallery on Front Street. It was a big success and it was there that she met the new man in her life, Noel. Noel was fiftyish and handsome and according to Lina, very, very masculine. He came on to her with all the fervor of an adolescent. He loved art and artists and affected corduroys, mufflers when the wind howled, and caps with little brims on them that needed constant rearrangement. He was a nice guy. Partridge liked him, too. He'd pop in and take Lina to lunch and send the odd bouquet of red carnations from the local florist directly to her at the frame shop.

Suddenly things were getting complicated and Lina was becoming concerned. To Partridge and her, it seemed that Dodge had clearly imputed more to his relationship with Lina than she had. He was now thinking of her as his special woman. Maybe even a sort of geisha—to complete his fantasy of being a tattooed Japanese ninja. Someone to be there for him when he visited the North Peninsula. Had she led him on? Here she was, entertaining Noel in Dodge's house and here he was, on the verge of coming back to fix Thanksgiving dinner. Now what?

Partridge tried to help. "Have you ever told him about Noel?"

"No, why should I?" she responded.

"Because, Lina, it's unethical to accept one man's hospitality while you're dating another man—one of the ten commandments of dating—it's called ethics, Lina—*ethics.*"

"Well, what difference does it make? I don't belong to him. I'm just caretaking his house."

Partridge persisted, trying to make his point. "But, you've got your dogs over there—three of them—in the house with you—I mean, he's got you set up—I mean, you've seen him—naked, Lina. You can't just walk away from all that. Now, he thinks he's got 'rights'. Know what I mean?"

"The hell he does," Lina responded. She was indignant. "Oh, my god. There's something I forgot about. I think I'm gonna be sick."

Partridge leaned forward. "Okay, spill it."

Lina turned pale. "Princess completely devoured one of his sofa pillows. I'm sick." Princess was a Doberman pinscher whose ears had never been cropped and who looked like a dejected SS officer caught in a rainstorm.

Partridge threw up his hands. "Lina, you're beyond help. Believe me." They looked at the shop calendar. "Okay, you've got exactly three weeks to get it fixed."

"But, what am I going to do?"

"Well, fix it. You used to be a weaver, remember? And not only that, how far are you along on painting the tattoos?"

"Ohhhhh, I haven't worked on them for weeks."

"Well, isn't Dodge going to want to see something for all those big bucks he's spending? Isn't that what he's coming up here for?"

Lina shrugged palms up. "I don't know. I'm sick about the whole thing. How did I ever get into this mess?"

"Look, Lina, if it's not too late to tell you, 'I told you so', I'll tell you now."

"Please, just what I need." Partridge twisted a discarded bit of framing material. "Okay, let's add up the damage. One. You've slept with Dodge—"

Lina looked surprised. "I didn't say that."

"You didn't have to. Okay, you slept with Dodge. Two. You've photographed every nook and cranny of his body. Three. You've moved into his house—with your *three* dogs. Four. The dogs have destroyed the interior of the house—"

"Ohhhh, no—"

Five. You've had all of your friends up there going through all of his things and partied and entertained and—"

"Wait a minute—"

"Six. He's paid all the bills, you know, utilities—and he's charged you no rent and he's wined and dined you, that's *seven* and he's given you cameras and—whoosit?—Bennett pictures and god knows what else and eight, nine and ten, Lina, you've had Mr. Whelky and his cruddy Army buddies up there at night with the neighbors peeking through the curtains and taking notes—"

"Now, wait. That's not true—that was just to sign divorce papers—"

"That's not what you said. You said they came over to watch TV and eat spaghetti. And twelve, or where are we? Twelve, at least—wait, wait—and then, you had Noel overnight, where you probably attacked him in his own bed—"

Lina clenched her fists in frustration. "Now, look, I didn't say that either."

'Oh, yes you did," Partridge went on. "And now your host, your kindly, generous and unsuspecting host is coming back to fix you your Thanksgiving dinner, wine you and dine you yet again—and maybe give you a ring, huh? Huh? A ring? And you don't feel you owe him anything? Is that it? Just because somebody drew all over his body with a ball point pen, Lina, doesn't mean he doesn't deserve some respect."

Lina was down but not out. She'd have the final say. "There's one more thing."

Partridge covered his eyes. "I thought the sofa pillow was it."

"Not quite," Lina continued.

"Okay, what is it?"

"Noel and I are going to get married. And, you're right," she blushed, "I've just checked him out and all his parts work perfectly." She smiled fiendishly.

Partridge was in shock. "Lina, what is this 'all his parts' business?" What's the matter with you? Are you crazy? You're getting yourself into so much trouble. Thank god, I'm not your father. Okay, so congratulations already and when are you getting married?"

"Well, as soon as we can. Maybe end of the month. Who knows? My divorce will be final in 10 days."

"Have you told Mr. Whelky?"

"Uhhhhm. No. Why should I?"

"Because you just divorced the man. He's grieving. I've seen him when he comes to town to bring you your mail. He looks terrible. His face looks like a Makah Pook mask. Seriously. He's going to think you left him for Noel. Know what I mean? Everybody else in town knows you just met Noel three weeks ago and just got his parts certified. And Dodge thinks you're promised to him because you photographed him in the buff or the *blue*, I suppose. You're in a mess, girl."

And she was. Lina didn't know what to do. She was very quiet for a couple of weeks after that and kept a very low profile. The gallery went on to other things. Then, one day Dodge called the gallery. Partridge answered the phone and the two chatted together for a couple of minutes. He asked to speak to Lina. Later, she came up to the front desk later, looking dejected. "I couldn't tell him," she muttered. "It was no good. He just kept on talking about Thanksgiving and butterball turkeys and orange-cranberry relish. What could I do?"

VI

It was the old story. Lina wasn't in charge of Lina anymore. She was always under the sway of somebody. In this case, it was Noel and Mr. Dodge. She was sleeping pretty regularly with Noel, now, and that relationship was dipped in bronze. But, what to do? Her plan was to keep Noel out of sight until after the big day and delude Dodge into thinking that she was his 'girl' for one more time. Noel wasn't happy with that, but he went along with it. When Thanksgiving day arrived, he went underground, so to speak. Lina had quickly gone back to work on the tattoos, just so Dodge could see that she was still committed to them. The bucks were big and she and Noel needed them now, more than ever. The dinner went well considering everything and Dodge even did the dishes, Lina reported. He was up to his tattooed biceps in detergent. He was beginning to feel quite domestic with her. It was unsettling.

Next day, Dodge visited his mother and completed more estate business with his Peninsula lawyer. His mother was finally set up at the care center and his father's house and worldly goods were squared away. The third day, Dodge made what was to be a quick trip to Seattle. He said he'd be gone overnight. Lina welcomed the respite and used the opportunity to make love to Noel on Dodge's living-room sofa and later that evening they made a run to the movies on First Street. As it turned out, Dodge completed his business early and decided against an overnight stay. He returned to the Peninsula early. To his surprise, Lina was gone from the house. Bored and restless, he jumped into his father's old Land Rover and went downtown to The Coffeehouse Café, next to the theatre. Who should he run into but Noel and Lina hanging on to each other coming out of the movies.

The jig was up. Lina introduced the two of them. Dodge smiled shyly, realizing the he had less claim to her than his imagination had supposed and the fantasies of his largess had entitled him. Surprisingly, Noel and Dodge hit it off. Dodge invited the two of them up to his house and made them Bananas Melba as an after movie treat, seating them on the same sofa which had been their steamy love-couch only three hours before.

Lina had made no mention of the impending marriage and the tattoos were, luckily, out of sight in another room. It was if Noel had never heard of them. Dodge spooned and then flamed the Cointreau over the bananas with great flair and they all made polite conversation until it was time for Noel to go home. Then, in a magnanimous gesture, Dodge made Noel a turkey sandwich to put in his jacket pocket. "Something for tomorrow," he said.

Lina finished telling all this to Partridge the following day.

"He made him a turkey sandwich?"

"Lina nodded. "Yup. I couldn't believe it either. They really hit it off."

"And he didn't guess that you had told Noel all about the tattoos?"

"Not an inkling. If he did, he didn't say so."

"Well, terrific," Partridge says. He'd finally run out of commentary on that phase of the love triangle.

"Yup. Now, I've got to get past the wedding announcement. You know—telling him about it. I'll do that at Christmas."

Partridge frowned. "Yessir, Merry Christmas, Mr. Dodge—now it's my turn to open a present—"

"Well, my gosh, why shouldn't I have a boyfriend? So what? He should be so lucky. I've cleaned his stove and—everything."

"And what'd he say about the sofa?"

"He didn't care, he *loves* dogs—isn't that perfect?"

"Oh, come on."

"That's what he said. Now, he's going back to Tokyo and he won't be back till Christmas."

As he said he would, Dodge left for Japan again. He didn't stop by the gallery this trip, but a few weeks later, he called from Tokyo to say hello to both Partridge and Lina. In the meantime, Lina went into high gear and mobilized Noel into a very quick church wedding with just a few friends and moved into Noel's tiny house. She left most of her things at Dodge's. Noel's place simply couldn't accommodate all of the furniture and personal possessions Lina had liberated from Mr. Whelky. She was even going to go back up to the Rat Hole, later, and dig up her roses. The judge told her she could have them.

Dodge's antique Japanese stamps were all framed up and they did indeed look beautiful. The new Japanese owners of the paper mill came in several times to look at them and translate. They were clearly owned by a philatelic aficionado. Strangely, Christmas came and went and no Dodge. They couldn't figure it. Lina was quite surprised that he didn't show. And Partridge was anxious to recover his up front framing money, so he billed Dodge at his L.A. address. No dice. No strange phone calls from foreign capitols.

Several months elapsed with no news of him. It was quite mysterious. Lina and Partridge frequently speculated about him. The gallery accountant was getting antsy. She insisted on having his outstanding invoice reconciled. Suddenly, Dodge called from Japan and asked Lina to meet him at the airport. Winter had set in pretty good on the Peninsula and snow and ice were everywhere. He apologized about Christmas, she said, and he told her he would explain everything later.

Lina wasn't that worried about an explanation. She was very happy with Noel and she flip-flopped back and forth between his house and Dodge's house, using it as an artist's studio. It was somewhere she could go to work on her art projects without having to set them up and break them down all the time. She alternated on painting his tattoos from the photographs with a couple of other commission paint jobs she'd acquired and receiving guests. It was perfect.

When the time came, Lina cranked up her stubborn Mazda and hauled out to the little commuter jet airport which served their area. She waited there for an hour, she told Partridge later. No dice. No Dodge. She was steamed and complained bitterly. Partridge calmed her down. Two days later, he received a phone call from L.A. It was Dodge. He was terribly sorry he said. He had the flu or something. He couldn't make it to the Peninsula after all. He flew through to L.A. to see his doctor. Partridge told him he understood and not to worry. He didn't mention the outstanding invoice.

"I don't know what's the matter with me," Dodge said. "I'm just completely knocked out. Flu or something. I can't figure it out. And I'm so tired. Walking pneumonia or something like that. I'd be no good up there. I'll be up in a week,—whatever." Then he asked to speak to Lina and repeated his story to her. Afterward, they exchanged notes.

Lina was elated, she could put off news of her wedding to Dodge one more time. She got off the phone and breathed deeply, leaned against the matt—cutter and thanked God.

VII

Two more weeks passed and Partridge was manning the gallery on one of Lina's days off. She had, by now, moved in completely with Noel and didn't connect with any of the neighbors who were watching Dodge's house. One of those was Walter. He was eighty years old and he was the one who had found Dodge's father dead six months earlier. He was very nosy and kept his eye on the abandoned house after that. On one of his usual walks about town, he dropped in to the gallery.

"Hi Walter," Partridge greeted him.

"Hello, there," Walter responded in a thick Swiss accent. "How are you, Mister?"

"Great."

"Well, it's too bad about Bill, ja?"

Partridge shrugged and rustled some papers. "Bill, who?"

"The one that owns the house that your whoosis is living in—that woman who works here. Bill Dodge. Didn't she tell you?

"Tell me what?"

"Oh, by golly, he died. Died three, four days ago. Maybe more. They had to break down the door to get to him. Oh, yes, it was terrible. The lawyer, he's been all around the house, checking it out and like that."

Partridge was shocked. He questioned Walter further and got everything out of him he could. Dodge's Peninsula lawyer had been notified and he went to Walter to pick up the spare set of keys to secure everything. Walter wanted to go on and on about the Bill Dodge's death and rehashed the death of old man Dodge in the bargain. On the third go 'round, Partridge ushered him out of the gallery. He couldn't wait to call Lina. She came down immediately and they carefully examined every aspect of the bizarre incident. Dodge had seemed healthy enough. Nobody had established what he died from. They reviewed Dodge's past behavior looking for some kinky angle. He was, after all, Partridge observed, not your ordinary every day kind of college professor. He speculated what the coroner must have thought when he saw the stripped cadaver of Dodge in the morgue. What a surprise. Even the Coroner to the Stars would have gasped a little at the sight. Lina was uneasy. "I've got to get my stuff out of that house, before they seal it," she said. She raced off to get Noel's van. Two or three trips should take care of it she'd said.

Partridge was certainly sorry about Dodge from several angles. Not the least of which was their unfinished business. The gallery owed Dodge money. Dodge owed him money. There were still a bunch of unsold Bennetts. There was the expensive frame job. It was a mess. Luckily, his gallery agreement and invoice were ironclad. Only the agreement to give Lina a Bennett of her choice was verbal. If she got the Bennett out of Dodge's house before it was sealed, so much the better. Another month went by before Partridge found out the name of the lawyer who was handling Dodge's estate. He called him and arranged to have all bills, agreements and statements delivered to him for forwarding to the California executor who turned out to be a woman with whom Dodge had an 'arrangement.' The lawyer told Partridge to expect Dodge's cousin in a few weeks to resolve the gallery details. He was coming from Virginia. He was to fly into L.A. to talk to the executrix and then head on up to the Peninsula.

Partridge breathed a sigh of relief. It would soon be over.

VIII

Fog coiled up from the Coho ferry dock, entangling itself in the iron hand-rails and wrought-iron lamp posts in front of the gallery. Partridge looked outside. Wouldn't be any good for tourists, he surmised. One of those days when passengers to Victoria would cling to the mall by the pier and not venture into the town a block away.

When the gallery door did open a huge man, about forty-five years old, strode up to the desk. Partridge had learned to eyeball his customers at a glance while he waited on others. The big guy was six-foot-six, easy. He had a big frame and a pot gut. He was ham-fisted and wore rimless glasses, somehow too dainty and delicate for his large features. Partridge guessed that he might have been a bit younger than he looked. Partridge finished waiting on one of the locals and asked the big guy if he had a question.

"Well," he says, "I hear you've been waiting for me."

"I'm afraid I don't understand," Partridge replies. He finished with the local.

The big guy extended one of the hams and announced that he was Bob Cox. Cousin of Bill Dodge. Partridge caught on. He was relieved. Now, he would get his money and be rid of the damned annoyance with his accountant. "Oh—sure. Oh, of course. Mr. Dodge's cousin? Of course. How do you do?" He looked at the giant in front of him. He looked like he was doing just fine. He slipped into low gear. Partridge wondered just what tack to take. He and Lina had waited a long time for this moment. He leaned into the squawk box and told Lina to come on up to the front desk. "So, you're Mr. Dodge's cousin. Well—I can't tell you how sorry we were to hear about Mr. Dodge. I'd just talked to him a day or two before he died. He told me he had the flu."

"Yup," Cox said. Then he smiled. "Well, when you gotta go, you gotta go."

That insensitive response set the tone for the rest of the conversation. Lina slid next to Partridge and he the two.

"Oh," says the big guy, "let's see—you the one who was living at Bill's house?" He sized her up quickly.

Lina giggled nervously. "Not now—I'm married. We're so sorry and we were so surprised. What happened, anyway?" She didn't worry much about introducing meatier queries to the big guy. On the off chance that he was still grieving for his cousin, such forwardness could have put him into shock. Partridge looked at her painfully. But the big guy, it seemed, was more than up to any interrogation and in fact, seemed to relish going over the lurid details.

Cox found somewhere to put his briefcase. He was wearing marine camouflage pants and kangaroo construction shoes with rawhide laces tightly tied as if to keep them from getting away. He rolled on the balls of his feet and threw back his shoulders in a military manner. He was well aware that his audience hung on his next words.

"Well,—he died of a rupture in his abdominal tract."

"My god, was he—struck—or hit in some way?" Partridge asked.

"Geeeeee," says Lina.

Cox placed all of his fingertips together and rocked some more on the balls of his feet. He looked enormously tall and forbidding. "Coroner hasn't figured it out," he said ominously. "But, hell, they released the body. So there's not much more they're going to find out there." He laughed nervously, looking from one to the other. "At least I don't think so. I brought him up with me. Ohhhh. The *ashes*. Bill's ashes. They're in a shoe box in my hotel room. Do you know they weigh twenty pounds? Twenty-five pounds? And the ashes—they look like cocaine." Partridge raised his eyebrows at the strange analogy.

"He wants me to drop the ashes in the strait at the international line. But, frankly, I'm worried that the captain won't let me—then I'll have to land with it and the Canadians will think it's cocaine or something. It'll take hours to explain it to them."

Lina nodded sagely. "What if you talk to the captain first? I bet they do that all the time."

"Well," Cox agreed. "I gotta do something. Yesterday, somebody I met over at Zeke's—that bar on Front Street? He took me out to the end of the spit. You know, right out there in the strait. But, hell, ever try to tack a sailboat out there on a windless day? I mean, we tried for five hours and couldn't get past the coast guard station—let alone the end of the spit.

"So what are you going to do now?" Partridge asks him.

"Well, I'm going to take the ferry and I don't care who tries to stop me. I'm gonna dump Bill onto the international line." He laughed easily again. "And, I don't think anybody's gonna have much luck with that."

Lina and Partridge looked at each other and nodded.

"Hell, he's not there ya know. I'm not being insensitive. Hell, he'd be the first one to laugh. I've been around death a lot. Vietnam. When it's over, it's over. Hey, I think it's funny just trying to get him blown away out there on the strait."

Partridge was beginning to feel a little more at ease with the big guy. Bolder.

"Well," Cox continued, "I guess I owe you some money or something, don't I? Or, heh, you owe me money or something." He looked back and forth at each of them, fingertips together and a look of hopeful expectancy upon his face.

Partridge went over the invoices and the gallery agreements for the Bennetts and they wound everything up amicably. They shook hands. Partridge still had some questions. He decided to go for it, and ask the $64,000 question.

"Well, Mr. Cox—your cousin was such a nice guy—mind if I ask just one little question about him?"

"Shoot."

"How do I put it? Well, just tell me—uhm—I don't know—twenty-five words about your cousin's tattoos."

The big guy looked very surprised. "Well how in the hell did you know about them? I only just found out and I've known him all our lives. Well, shit, excuse me ma'am—sure I knew he had a few—but, I'll be dipped—how'd you know about them?" Lina gave her patented shrug and Partridge just smiled.

"Well, I just *did*," Lina answered enigmatically.

"Hell—don't answer that," Cox responded grandly. "It doesn't matter and I don't care. Well, okay—it's right here in his will." He looks for his briefcase and starts to open it.

"No, no," Partridge motioned. "You don't have to show me the will. I was just curious, that's all."

"No, hell, here it is—right here—Item Four—He says right there in his will that he's tattooed all over his body in the Japanese fashion and he wants to be *skinned* and the skin to be cured and sent back to Tokyo to a—let's see here—to Mrs. Juhn—I think she's Korean—not Japanese, or something." He looked to see what effect his words had on the others. Partridge and Lina shuddered. "Hell, he had books full of business cards in those little plastic gizmos—books and books of them all over his condo. There are tattoo aficionados all over the world. It's amazing."

Lina winced. "Skinned. My god, why would he do that?"

"Or, better yet, who could he get to do it?" Partridge shuddered.

"Oh, hell," Cox continued, "in Japan somewhere, they've got like Madame—whatever—Tussaud's—whatever—only with fully cured skins of ninjas in them. It's sort of a ninja code to be tattooed all over like that. Macho. I guess that's what Bill was into." He giggled a strange high giggle for a man so large. "Then he had boxes and boxes of those little cards from South Africa, Germany, Japan, Korea—and the Philippines—from all over. Really weird and interesting." He became quite intense as he re-lived the discovery of the cards. "And a lot of books of Japanese ladies—bath-house ladies, you know? Who wash you all over and do whatever you want them to do to you." Lina reddened. "Well, excuse me ma'am, that's in their culture, you know what I mean?"

Partridge nodded. He could be as sophisticated as the next gallery owner.

"And—lemme see—oh yeah, lots of strange books in his collection, too. Boxes and boxes of them—all written in Japanese. Hell, I couldn't read them, but the pictures were pretty explicit." Lina looked uncomfortable.

Cox was definitely warming to his theme. He seemed to want to tell all he could. Luckily Partridge's forecast about the tourists held up. There weren't many customers. It was fascinating to hear Cox tell about his cousin. He leaped in with questions from time to time and Cox would pour forth. Lina told him about the photo sessions and agreed to send him the prints. Cox was curious to see how his cousin looked in the buff and was ecstatic about the incredible luck of running into Lina. He went on.

"Well, sure, I gave away some things to his co-workers. Cufflinks and things like that to his buddies at UCLA. Nobody knew about those damned tattoos."

"How about his mother? His father?" Partridge asked.

"No sirreeee and that's the thing. Don't know what I'm going to do about that. There's his mother up there in the home, you know, on the hill? She's bright and sharp. Sure, she's old and she's in a wheelchair and needs full time care. But she's sharp. She wants to see the will. How can I show it to her? I don't think she should see all that tattoo stuff and particularly about being skinned. Might kill her. Kill her. So I can't give her the will."

"What about putting white-out over Item Four and then photocopying—or retyping it?" Partridge offered lamely.

"Thought of that—can't do it—well, maybe—but—she's sharp. She'll get wise if I 'X' out Item Four. There's items five and six—you know—it'll look *doctored*. Oh, boy."

"Yeah—terrible thing."

"I took Bill over to Zeke's last night. All twenty-five pounds of him. Fifteen pounds? I don't know. Anyway, I plunked him down on the bar at his favorite stool and bought him a beer. He would have liked that. Zeke didn't, but he didn't say anything. Bill and I used to drink there when we were in college. You know the importance of that guy to the science of demography? I mean—you can't overestimate it. The Israeli government and the South African Government and the Japanese and the Swiss all used him." Partridge nodded. He had work to do and the big guy seemed never to wind down. "Look, this is how important he was—his formulas could predict to the South Africans when—and I mean to the minute—when the blacks—you know based on all the scientific evidence and like that—when the blacks—population-wise—get me?—when they would like—overtake the whites in terms of swamping society—you know, use up welfare resources and such—things like that. It was like he could look at a population time-bomb and tell you when it would go off. He did the same kind of work for the Israelis—you know the Palestinians? Well, Jesus, you know they all breed like flies—and the Jews gotta know when that time-bomb is going to explode. His formulas were that important."

Partridge nodded some more. Where would it all end? He remembered the formula tattooed on Dodge's ankle, upside-down for discreet viewing, say, in a meeting in the Israeli Knesset, or something.

Cox continued. "He had about four books going simultaneously. One guy called me from South Africa while I was in Bill's condo and he says he needs some stuff Bill had real bad. What a mess. I couldn't help him. And thousands of collector stamps sitting loose all over the place. What a mess. And then, in that little house of his mom and dad's over here on the Peninsula." Partridge perched on the counter top and scanned the doorway. It was still gloomy out. No customers. "Now, how come more people didn't know about his tattoos?" he asked Cox.

"Well, that's got me, too. You know I've been in Virginia for years and I only wrote letters now and then to Bill. You know we didn't go skinny dipping together or anything. He was a little older than me. Apparently he kept it a secret. Secret sort of life. I knew about some of them, but not to that extent. Whew. He'd run to the bathroom fully clothed and leave it the same way when he took a shower. One of his few relatives, an uncle, asked him how come he papered up all of the windows in his father's house after he died and his mom went to the home. Well, he says to his uncle that he likes to run around the house in the nude and he didn't want anybody peeking in. Must have been some sight, huh? A fully tattooed man in a little burg like this running around naked in his house? Whoa."

Lina laughed and Partridge shook his head, listening for more.

"But, it's okay with me. I'm an ex-Marine ranger and I'm pretty tolerant of what you call extremes, yeah? As long as you don't hurt women and kids, I don't care what the hell you do. Bill and I were going to move in with each other. He was going to take an early retirement and we were going to buy Zeke's beer bar—it was all set up—and just work it during the summer and take off all winter. Fish for salmon—steelhead ya know—Coho—whatever it is you folks got in your waters up here. Well, I guess we won't be doing that now."

Cox looks at Lina. "I really want to thank you for those pictures. I'll pay you for them as soon as you tell me how much. Just ship them out to me. Soon as I heard about it—soon as the coroner told me—I wanted to—you know, why not? He's my cousin—can't I be curious like everybody else?"

"So you never saw him nude, then?"

"Nope."

"Well," Lina says, "if you ever wondered whether he's tattooed *all over*, the answer is—*yes*—and I mean all over."

"You're *serious*?" Cox said. "Geeeeez. Yeah, I did wonder."

"And he said it hurt worse when they tattooed him on the butt and under his arms," she added indelicately.

Partridge hopped off the countertop. A customer pushed through the front door. It was time to get back to work.

"Ohhhh," says Cox. "I don't know if I believe that."

Partridge orchestrated a quick end to the macabre reminiscence, got Lina to hot foot it back to the frame room and somehow shoe-horned the big guy out the door.

IX

Two days later, Partridge was sweeping his entry way and checking out the weather and the tourist activity at the ferry dock. Cox lumbered around the corner in his camouflage-wear and kangaroo boots.

"Well, I did it," he told Partridge.

"Terrific. Did what?"

"Yeah. I dumped Bill overboard. Right at the international line. No problem."

Partridge nodded conspiratorially and leaned on his broom. "One last question, Mr. Cox."

"Shoot."

"Well—sounds stupid—but considering all the blue ink pumped into your cousin—Mr. Dodge—the ashes—were they even tinted blue? I mean—you know—silly question—"

Cox laughed. "Oh, hell no. Not stupid. Hell the ashes were white—like cocaine—like I told you."

Partridge shrugged. Cox showed no signs of moving along. Partridge took a deep breath. "So, uh—then nobody asked you any questions?"

"Well, two deck hands came towards me. I just stood up and dumped Bill over the side and then the box after him. And then I pulled out a bottle of Jack Daniels and said, 'Here's to you, Bill, and took a slug for each of us and then tossed the bottle overboard. I mean, what were they going to do? Arrest me for littering? Let 'em try."

"So, it's all over, then?"

"Yup. It's all over. I've gotta go over to the bank. Bill's mother wants to see some bracelets and rings from her safe deposit box. I'll be leaving tomorrow. But I'll be back. I'll look you up. You been swell. You and Lina. I want to thank you both."

"Well, then. Have a great trip. Sorry it wasn't more pleasant for you."

Cox extended a giant arm and brought it to rest against the brick facade of the gallery. Leaning comfortably, he crossed his ankles. Partridge winced. Cox was settling in. "Yeah," he said, "you know especially that part in L.A. There's something weird about the people down there—I mean when I got to the condo—." Partridge got the picture. Cox was enjoying his celebrity status.

Partridge paled. He was through now. He looked up in the sky for a hook to save him from the talking ex-Marine. There was nothing. He thought he heard the telephone ring in his office. "You'll have to excuse me—I've gotta run," he said lamely, "have a *great* trip."

There was nothing more he wanted to know about Bill Dodge or his tattoos. The gallery door bonged shut behind him.

The End

THE WHITE DOVE

Vernon tried to guess what time it was. A high pale moon and buttermilk clouds moved quickly past. There was a low pressure system cooking up overhead and the chink of sky he could see through his broken window told him there'd be rain tomorrow. Another beer bottle hit his trailer. He wanted to get up and mow them all down with an AK-47 assault rifle, but one didn't do that to one's neighbors. Especially if the neighbor was your landlord. Vern remembered the conversation.

"You in exile, man? Witness protection program? What you want to live out here on the res for? This ain't no way for no white man to live." Rudy laughed. He was half-Indian and he had a little string of trailers all lined up in a row, as far up on the northwest tip of the lower forty-eight as you could get. "I *mean* it. You an exile, buddy?" His inflamed eyes passed over Vernon, trying to read him like a UPC hand-scanner. Vernon could almost hear the electronic beep of approval. "But, hell, man, your money is as good as anybody's. You take that tin can over there. You be next to me, man. That's my bus."

Vernon looked where Rudy pointed. A large yellow school bus with flaking paint dominated a row of half-a-dozen scuzzy trailers, each one looking worse than the one next to it. Dingy café curtains barely showed through mud splattered windows.

"I can keep my eye on your stuff, man, you know? I'm the heavy 'round here." He winked, looking around at bunch of native-American losers squatting in the distance. "You know man, you gotta watch your stuff. Everybody up here on the res is cousins, man. *Cousins.* What's mine is mine and what's yours is mine, too. Except for women." He laughed an ugly, obscene laugh. "The law of the res, buddy. You got yourself a woman, or you alone?"

Vernon shrugged. "Well—."

"Gotcha, buddy," Rudy smirked. Rudy's alcohol breath reminded Vernon of how he used to smell. It was like looking in a mirror and seeing himself. Recovery was like that. Everywhere he looked, there were lots of little Vernons puking behind the rocks, trying to straighten up in time for a night's beer bust in the woods, or in somebody's rent-party trailer. But the big Indian was right. Vernon was exiling himself in a sense. Rudy Bill was an astute observer. Vernon just needed some space. Affordable space. He'd just left another trailer way down on the Strait, where all the retired somebodys with nothing to do hung around his place and watched him carve his rock sculptures. It bugged him, with them all of the time asking him what he was working on. He just needed to get away. Get away to somewhere new. See new people. Get new input. Away from the annoying rubberneckers. Maybe this wasn't it. Who could know? Fact is, he was burned out. He drove up here to the wild coast of Cape Flattery where the coastline terminated gracefully with Tatoosh Island and its lighthouse, a white explanation point at land's end. America the beautiful. He fell immediately in love with its picture-postcard coastline. There were plenty of his kind of rocks for carving. Sandstone, granite cobbles, iron pyrite. They were everywhere, and all within easy walking distance on the rocky coastline, north and south of his designated trailer. All free for the picking. He could see that much at a glance. The sea was spectacularly inspirational. Just above the shoreline, a row of picturesque, oxidized Airstream trailers, looking like a caravan of aluminum millipedes, uncertainly gripped the bluff with a couple dozen blown, bald tires. In a shanty, fifty feet away from the trailers, were communal showers and a chronically puddled laundryroom outfitted with several leaking coin washers. Rudy;, the owner, called it Deer Park Campground. His Indian ancestors would be ashamed of it. Vern shook his head. The place looked like the kind of dysfunctional heaven he was used to.

Rudy's voice hammered. "Sure, man, you can have your cat. What's his name?" He looked into the cab of Vernon's truck at a striped tabby.

"Sam. His name is Sammy." Vernon smiled weakly.

"Sam. Hey, buddy, I like that. I had a mess sergeant once named Sam. He was a bastard. Okay, done deal. One fifty a month—in advance—no checks."

Vernon took it. What could he lose? He threw his doublewide sleeping bag and blue ground-tarp on top of the sour mattress in the rear of the trailer. He knew he would never touch the striped ticking with his skin. Radiating amber stains, successively overlaying each other, were indelibly imprinted on it—a Jackson Pollack dribble—from who knew how many dozens of random human leakages. Sweat. Urine. Blood. Semen. Tears. The works. He shuddered. He hauled in his six surplus-store 50-calibre ammo cases. They held his most private possessions. He stacked them neatly, two by three up. He lugged some of his stone carvings inside and swept out the place and, when he was done, he placed his prized white Carrara marble dove on the kitchenette Formica table. The Carrara marble was from an expensive art supply catalog. Imported from Italy. Those were the days. The dove's outstretched wings, pushing for takeoff, seemed to bless his small space. He blew the dust off it, knowing it would be the last piece to go. Every artist held something back until the end. It was a good piece and he was proud of it. He wouldn't trade it away for cigarettes or booze or dope. Those days were over.

The interior of the trailer smelled as foul as a discarded can of cat food. He left the door open and hoped for the best. It was damp and mildewed. He flipped on a small electric wall heater and sat down in the cold Naugahyde booth of the luncheonette that would become his dining table, drafting table and rainy day, indoor workbench. He counted his money. There was not much left. He'd have to sell some art soon. For sure. The three big tourist months were coming up and if he worked hard, he could have sculptures in most of the galleries on the Peninsula. There were potential customers waiting for them. Always had been.

Sam jumped onto the table and watched Vernon's pencil move about the uniform gray surface of the want-ad section of the newspaper. Vernon, dreaming, drew the whorls and curlicues that would become his next rock sculptures, shading them so that their one-dimension seemed like two, and their two-dimensions seemed three, and some ordinary forms, a bird, a bear, a cat, were raised to a satisfying level of abstraction. All illusions. Sam was accustomed to a routine. He waited for Vernon to wad up the drawing and toss it for the chase. The cat took a swipe at Vernon's pencil tip. Vernon caught his paw and squeezed it gently. His transistor radio spattered some country western about the room. Home.

After a month, Vernon's routine more or less settled in. Only a couple of people in Port Angeles, a hundred miles away, knew he was living on the reservation. He set up his outdoor workbench and turned out several abstract sculptures from river rock, beach stone, and marble. But, just as before, his workbench, just outside is door, attracted more and more attention and the Indians began to hover around him to ask questions and shoot the bull—and he was losing the privacy and concentration he needed so desperately. Worse, their non-stop partying drained him of needed quiet, fracturing midnight to dawn into restless nightmarish intervals. Screaming, knifings, rabble-rousing, and then, gunshots, fired far into the low-hung night sky, disrupted his rest nearly every night. He felt imprisoned. The res cops, Indian brothers like themselves, were regular visitors. They lightheartedly hauled off brawling men and women and dangerous, stoned teenagers only to release them hours later. The annoyances never ceased.

Two more beer bottles hit the trailer with loud frightening thumps. Sam was terrified. Vernon pulled him into the sleeping bag next to him, and he held him close to calm him.

Next day, Vernon went over to Rudy's yellow bus and asked him to put a stop to the nighttime ruckus, but it was no dice. Rudy looked down at Vernon from the top bus step. "Hell, pardner, like I told you, they all be cousins. Can't put them out on the highway. You know how it is?" Rudy was smooth as silk, scratching his privates indulgently. "Look, when times are tough, people party. You gotta learn to relax—stay loose, pardner—roll with the punches." He laughed sardonically once more, and Vernon knew he wasn't making any headway. Rudy climbed down out of the bus and pissed on one of the rear bus tires. It was noon and he was hung over. His woman, LaShanna, hollered out the back door that his breakfast was ready. Rudy ignored her. "Look," he said to Vernon, "I been looking at your stuff. Them rocks. What do they go for?"

Vernon saw no reason not to answer. He was proud of his art. "Seven hundred bucks in the gallery—depends. Some up, some down."

Rudy whistled through his teeth and his bloodshot, hung-over eyes flashed over the commercial possibilities. He adjusted his dirty-gray jockey shorts and spat. "Tell you what, pardner, I'll trade you six-months rent for three of them—whatever they are." He had his own idea to sell them down the coast, maybe at Ocean Shores. Gallery owners would buy anything from a real Indian.

Vernon was tempted. He was low on dough. Rent was always a problem. "To tell the truth, Rudy," Vernon countered, "I can't even think in this place here—people on my ass all night—can't sleep—throwing bottles at my trailer—hollering—fucking gunshots—police."

Rudy became very paternal. He wanted to protect his new investment. "Look," he said, "—you don't worry about my people—I'll talk to them—you don't worry about them." He was the worst offender. He and his woman screaming at each other all night ten feet from Vernon's ear. He spat again. "We'll talk—we'll talk. Oh, buddy—I noticed you got a broken window there—I'm gonna to fix up that pup—tomorrow." He tried to mollify Vernon. "Oh, and buddy—that honcho up at the store?—He says he might like your stuff too—I told him all about 'em. He told me to tell you to bring some pieces up to him—he'll put 'em on consignment, pardner—but I want my pick first. He gets *some* tourists up there." Rudy was railroading him with attention. Vernon wasn't stupid. "We cookin'?" he asked him. He didn't wait for Vernon's answer. Vernon looked at the tire of the flaking school bus, still moist with Rudy's urine. A res dog wandered over from under the bus, sniffed at it, and backed away. He could hear Rudy inside the bus shouting at his woman and he saw the bus lurch when Rudy flopped back onto the sweaty sheets of his day bed and cranked up the TV. Well, Vern hadn't signed a lease. You don't sign leases with guys like Rudy—and his string of tin can trailer shanties. He could leave whenever he wanted.

A hundred yards away, the Pacific was roiling with whitecaps. Overhead, gulls screed, scrounged and scavenged for gut scraps washed ashore from salmon seiners. Puffins were diving off the cliffs into the salt spume and a bald eagle was shredding something on a snag nearby. Vernon looked back through the clutter of the trailer court. Dogs were running everywhere, checking everything out. Nobody feeds dogs on the res. There aren't any scraps for them. Not on the res. Vernon took a deep breath of the cleanest, bluest, coldest air anywhere in the world. Nothing was real any more. Life was a compromise. He'd think about Rudy Bill's proposal. But *three* of his sculptures? There was no way.

.. ..

Eddie Stroble's family owns Stroble's Foods. It's the only market on the reservation. Last winter, a fire of suspicious origin had burned it down—but completely—and the Stroble's had just opened a modern new replacement to great hoopla. Called it Stroble's Trading Post. Fancy. Eddie is a white guy who befriends all the Indians and extends a line of credit to just about everybody on the Cape, probably including the unknown firebug. He just laughs it off. It's good business. He's the third-generation grocer to the res. He is to the res what Fred Harvey's was to the Southern Pacific and the Navajos. With more and more affluent tourists coming up to the Cape, he decided to open an Indian craft alcove inside his store. Bear grass baskets. God's eyes. Masks. Carvings. Stuff. It was doing quite well. Vernon liked Eddie and Eddie liked Vernon. They hit it off immediately.

Vernon hauled three of his best stone sculptures up to Stroble's in a cardboard box. They were wrapped in old T-shirts. Vernon laid them out on the counter for Eddie to see. Eddie, swigging on a liter of Diet Pepsi, had a big sunny uncomplicated face. Vernon knew he'd like his work. He unwrapped each one, dusting them off with a T-shirt. When he was done, he stood back, nonchalantly, like a Mexican street merchant selling papayas. Eddie sucked in his breath and held it for a tantalizing second of suspended artistic judgment.

"These are great—just great." He smiled and complimented Vernon. "What's this one? It's a *what*? A cat? A panther?" He stroked it.

"Well," Vernon nodded, "uhmmm—cat-like—cat *essence*—I guess. Whatever." He was not *arty*, the way most artists were. He disliked explaining his work. Eddie sensed his reluctance to open up and didn't push it.

"*Dyn-o-mite*. And this one—it's a—a—*sure*, I *see* it—it's a bear on a rock, right?" Vernon nodded. "And this one," Stroble enthused, "it's a—*very* abstract—"

Vernon saved him the trouble of speculating. "It's Portuguese pink marble—I call it *Puffins*—or maybe *Snow Birds*. He shrugged. "Anything you want." Two very sensual, conjoined, pink figures composed the sculpture. One of them had a magnificent set of Dolly Parton boobs. Each of them had a marble circle forming a kind of head. They looked like anything but puffins. He was suddenly aware of someone standing beside him.

"*Love Handles*, I'd call it."

Vernon turned to include the new person. A native-American woman smiled at Vernon's narrow face and his very sad, protuberant, extra-terrestrial eyes. He was no Cary Grant. He gave her a sweet, melancholy smile. "Well," he said, "you could just about call it anything you want. As long as it sells." He turns to Stroble. "Sure, call it, *Love Handles*." He made a nervous chuckle.

Eddie smiled. "Sure, no prob—this baby'll sell. How about a price?"

"I was hoping for maybe four hundred each—that's for me. And seven fifty for—*Love Handles*, here. It was a lot more work. You can do your own markup." His eyes met Eddie's.

"Sure. Sounds fair. It's a deal—no problem," Eddie nodded him with growing conviction. "Well—they're not cheap—."

"Fine art—."

Eddie's head nodded again. There was something about Vern that Eddie Stroble liked. "Give 'em a week—they'll be outta here. You seen our tourists? They're loaded. They're always looking for something new?" Vernon nodded. "Yesterday I sold a Makah mask for Rudy George—twenty-five hundred bucks. Collector up from Palm Springs. Didn't bat an eye." He drilled Vernon with a look. "Problem, though, your stuff's not *Indian*, buddy. You're white, right? I can't sell any of it as—you know, *Indian*. You know what I mean? Indian art brings top dollar. Your stuff—I've got to sell as Indian-*style*, get me? Non-tribal affiliated. Big federal fine for misrepresentation." He looked admiringly at the sculptures. "You're in other galleries?"

Vernon nodded and cocked his thumb toward the strait. "Port Angeles. North Light Gallery."

"So you understand about this Indian thing?"

"Sure," Vernon nodded, "no problem. I'm *not* Indian and my stuff's not *trying* to be Indian. It's just my work and it's what I do. That's it." The tried not to sound defensive.

"Okay, great. But you could do a bunch of say—salmon for me?" Eddie pulverized a toothpick with his teeth and thoughtfully took another swig of Pepsi.

"No way," Vernon complained. He took a couple of steps backward in mock horror. "*Salmon*?"

"What's the matter? I could sell all the salmon you could make." It was like he was ordering a case of produce. "Do me some salmon in this pink Portuguese—what is it?" He fingers it. "Marble? What did you say it is? I could sell all the salmon sculptures you could make."

Vernon attempted a rare and wry smile. "No thanks. I'm really tired of salmon—no challenge—it's not art. Too easy." He made a nervous laugh. "Me—a little salmon factory?" He runs his fingers through his thinning hair. "No way. I've got new some ideas I want to try out." He taps his temple. He knew he should have said yes. He needed the dough that bad.

"I get it—okay—okay—no problem—an *arteest*." Eddie was smart. He wouldn't force it. He'd catch him later, when he was hungrier. All artists get hungry.

The Indian woman stroked the newly named *Love Handles* with long elegantly groomed, tapered fingernails. "They're all three lovely," she complimented Vernon in a rich throaty voice. "And the loops on this one *are* just like handles." She smiled and ran her forefinger around the inside of each pink marble loop and unselfconsciously stroked the prominent pink marble breasts with the tip of her little finger. "And the finish," she observed,"—it's almost like flesh."

Vernon flushed and cleared his throat. "I finish them up with 2000 micro grit—all by hand—it's a lot of work getting them that way." His hands were callused and his knuckles enlarged and bony.

The woman said, "They're excellent sculptures and well conceived. Have you heard of Brancusi?" Vernon was embarrassed. She looked and spoke like no Indian woman he'd ever seen or heard. She was a knockout. He picked absently at Sam's cat fur on his scuzzy Polartec sweater.

"No, ma'am," he lied. Next thing she'd be telling him his work was just like Brancusi's. But, his work was unique. He copied nobody.

Eddie stepped away to deal with a beer deliveryman, saying, "Vernon, this here is Soonie—say hi. Soonie, meet Vernon the sculptor. Be right back—don't go away."

"Ma'am," Vernon said.

"It's a pleasure. Your work is wonderful. Do you have any more?"

Vernon was entranced by her. She was tastefully made up. Her eyes were jet and her hair fine and black, combed into soft waves unlike any of the Indian women around the reservation whose hair was coarse and straight. Vernon ignored her question. "Are you a tourist?"

"Oh, no," she said. "I raise horses. A friend of mine has loaned me a few acres down here to breed my mares." She laughed. "I'm *not* a tourist."

"Oh," Vernon replied woodenly. He became very self-conscious and continued to polish his sculptures with feigned concentration.

Eddie came back with an artist's agreement form. "Let's see, now. You live down there at Rudy Bill's place?" Vernon nodded. Eddie made some notes and then looked at the Indian woman. "Soonie, you live down there somewhere, too, no?"

"Across the highway," she smiled. Her fingers stroked Vernon's sculpture of the bear on the rock.

Vernon asked her, "You know Rudy?"

Soonie frowned. "Doesn't everybody?"

Eddie Stroble looked at Vernon and laughed. "How in the hell do you get any work done down there?"

Vernon smiled back. It was nice knowing that someone knew what he had to put up with. But he was cautious. "Well," he said, "it's okay—the rent is right—I guess." He shrugged.

Eddie bent over the consignment agreement with his Bic and, without looking up, he warned Vernon to watch out for the riff-raff down at Rudy's picturesque trailer park. A young Indian gave him a couple of dollars and change for a liter of Coke and a package of Cheez Nips.

Soonie looked at Vernon. "Seriously, do you have any more pieces? I've got a lot of friends."

"Sure," Vernon nodded obligingly, "Sure, c'mon down. I got five or six I can show you any time."

Soonie gave him a lavish smile and Vernon felt giddy.

Eddie asked Vernon for his social security number. "In case," he said, "you sell over six-hundred bucks worth of art here—I gotta send you a Form 1099." Vernon shrugged. He knew that. "Just so's you know. It's the law, sir," he joshed. "Sign here, and good luck. Okay, let's *sell*. That's the name of the game." He gave Vernon a handshake and placed the three sculptures in prominent positions on a small, black-velvet draped table in his tourist folk art alcove.

Soonie stroked *Love Handles* lingeringly. "They look great there," she said to Vernon. "Well, maybe I'll see you around."

Vernon looked at the beautiful Indian woman. He hoped he would see her around.

.. ..

Vernon walked the mile back down the highway to his trailer in a light, bracing, drizzle. He felt good about the day. Stroble's wanted his art and he'd received some compliments. The prospects of sales were at least encouraging. His good mood lasted only until the door of his trailer. It was wide open when he pulled up in his truck. The metallic squeak-and-slam of trailer marked time in the wet, late spring wind that rattled about Deer Park Campground. The appearance of the place was off. He'd been robbed before. His scalp tingled. He leaped out of his truck and saw Sam, crouched under the trailer, looking soggy and mournful.

Vernon took a look inside before he climbed up the corrugated metal steps. His place had been trashed. The ammo cases had been pried open and their contents spread carelessly around the floor. His aborted journal. Divorce papers. The works. He wiped muddy footprints from a photograph of a blond child. Nothing to tempt a thief. Art books. Hardly. He had got rid of all his valuables a long time ago. What there was left. It was just the annoyance factor and the sense of trespass. He picked up his papers and put them back into their respective ammo boxes. Sam's food and water had been stepped on and his bowls overturned. The sleeping bag was tossed around. Thieves generally went for the sleeping bags. Cops said that they seemed like good hiding places for valuables, but he had none. His pistol was hidden in his pickup—so that was not an issue.

Vernon looked about in disgust. It was then that he noticed the white dove was gone. And his transistor radio. He hit the table with his fist. He examined the latch where the door engaged the mainframe of the trailer. It was a sorry connection and wouldn't have kept out a determined five-year-old. He swung down into the mud and he went around to the other side and banged on Rudy Bill's yellow schoolbus door. He could hear the television, overloud and stressful.

"What do you want?" Rudy's voice reflected annoyance.

Vernon hollered into the door, "It's me."

Rudy lumbered to the opening. "Hey, what's up, man? You go on up to Stroble's like I told you to do?"

"Maybe I did, Rudy, but that's not the problem." He felt his face flush. "Somebody's fucking trashed my place. If I remember right, you said that you were the main watchdog here, and we gotta all watch out for each other—what's yours is mine—and what's mine is mine—and all that bullshit. You got any ideas, here, about what happened to my place? Ten foot away? You see anything, or should I call the tribal police?"

"Ohhhh, man, buddy, not the cops again. Look, what did they take? Tell me . . . tell me. Me, I didn't hear nothing."

"A five dollar radio and a piece of my sculpture. I didn't make an inventory."

"Well, no shit? Hey, lemme go pull on some pants. I gotta see this. Probably fucking kids."

"No." Vernon raised his hand. "You don't have to come on over. But, you can put the word out that I play rough. If I catch anybody in my place—anybody at all—that I didn't invite—there's gonna be trouble. And, I'm reporting this to the cops. I don't give a godamn if they do come on out here—or whatever—I'm reporting this shit—and it's going on the record. I'm not saying that you know anything about this, I'm just saying you can put the word out—you know this place and I don't. I can't live like this."

"Well, shit, man, I got no idea anybody got into your space, and I sure as hell got nobody to *warn*. This here is sure one sad day for Deer Park Campground." His response lacked conviction and he didn't sound very contrite to Vernon. He spat a stream of SKOAL into the mud. "Look, buddy—Vern—you need any help cleaning up or anything, I'll send over my woman, LaShanna—she help you out."

Vernon was pissed. Rudy Bill knew plenty, he was sure of it. "You can thank LaShanna for me—she's probably got all she can handle right now." He knew the irony would be lost on the Indian. He turned and picked his way back through the mud to his own place.

.. ..

Vernon stepped down from his trailer and checked the day. The light was a flat monochrome, but it was early yet. He walked over to the bluff overlooking the shoreline. A gray sea stack, eons old, was mirrored in the water there, as if floating in the low tide. Another sea stack, a smaller one, loomed near it and it too appeared suspended an inch above the receding, reflective, tidal waters. Blue spruce trees bit into the sea stacks at deliriously odd angles, as if hurled by drunken *picadors*. Vernon wondered how they managed to hang on during foul weather. He took a deep breath. It was beautiful.

On the horizon, the white peaks of early-bird sailboats appeared becalmed. The air was still, and the far-off voices of playing children were clear and undistorted. An almost tangible scent, moist and salty, sent shivers up Vernon's spine. In the distance, he watched a horse and rider emerge from a wisp of ground fog to pick their way along the craggy shoreline, stopping here and there, to scrutinize some interesting flotsam.

Vernon skinned on down the foot trail that led to the beach below and walked nearly out to the sea stacks in his Hush Puppies. Their shallow imprint in the low tide followed him until by degrees they slowly filled with seawater and vanished. Something had caught his eye. When he returned, he was holding a thick, green, glass float. He examined it with great interest. He would add it to the growing pyramid of viridian floats beneath his trailer. When he turned back, he saw that the horse and rider had stopped at the top of the trail. It was Soonie, the Indian woman who had admired his work. She looked down at him with her arms crossed peacefully. A hint of breeze teased her hair. He greeted her at the top of the path and showed her the float. He explained that it was neither a molded float nor a plastic float, and he smiled with the pleasure of a child who had just found a dime under his pillow.

"Look," he explained to her, "it's actually blown glass—you can see right here—where the blow pipe was broke off. It could be twenty-five years old—who knows?" He gave a little laugh of delight. "Most floats are molded, these days, you know." Soonie did know. "You can see the seam real easy on the ones that are molded," he said. He turned it back and forth in the weak sunlight.

Soonie didn't try to butt in. She put her hands on the pommel and looked down and listened to him carefully, because that was her way. She smiled at his pleasure and when he was through speaking, she said, "I thought about your invitation." Vernon had forgotten. "To see some more of your pieces," she clarified. He didn't tell her about the break in.

Vernon patted the horse on the jowl. It had three white socks and a blaze. It moved away from him. Soonie smiled and said, "Just breathe on her nose. She'll be your friend for life."

Vernon looked dubious. "You sure about that?" He did as she suggested. The horse raised its powerful neck in quick, jerking movement and almost clipped his chin. Soonie reined her in and spoke soothingly to her.

She leaned over and handed Vernon a plastic bag. "I brought you these," she said. Her long fine fingers were purple and her fingernails were dark from berry juice. "I've found a secret stash of blackberries."

She pointed south along the coast. "About a half-a-mile back that way."

"Blackberries," he said, and he smiled owlishly at her. A memory triggered for him from another place. "I like blackberries—thanks." He didn't know what to do next. "Well," he said, "come on. Come on in—it's not very fancy." He looked up at her. "A trailer. Just like one of those—over there." They looked in the direction of the sorrowful string of battered Airstreams. He turned around, and led the way up the trail. He was surprised at how heavy the bag of berries seemed. He imagined it would be light. He didn't know why. But they had heft. He held the bag up to the gray sky, to where the sun would be, to see the purple. They were beginning to liquefy and he thought he could taste them in his mouth. He grinned back over his shoulder when Soonie's horse seemed to be nudging him to move along. He could hear her communicate with it, using clicks from between her clenched teeth.

Soonie tied her horse up to a skinny alder next to his trailer and dismounted. He wondered how his place would look to a woman. A woman like her, so beautiful, so cultured. Would she notice that it smelled of cat food and litter box? He winced, brushed his hands clean on his threadbare Levi 501's, and pulled open the aluminum door. "Come on in," he invited her. Soonie boosted herself up the wooden steps leading to the flimsy entrance and took in the interior of the trailer with a glance. Vernon rubbed his hands together nervously. He could see Soonie politely fix her gaze on the strengths of his sparse decor, his treasured Navajo blanket tossed over a stool, and his couple of books. She didn't dwell on the mess of the tiny, stainless steel kitchen sink or the clothing strewn about, or the pool of dried spaghetti sauce from a previous tenant, still peeking from under the stove. "It's not much," he said. "It's all I need."

"It's nice."

Vernon looked at her. "Go ahead, sit down, sit down." With his sleeve, he wiped clean a small space on the table. Soonie slid into the Naugahyde nook opposite the clean space.

"Look," Vernon said apologetically. His voice was dry and crackly. Hesitant. He wasn't much of a talker. "I drink tea, now. Do you like tea?"

Soonie smiled to put him at ease. She could tell by looking at him that he was probably in recovery. "I love tea." The corners of her black eyes crinkled.

Vernon rustled about the compact butane stove, heating some water in a saucepan.

Soonie pointed over Vernon's front door to a cluster of feathers. "You've got power feathers?"

Vernon looked at them and shrugged. "Didn't really know that," he said. "They were here when I moved in." The feathers were covered with dust. He hadn't noticed them there or he would have tossed them out. The heated water started a rolling boil and he began to prep their tea. He hoisted a box. "I got Lemon Lift." Then he showed her a little brown bag. "And, I got—uhm—hibiscus tea." He chuckled. "Now, don't laugh—I'm working my way down the shelf at Stroble's. Mint is next." He smiled. "Then, maybe cinnamon tea." He knew he was talking too much. Talking nervous. "This here's *bulk* hibiscus. Not in bags. Don't come in bags. It's pretty good." He looked at her expression. "No," he laughed, "It's *real* good."

"That's what I want," she said. "Hibiscus." She watched him shake some faded maroon petals into an infuser. She looked at several of the work-in-progress sculptures that the burglars had ignored sitting on the table before her. They talked, passing the glass float back and forth, examining its scratches and markings, and imagining where in Japan it might have come from. Soonie's stained berry-purple fingers, moved gracefully, and whispered over the curves and planes on each of his sculptures.

Vernon felt an ache. "You know," he said, "I hope you don't take this wrong—but you are one beautiful woman." Soonie laughed a good-natured laugh and her dark eyes flashed at him. He felt his knees touching hers and he pulled them in to give her plenty of room.

"Well, aren't you nice?" She laughed a throaty, musical laugh. "What a nice thing to say."

They sipped their tea. Vernon liked the way she didn't feel threatened by him. She had class. It was as if he were visiting her in *her* place, rather than the other way around. She made him feel so comfortable. So alive. A blue-and-white lace garment of some sort showed beneath her red sweats. It peeked out from beneath the cuffs at her wrists and from the vee at her neck line. He was transfixed by her exotic native-American femininity.

Vernon told her about Rudy and the handguns going off at all hours, and he told her about the beer bottles and about the coarse people who lived in Deer Park Campground. It felt good to talk to a woman again. She made him feel good in a way that no man—no buddy—could ever make him feel. He lit a cigarette and she asked for a puff of his. It was more for politeness—for bonding. He noticed she didn't inhale.

"I don't smoke," she told him, "but I love that first fresh *whiff*." It tickled Vernon, the way she pronounced the word, *whiff*. Warm and rich. She let the smoke wisp slowly from her lips.

Off the res, cigarettes were over forty-bucks a carton, and rising, but cheaper on the res, Vernon splurged on Marlboros. Soon enough, he'd be down to buying singles at a quarter apiece. He told her about Rudy, and LaShanna, and the wild res dogs and the robbery. She nodded. He suspected she knew about this life of his. Sam jumped into her lap and purred. Vernon looked at this beautiful woman and he wanted her.

"You from around here?" he asked her.

"Well, not right now. I've got some mares. That mare out there, she's my baby. She's not in heat right now. The others—three of them, I'm going to breed. She just came along for the ride."

Vernon nodded. "So, you don't live here, then? You're not from this tribe?"

"Oh, no."

Vernon looked at her skin. It was light and alive. "But you *are* Native American?"

"Oh, sure." She enjoyed the game. "Not this tribe. I'm not northwest. I'm Assiniboine. My people are plains Indians, out of Canada years ago. Right now, we're out of Montana. Fort Belknap. Why," she asked, "does that bother you—me being Indian?"

Vernon smiled at her. "No way." They sipped their tea and watched the cat. "If old Sammy, there, is bothering you, I'll run him off."

"He's sweet," Soonie said. She glanced casually about the trailer. "Cats are the embodiment of the female spirit—cat energy is very strong." Vernon nodded dreamily at the sound of her voice. After a few minutes she said, "I know I'm keeping you from your work." Before Vernon could say no, Soonie was alerted to the sound of her horse. She twisted her way out of the booth and ran outside. A small group of curious Indian boys clustered around the horse.

Vernon scrambled to the door of the trailer. "Go on—get outta here—get away from that horse," he hollered. Soonie hurried to where the mare was tied up, just in time to see her kick out savagely with a rear leg at one of the boys. Soonie brought the horse up to Vernon's trailer door. She was very placid and in control, stroking the mare's neck.

"You know what you need? This *place* needs?" Soonie asked him. Vernon laughed at her. "No, what?"

"You were right. This place—it's terrible. It needs to be *smudged.*"

"Smudged?"

"*Smudged,*" she repeated. "And the sooner the better.

"What the hell is *smudged?*"

"You'll find out tomorrow." Soonie told him. "For starters, take those *power feathers*—the eagle feathers over the door—and bury them somewhere nice and say a little prayer over them. Return them to the earth." She mounted up and then looked down at him. Her horse fidgeted and she reined her in. "Promise?"

What did he have to lose? "It's a promise," he told her, "a *proper* burial."

.. ..

It was drizzling. The Olympics, roughened by dark wet forests, drew a craggy uneven line across the horizon over which a brisk westerly shepherded errant rain clouds. Weeds flourished in the rich soil of the embankment below Vernon's trailer and their ripening seed heads bent under the weight of the rainwater. Just beyond them a limitless supply of raw material for his sculptures.

Vernon looked up from burying the power feathers along the trail when he saw Soonie at the top of the bluff looking down on him. He waved and hustled up toward her. Hatless, she shook the water out of her hair. The rain pelted the tops of the aluminum trailers and created a soft cacophony. The campground dogs huddled beneath them slapping the moist earth with their ratty tails when anybody walked past them. Nobody bothered much about the rain on the peninsula.

"I drove over," Soonie told him. She pointed to her camper. "Rangers flushed a couple of black bears out of town—up by Stroble's trading post."

"Better get you inside, then," he laughed. "Just planted your sacred power feathers." What was it about her that drove him crazy?

She carried a bag. "And this is for you."

"Doughnuts."

"And *this* is for you." She extracted a brown paper sack from her shoulder bag and handed it to him.

Vernon looked inside the sack at a couple of ounces of dried leaves. "Oh, oh," he says. "It this stuff legal?"

Soonie laughed. "Of course—it's not *weed*—it's sage and sweetgrass. We've got to do our smudging." Inside, she slid into the red Naugahyde booth. He looked mystified. "You really don't know what smudging is?" she asks him. Vernon looked bemused. He dunked a donut in his tea. "Okay," Soonie explained to him, "This place you live in has negative vibes for you—your neighbors—your burglary—all of that stuff—we're going to put it all in balance. What I want you to do is get me a pie plate or a pie tin, you know, first of all—and then I want you to make a sacred rectangle around your trailer using—let's see—something personal—something of yours. What have you got?"

"Like what? I don't have nothin'," Vernon laughed.

Soonie's black eyes looked right at him. "Sure you do—just think. I've got it. There's a whole pile of chips from your sculptures out there on the ground beneath your work bench." Vernon squinted at her, listening to her attractive voice, trying to figure her out. Those chips are part of your art—very powerful." Soonie extracted feathers from her bag and began to fix them into a new ceremonial wand. "These two are golden eagle," she told him. "These are raven." She wove an intricate webbing of colored string about the ends of the feathers. "Yes," she instructed Vernon, "gather those rock shards and make a line, and little piles of chips every few feet around your trailer—in a rectangle. All around it." She looked serious. "Don't cheat, now—this is major."

"And, this is *smudging*?"

"You want to be in balance? In harmony? Trust me," Soonie admonished him. "Now—I need that pie plate." At that moment, the sun chose to burst through the overcast. She looked up, shading her eyes. "This is good—we have no time to lose."

"But wait a minute—is your Assiniboine magic going to conflict with the magic of this tribe on *this* res? I mean I don't want to get in any trouble with these birds—I got enough problems."

Soonie cocked her head and smoothed her hair. "Don't worry, Babe, this power has been around for thousands of yeNative peoples have been using it for that long—you got to have faith. It isn't going to screw up now."

After a few minutes, Soonie joined Vernon outside the trailer. He had made a line of shards, useless chips from his sculptures, all around his trailer and every five feet he made a small pile like a miniature cairn.

"Perfect," Soonie observed with satisfaction. "Perfect—you do good work," she smiled. When he had completed his task, she brought out a pie plate of smoking sage and sweetgrass, and a saucepan of steaming sweetgrass tea. She handed the tea to Vernon. "I want you to drip a fine line of this sweetgrass tea just ahead of me and try to get it on the shards," she told him. Vernon did as he was told and she followed behind him, chanting softly. She stopped at each cairn and invoked the cardinal points of the compass and the Prophet of Direction. The smoke from the smudge wafted about, consecrating the area. After a while, large clods of dark wet rain-clouds parted as if by design. After the two of them had encircled the trailer, Soonie covered the pie plate with another aluminum plate to contain the smudge. Vernon watched her performance with fascination, dribbling away the last of the sweet grass tea on to the cairns and shards.

"We're going inside now," she told him. We have to smudge the interior of your place."

Vernon gave her an elbow up, coming up close behind her. Her own wonderful fragrance commingled with that of the smoldering herbs. Inside, Soonie wafted the smoke from one end of the tiny abode to the other, again paying attention to the Four Directions. She sang aloud in a riveting, haunting voice and, when she was finished, Vernon asked her what it was she sang.

"Assiniboine—" she smiled, "I told the Great Spirit that we honor and acknowledge the harmony He possesses and disperses."

"You said all that?"

"Of course. I was moved to sing aloud—the spirit just came to me to do it." She laughed. "Was it bad?"

"It sounded great." Vernon didn't know what else to say. He assumed she was finished. "Thanks," he said.

Soonie inhaled the fragrance of the smudge. "Okay," she instructed Vernon, "now you have to get undressed." Vernon looked surprised. "Come on—hurry up before the smudge is all gone."

Vernon mildly protested. He was embarrassed. Soonie reached over with her free hand and began to unbutton his shirt. "C'mon," she said, "let's go—this is no time to play the shrinking violet. This is serious business."

Vernon laughed nervously. "What about my tattoos?" he joked.

"What about them? I've *seen* tattoos." Soonie breathed in the wisps of smoke.

Vernon disrobed in amused disbelief.

"Shoes, too," Soonie ordered. Vernon kicked off his shoes and stood stark naked before her in the gloom of his trailer with his eyes closed. He raised his face to the ceiling. Soonie took the eagle feather whisk she had made earlier and, using it as a fan pushed some smoke toward Vernon's face and then, stooping, she smudged the entire length of his body. "Lift your arms," she told him. She blew the aromatic smoke under his arms and again into his face. She began to chant again in a strong rich contralto. Vernon was transfixed. When she was finished, she told him, "The guardian spirit of the eagle gives you sight and insight. You are now purified. You are in balance and your neighbors are in balance—and they will honor your boundaries."

Vernon shuddered ecstatically. "Whew."

"There, that wasn't so bad was it?" Soonie asked him. She set the dwindling embers of the smudge pan on the tiny stovetop, where it burned itself out.

Vernon pulled her gently down with him to his sleeping bag. "I hope I'm not too pure to be doing what I'm thinking of doing," he whispered to her.

.. ..

Vernon hadn't seen Soonie in two days. He had no telephone and she didn't leave her number. The weather had lifted away and the days were crisp and clear. He worked outside on his workbench, thinking good thoughts about the restorative effects of hard labor. It seemed odd to him that he wasn't attracting annoying *looky-loos* and when Rudy Bill walked past his trailer he waved in a friendly manner, taking care not to cross over the lines Vernon had made with his shards. Before, he'd have walked diagonally across his space and maybe banged on Vernon's trailer as if it were a Caribbean steel drum, hollering, 'Whoa, babe'. Rudy's other renters, his logger buddies, his so-called cousins, who came to see him, were also careful about not stepping inside the boundaries of his sacred area. Vernon thought it was his imagination, or, the power of suggestion. He began to pay serious attention to the phenomenon of Soonie's Assiniboine smudge lines.

Vernon ran his thumbs along a curving ridge that formed the beak of a recumbent blue heron he was working on. It was smooth as glass. He was satisfied. A group of noisy kids from the campground ran past him down to the beach without first hassling him. He felt their joy in the warmth of the sun and the electrical energy of the natural world. He waved to them before they disappeared over the rise of the embankment. Things definitely quieted down a bit. He had even slept well for a couple of nights, keeping his demons at bay.

Vernon hung up the new whisk of eagle power-feathers just above the door to his trailer, exactly as Soonie had instructed. He wanted to talk to her—and hold her. He wanted to tell her how it was going—and hold her. He wanted to hold her and tell her how the sacred area she defined around his trailer was just like when he used to lay carpet. In a sea of same-colored carpet, sometimes, a decorator would have him lay in a square yard of yellow carpet, or some other high contrast color. He used to notice then, how all the detailers and contractors would walk around the yellow square set within the sea of gray carpet. The little patch was something special. Unconsciously, everyone stayed off it, hopped over it, walked around it. There was no explaining it. It became a special, inviolable place. The space she made for him was like that. The same principle, he thought. A protected space. Maybe her magic worked.

It was evening. Vernon ate a can of hash for dinner and then hopped into his pickup. He drove up to the highway looking for Soonie's horse breeding farm. He didn't have far to look. A mile down the road he saw the white fences and barns just off the highway. On a chance, he took the long one-lane blacktop up to the barn area. A tall rancher came out to greet him. He was native-American. His face was solid, with flat cheekbones. He had pleasant and almost Asian eyes. His voice was husky. Black quarter horses grazed the pasture behind him.

"Yessir, bud?" he queried Vernon.

Vernon stayed in his truck. "Howdy," he said. "I'm looking for a gal named Soonie. Would you happen to know her?"

He shook his head. "Sure. She was here, but we finished up with her mares on Wednesday. Sorry." Vernon tried not to look astounded.

"She took off back to Montana. You by any chance that artist friend she met over there at Rudy Bill's trailer park? You do rock carvings?"

"That's me."

"My name's Teaser. Teaser Greene." They shook hands. Greene called a boy out of the barn. Vernon heard him tell him to get something out of his truck. "Soonie and I are friends." He grinned at Vernon. "We breed—horses." He did a pregnant pause. "She has some great stock." He pointed to a beautiful all black stallion behind him and made a chirping noise to beckon it. The animal came up to the fence. "This is my buddy, Misty. Soonie's mares like him too." Vernon nodded. He looked at the handsome Indian. Had Soonie *smudged* him, too? The boy returned with a cardboard box. "I'm a little late—Soonie asked me to drop this off to you when I got around to it. I haven't been off the ranch since Wednesday, or I'd have brought it over. She said you'd be happy to see it. You saved me a trip." Teaser handed the box to Vernon. He lifted a corner of the flap. He could tell by the heft what it might be. When he saw his stolen white dove sculpture, he could only shake his head. "Soonie said some kid sold it to her up at the district—outside Strobes' market—thought she was a tourist—she bought it and wants to return it to you. It's a beauty? You make it?"

"Yes." Vernon kept shaking his head. "Unbelievable—thanks. We had a little break-in at my place. I never thought I'd see this again. It's my baby." He smiled his half smile.

"Looks like nice work to me. Sorry I took so long getting it back to y'all."

"That's fine," Vernon thanked him. "Come on down to Deer Park when you feel like it and say hello. I'm just across the highway. If you see Soonie, tell her it looks like everything's going to be fine."

"I'll be sure to do just that," Teaser says and he touched the brim of his Stetson.

Vernon saw Teaser and the boy watch him hang a U-turn and head west out of the breed farm. The sky was gray where the evening fog rolled in and a yellow patch defined where the sun was setting on the horizon behind it—a special place.

The End

THE WOMAN WHO NEEDS SPECIAL SURROUNDINGS

A
Performance
Monologue

Hello? Hello? Who *is* this? *Hello?*

Oh, those *damnable* phone calls. I hurry in to lift the receiver, you know, and then, oh—just—*silence*. It drives me *crazy*. What gives? I just picked up my mail at the post office. Oh, sure, I have a box. Box 1965. Well, *forget* that. I didn't *tell* you the number. I *have* to have a box at the post office. You really don't know when some *crazy* will try to do you harm, isn't that right? Receiving unspeakable things in the mail? I've read about all of that in the papers. It's everywhere. Very pervasive. Victoria's Secret catalogs and so on. Victoria's only secret, if you don't mind my saying so, is that she *has* no secrets. The shame of it. I've filled out a card and mailed it back to them. Do not mail me *any* of your disgusting material. Those organizations buy and sell mailing lists and make impertinent generalizations about what your interests are and before you know it you could fill up a cardboard box every week with distasteful advertising—junk-mail is the perfect name for it. Well, I just don't want my address out there for all those sleazebags to exploit. What's wrong with that? I don't feel as if I have to rationalize it. I saw something advertised in a magazine—oh, I don't know what it was—which one. *So, I sent for it.* Just to check it out. *Filthy.* For adults only. A catalog. And, I'm not talking Victoria's Secrets, here. I looked at it and it made me *want to throw up.* Now, I receive many similar catalogs. Catalogs of people's fetishes and perversions. I look at this stuff and I'm horrified, really—and I write a card to the postmaster: Sir, *do not deliver to me any material from this or that sorry source.* Where is our civilization headed that I should receive these things in the mail? Unsolicited. Thank god, I have a P.O. box. Imagine somebody using that information to stalk you at your *home*—where you *live.* Even in the post office, somebody could just be eyeing you casually, say, over there, by the copy machine or the stamp machine—you don't know—you don't *notice*—mailing something to your box number and then waiting for you to pick it up—spotting your box number—then following you home. Oh, don't look so surprised. It happens. Believe me, I look around me when I go to the post office. Where are we headed, our civilization? Into a black hole, that's where—compressed in upon ourselves waiting to be sucked up inside some cosmic maelstrom and spat out on the other side like a bit of debris expectorated from the tip of this—cosmic tongue? Isn't that it? Our society is *sick*—and the media—oh, the *media*—they *spread the sickness* all over the land with an electronic spatula. Junk mail. Spam. TV ads.

My telephone? It's *completely* unlisted. I've seen to that. That's even more important than a P.O. Box. An unlisted telephone is, in a way, just like a P.O. Box. *Nobody can crack your privacy.* Nobody. I look through the telephone book all the time and I can see that it's filled with literally hundreds and hundreds of names with no addresses—just a first initial and a last name—no address. Forty or fifty of them per page. I expect that sometime, the whole telephone book will be filled with just initials and last names and no addresses *whatsoever.* People hiding. Do you know what I mean? The siege syndrome, I call it. And then—and then, dropped in among all of them are the married couples *flaunting* their married status. *Such a big deal.* The man's name *first*, of course. In any case, how do you look up the name of a woman who is simply *unacknowledged* in a telephone listing behind her husband's name? As if she didn't exist. Mr. William Wienowski. 205 Laurel St. You *don't know* from that listing if he has a wife and ten kids. A certain arrogance. He's probably got a faceless, nameless wife. I know what I'm talking about. In his case—Wienowski's case, *I can see* his wife and kids. They live across the highway from me. She's *there* all right. *And her kids.* But she—Mrs. Wienowski—is not listed in the phone book. Insufferable male arrogance. It may seem like a little thing—but it *irritates* me. He's probably the kind who clutches the remote control for the television as if his very life depends on it. Or his *identity*—same thing. Who's fooled? Please tell me that. Who's fooled by those initials followed by a last name? I mean it's a formula, isn't that right? Those telephone listings? E. Smith. K. Blackburn. L for Linda. E for Evelyn. K for Katherine. I mean *really*, who's fooled? If some *sicko* with *raging testosterone*—and they're out there, *believe me*—I see them looking at me in the market and the drugstore—on the bus—if one of those is going to make an anonymous obscene call wouldn't he pick one of those names? X for Xenia? M for Millicent? Everybody knows those initials represent a woman living alone—maybe *terrified*. E. Smith. K for Katherine Blackburn. I'm not stupid. My number is unlisted.

It will *always* be unlisted. I'm not in there with an initial. No way. I don't want *any surprises*. The male of the species and his insistence on dominance is pretty obvious in just the telephone book example—let alone *everywhere else*. Believe me—*I spotted it right away*. Just look at those lists of names and make up your own mind.

It's frustrating to be a woman alone. I bring this up only by way of illustrating that trying to find a home to rent here in this godforsaken mill town is tough enough in a tight rental market. But when you have as many allergies as I have and you are as hypersensitive to the environment as I am, the rental search can be a full time job. I need to move right away. I'm really facing a *crisis*. I become terribly, terribly ill under certain environmental conditions and I'm really restricted to where I can live. I've got to vacate by Thursday. It's so tough. I can't live in a home with paneled walls treated with, say, formaldehyde. If I even *enter* a home with strong odors or freshly cleaned carpets, I get terrible migraine headaches and I have to go to bed in a darkened room for *days on end*. Tension headaches. Even tap water—filled with *crap*—can't even filter it—.01 microns—whatever. The doctors are still trying to find out just what *is* wrong with me. Seriously, I don't think they'll *ever* find out. My symptoms change like lightning. They just can't pin them down. I can see their faces when I go into the clinic. I'm looking for a female doctor now. I really think they're more perceptive—more *intuitive*. They can take my symptoms, you know—flu-like signs, achiness—achiness all over—and fatigue—floating pains—terrible fatigue—*my brain actually swells*—I'm sure of it—and I turn into a *zombie*—they can take those symptoms and come up with a diagnosis. I'm uncomfortable with a male doctor. I really am. The horror stories I see on all the talk shows. The dentists. They put you *out* with sodium this, and amytal that, and you don't know from *anything* what they've *done* to you. **60 Minutes**. It's all on **60 Minutes**. You've seen it. You know what I'm talking about. It's just a matter of time. I'm sure of it. Trust me. Your number comes up. It's your turn. Understand? Unspeakable things in a dentist's chair. You wake up. You don't even know.

You asked about my landlord. He's very strange, what else? I saw him the other night. A little white dog at his heels. I'm sure that's for *cover*, if you know what I mean. I see him out walking around, late at night, in the pale moonlight. I'm sure he's peeked through my windows at me. I'm *sure* of it. You just have that *feeling*. Look, his name is *Beryl Creech*. With a name like that, what *else* would he be doing out at midnight? I keep my lights low. Sometimes, you wouldn't even know I was in my trailer. I don't dare keep my lights on bright—all of my windows are on eyelevel, you know. Well, I saw him through the Venetian blinds—flipped the lights off and just peeked out. Saw him several times. Just last week, it seemed as if he was walking away from my trailer into the dark, through the shrubbery with his little white dog—back toward his own house. It's on the lot next to mine, and no fence between us. No hedges. I went to the front door and cracked it and I cleared my throat *very loud*, so that he would know that I'd seen him. His screen door creaked and I watched him go inside without looking back. It was the next day that he told me I had to be out of here by *Thursday*. No explanation—well—he's a peeping Tom—I caught him at it. So, I don't know if he can do that—throw me out like that. I'm going to have to look for an ombudsman to negotiate if I can stay a bit longer—until I find a place. I've heard that you can stay up to ninety days, *legal, without paying rent*—renter's *rights* or something, you know, while your complaints are being negotiated. Well, I'll have to look into that. But, I would never take *advantage*. I'm not *like* that. They wouldn't have the nerve to call me a squatter. But I do know my rights. Beryl Creech is a *pig*.

Like I told you, I have environmental sensitivity and I can't go just anywhere. I have to be very particular about where I live. I've learned a lot in the past few months. I need to be in a remote location. The house must be situated back at least one mile from Highway 5 and away from constant wood smoke. Wood smoke is a killer. Why do you think they prohibit wood fires during certain weather conditions? Like low-pressure conditions—or whatever it is. I agree it's beautiful. Looks nice. Picturesque. That first *whiff* and all that. But like everything else, there is a hidden agenda, if you know what I mean. Contaminants in wood smoke. Miserable for people like me. Like I said—a killer.

It's very depressing—going through rental advertisements in newspapers. Even the ink makes my hands swell when I touch it. I'm *very* reactive. *Very*. I have to wear special gloves and I breathe through a carpenter's respirator when I'm around chemical inks and dust and pollen. All papers should be using soy-based inks, by now. *Everybody knows that* and nobody does anything about it—except for the so-called green presses—the little literary presses. All those little magazines filled with the poetry of repressed and frustrated feminists. How many of those poems can you read without *going crazy yourself?* Those are the only books printed in soy-based inks and acid-free paper, I'm telling you. I went in to a gallery the other day. Just took a deep breath, you know? I should have telephoned, instead. North Light Gallery. You know it? I asked the man in there, you got any pictures made from soy-based inks? You know, I wouldn't mind to have a picture on the walls of my trailer. Something pretty to doll up the place. He looks at me as if I'm *crazy*. Never even heard of soy-based inks. And he is a gallery owner. He should know. It just proves my point. He'll check into it, he says, but he didn't even take my name. You can't really get service these days—nobody wants to put himself out. Meanwhile, I'm almost gagging from the fumes from the gallery frame shop. I got out of there fast. It's *horrible*. My eyes run and I cough. I sneeze. Sometimes I have to wear my respirator to bed with the shades drawn. Can't roll over—can't get comfortable. *Ever*. Well, it seems to help some, the respirator. Except when I get a magazine with a perfume strip in it. I can't *stand* that. A perfume strip. The audacity, really. I have to go to bed *immediately*. The world is upside down. Even men's magazines now have perfume strips in them. GQ—all of those. And, what is it with men these days? They all smell so *fruity*? My father never smelled like a French whore. He smelled clean like sun-dried wash and Lifebuoy soap—you know, strong *carbolic*. Even on the bus these days. I can't sit anywhere near anybody. Stale cigarette smoke. All that shaving lotion on the bus driver. I've got to write a letter, *really*. The city bus should have more sensitivity about that. I could *scream* to get on a bus. It's excruciating. A captive to perfumes and essences. My eyes puff. Sometimes I have to get off. Catch the next bus. Hope for the best. Now, I understand that Time magazine—well, you can tell them to *not* send you an issue with a perfume strip in it. Can you believe that? You can ask to *not be polluted*. Well, that's *fine*, but what can you do if you don't subscribe to Time magazine and you just pick one up in the market and *all of them* have a perfume strip in them? I can smell them standing in line at the checkout counter, you know, next to the tabloids. But, don't get me started on *that*. My sinuses swell immediately with those strips. It's torture, *believe me*—when you have my condition. I can't wear my respirator out to the market. I'd look like some kind of fool, an insane person. Outer space. A mad bomber. What can you *do*? And really, why is it necessary to pollute the environment like that? Those strips are *destroying* our ozone layer and what *for*? So Liz can put another notch in her corporate garter belt? What is it? *White Diamonds?* I don't know. Make another trip to the bank? There has to be *something more important* than an eighty-year-old *has-been*—with a teased beehive hairdo—fixed with atmosphere-destroying lacquers and other god-knows-*what* pollutants—oh, and another thing—who or what did they have to *kill*—how many? How *many* laboratory rats or capuchin monkeys did they kill to test the toxicity of the eyeliner crayons Liz uses for her *violet eyes*? And to that you could probably add her strange little friend Michael whatever-his-name-is, with the bleached skin. And about her eyes—which I think they are probably a *false* rumor anyhow? A damned *urban legend*. About the *violet* color, I mean. I don't even think she's *that* beautiful. Really, don't get me wrong, I *loved* her in National Velvet—but somebody should wake her up and tell her *the race is over*. You understand? The race is *over*. Her voice is a *foghorn*, already.

If only my *own* dilemma could be over, even. I contacted a dozen real estate agents up and down the peninsula, looking for suitable rentals, but, so far, nobody's found *anything*—they don't even call me back? What *am* I, a pariah? You want to know why they don't call me back? Sure, they're interested in *hot California transplants* with big dough. The hot markets. How much commission do you think they'll make off a rental from me? What do they care about my problems when they are probably getting *double* commission off a $300,000 dollar house, *buyer's and seller's*—at 6% each—that's the going rate. Nope, they *don't even call back*. I'd be grateful if anybody would help me out of this mess I find myself in. And then on top of all this, I've got food allergies and I hate to say it, the 'L' word, *loneliness*, which I really don't like to talk about—but it's *unavoidable*. I've got to shun foods that have been chemically treated or sprayed with pesticides or chemical fertilizers. I get sick from them. *Sick*. I get sick when I'm around some clothing—you know, *certain fibers*—to say *nothing* about underarm deodorants, hairspray and *residual detergents in clothes*. And I've got to avoid people, too. Oh, a couple of people have *tried* to be friends with me, but they *didn't last*. I have *very high* standards when it comes to friendship. High *expectations*. I can't be a friend with just anyone. There is no *way*. I'm really on my guard there. And, don't you suppose that I'd like to have a pet? A dog or a cat? Feel the touch of someone, *something* on my arm? A dog nuzzling my cheek? Don't you think I'd like to hear a cat purr? I can't even respond to such a question.

I can't go to any social functions. Now *can* I? You can *see* that. I can't find any comfort in church because of my allergies. Yes, I'm *allergic to church*. Furniture polish—*dust in there*. Musty hymnals. Communion wafers. Communal wine cup? *Never*. Even the tapestry-cloth which covers the grill of the confessional booth—ugh—*raging* with germs. The *works*. So, sure, I have bouts of depression, who wouldn't—and there's nothing the doctors can do about loneliness. Is there? Tell me if you know. Write a prescription for friendship? RX: Take *two friends and see me in the morning*? I've looked at those singles ads in the newspaper and so on.

Frightening. Coded messages for debauchery. They talk about walking on the beach, fine wines and dining, getting-to-know-you-picnics, loving, single, intelligent, sensitive, men—firesides, hugging—hand-holding—all of those disgusting *buzzwords*. I can imagine myself having a reaction to the sulfites in a fine wine, let *alone the alcohol*—and probably *drunk from a bottle*, right? Styrofoam cup? I'm not a beach blanket bimbo, as we used to say—not by a *long shot*—and I *know* what these sensitive, poetical types are after—I'm *no fool*—and so much for sensitivity and *fine dining*, no? Drinking from a bottle? And me—passed out and probably raped and left to die on a remote beach somewhere. Who are these women who answer these ads? What is their *problem*? That kind of fun, I don't need. Look, *even in the summer*, I've got to wear a wool hat pulled down up to my eyebrows, wool slacks with a rubber band around each ankle to keep out dust from the roadway and turtle-neck sweaters and a long wool overcoat and so on. Wool mittens—in the hottest summer. I'm photosensitive, too. I've got to wear my dark glasses even in the trailer. My skin can't be exposed, you know what I'm saying? Wouldn't I make a great looking date? Imagine me with my carpenter's respirator and dark glasses on? Does it even make *sense* that I'd write one of those singles want ads? It's bad enough just to *read* them. So disgusting. And they're in there *every* day. Look, right here. *New* ones. Every *day*. GWF. SWM. Believe me, GWF doesn't mean Grandma With Fortune. Listen to this one: Asian Women Desire Romance. And this: The Gypsy Exchange for Artistic Singles Who Like to Travel. Confidential. Oh, and get *this* one. Women Loving Women. Discreet letters. Five dollars a sample. Well, at least if I wrote a letter *nobody would know I stutter*. Isn't that right? Such *filth*. So, I stutter a little bit. You've noticed? That puts people off. And *wouldn't* it? Let me tell you, even *stutterers* are annoyed by stutterers. *Believe* me.

Look, I'm *constantly* on the alert to the environment. Finding foods I can eat. You know, survival is a *full time job* for me. Every *moment* of every day I have to fend off something. *Something*. You can *imagine*. Oh, don't get me started on celiac disease.

Sorry, excuse me. There's the telephone.

Hello? *Hello*? *Who is it*? Who's *speaking*? Who's there? I can hear you *breathing*.

So *damned* irritating. Such a nuisance, really. Sometimes I get two or three of these a day. I just know it's somebody who's seen me in the market. Or that Beryl *Creech*—my landlord. Would not *surprise* me. Him and his fleabag pooch.

And another thing—before you go. I've been concerned about surviving the mercury in my dental fillings. Have you read about that? It was in **Star**. You know some people claim they have received radio broadcasts right in their teeth—through their *fillings*—political *call-in* shows—things like that. If you read *anything* about that let me know. Now it comes out—*now*—that the mercury in your fillings may be causing—can you believe this?—may be creating anti-biotic resistant *bacteria*. *Okay.* You know that really rings a bell with me. Soon as I read it I knew it applied to me. One of my doctors even said to me that the shots he's been giving me don't seem to be working—which of course is what I told him. *Nothing* works on me. He's thinking of sending me to a *specialist*. Well, don't they *read*? Don't they keep up with their medical journals? Do you think I should have to find this out in the **STAR** at the checkout counter at Safeway and then report *back* to him? He's been pumping me full of crap antibiotics or whatever, and all along, my *fillings have been canceling out all the benefit.* What am I a *money machine* that he should pour all those *antibiotics* down the drain like that? Down my throat? You can imagine this is the age of eighty-four dollars for two aspirins in the hospital *and the doctors don't even flinch at it.* I wish those fools in Washington the best in reducing costs of hospitalization—with doctors and lawyers fighting every step of the way—calling the shots, so to speak—ha ha. Hillary Rodham Clinton couldn't pull it off when she was first lady. But, don't get me started on that. At least, she had the—what do they call them? *cojones*? to try—you know what I mean? So, I don't know. What *is* this already? Now, am I going to need to have all my *fillings* removed for god sakes? And, believe me here—yes—I'm beginning to hear voices—really—*voices*. I don't know how much more I can take. I'm making a dental appointment—what else can I do?

Excuse me, there goes the phone again.

Hello? Who *is* this? Will you *stop* calling me? Just *stop* it.

So *annoying*. Do you see this whistle here? It's a *police* whistle. If that sicko calls me *one more time*, I'm going to *blow this whistle* as hard as I can into the mouthpiece of this telephone. I always keep it on this cord around my neck. You *never* know—somebody could be *following you to the bus stop*—whatever. This whistle should take care of him. It should *destroy* his *hearing*. I guess I'm going to have to get caller-id. Another expense. Just to keep the world out. I have no choice.

Excuse me, are you wearing some sort of perfume, here? It's so *strong*, I think my eyelids are beginning to puff. Oh, you have to go? So soon? Well, don't blame yourself. It's cold here on the porch. I should have asked you inside. Silly me. Damn, there goes the phone again. Well, goodbye then, I'll talk to you later. Maybe, next time you could come on *inside*? We could *really* chat. I would love to do that. Talk to someone-you know, intelligent. Oh excuse me, here goes the damn telephone again.

Hello? Hello? Who *is* this? What do you *want*? *Don't think I don't know who you are*—.

The End

AFTERWORD

During the Great Depression, my mom became a single mother with three children under the age of ten. A depressing time indeed.

My lawyer grandfather soon died. Financially strapped, my grandmother sold his law library, automobiles, their Seattle home, and her wedding rings and caught the train to Southern California to help raise her grandchildren. Born in 1883 to a country teacher, she had all of the skills necessary to bring the art of literature alive to her grandchildren.

Every evening, after dinner, bundled before a gas heater, grandmother read to us from Charles Dickens, Robert Louis Stevenson, Louisa May Alcott, L. Frank Baum and other famous children's authors. As we could, we took turns reading in rotation, chapter by chapter, sitting cross-legged on the carpet; here, we learned the feel and taste of words on our tongues and heard gentle corrections to our halting pronunciation of complex multi-syllables. All this before the invention of television, cell phones, Internet, iPads, Wii and what have you. In time, our grandmother introduced us to tales of her own, *Chipper the Chipmunk, Rastus the Squirrel* and a dozen others. Whenever she traveled, she was sure to send new adventures of these rustling rascals to us by mail. We were of course delighted—and recognized the possibility of potential authorship that she unknowingly planted within us by writing little amusements of our own devising. We soon graduated to the carpet in front of the 'story lady' at the local library and from there to the shelves of printed riches accessed by that *open sesame:* the library card.

Thanks to her patient and loving guidance, I have been able to amuse myself in this formidable art of literature and perhaps, someday, amuse my own grandchildren as well.

Ed Robison